Praise for GWEN~~~~~~

D1342175

author of The Jane Austen Book Club

0060379731

Praise for GWENDA BOND

"With whip-smart, instantly likable characters and a gothic small-town setting, Bond weaves a dark and gorgeous tapestry from America's oldest mystery."
Scott Westerfeld, New York Times bestselling author of the Leviathan series

"Weird, wise and witty, Blackwood is spectacular."
Marcus Sedgwick, author of Midwinterblood and White Crow

"This haunting, romantic mystery intrigues, chills and captivates."
New York Times bestselling author Cynthia Leitich Smith

"Miranda Blackwood's battle against her own history is utterly modern – and utterly marvelous. She's truly a heroine all readers can rally behind."
Micol Ostow, author of family and So Punk Rock

"A deft and clever debut! Bond takes some reliably great elements – a family curse, the mark of Cain, the old and endlessly fascinating mystery of the Roanoke Colony – and makes them into something delightfully surprisingly new. How does she do that? I suspect witchcraft."
Karen Joy Fowler, New York Times bestselling author of The Jane Austen Book Club

GWENDA BOND

BLACKWOOD

STRANGE CHEMISTRY

An Angry Robot imprint
and a member of the Osprey Group

Lace Market House
54-56 High Pavement
Nottingham NG1 1HW
UK

www.strangechemistrybooks.com
Strange Chemistry #1

A Strange Chemistry paperback original 2012
1

A catalogue record for this book is available
from the British Library.

ISBN 978-1-908844-06-4
eBook ISBN: 978-1-908844-08-8

Set in Sabon by THL Design.

Printed and bound by CPI Group (UK) Ltd, Croydon, CR0 4YY

JUBILEEWOODS.ORG.UK

For my parents (principals but never fascists)

and

for Christopher (my partner-in-crime)

Entry from
A Brief History of the Unexplained

The Lost Colony of Roanoke Island. In 1584, Sir Walter Raleigh began his push for English settlement in the Americas. Establishing a settlement in North America was attractive to both Raleigh and Queen Elizabeth I – sure to bolster his influence and power as well as England's by opening access to a New World believed to be full of riches and by providing a staging ground for privateers to capture Spanish treasures on the high seas. Raleigh was granted seven years in which to make a successful colony in the lands then known as Virginia, after the virgin queen herself. The effort instead yielded one of the most enduring mysteries of the modern age.

After earlier trips proved largely exploratory, more than one hundred would-be colonists signed on to a 1587 voyage designed to finally create a permanent settlement on what is now Roanoke Island, part of North Carolina's Outer Banks island chain. But the journey proved harsh, as did the colonists' new home. Unfavorable conditions for cultivating crops and growing hostility with local Native American tribes made their future in America look bleak, especially without the hope of fresh supplies from England. Governor of the settlement John White – an artist by training whose daughter Eleanor Dare had just given birth to Virginia, the first English child born in the Americas – was chosen to go back to their homeland and petition Raleigh and Queen Elizabeth for help.

Unable to return for three long years, when White reached the site of the colony he found no sign of those he had left behind – save for a single word carved into an oak tree: CROATOAN. But a trip to that nearby island turned up no further traces of the missing colonists. The disappearance of the one hundred and fourteen men, women, and children of the Roanoke colony, known now as the Lost Colony, remains unexplained to this day.

For what we sometimes were, we are no more;
Fortune hath changed our shape, and Destiny
Defaced the very form we had before.

Sir Walter Raleigh, PETITION TO THE QUEEN

1

Miranda

The first time Miranda Blackwood checked the back of her closet for a portal to another world she was eleven. That was the year her mother died. After the closet, she tried other places. She wandered small patches of woods, seeking doors hidden in twisted trees, and peered into mirrors, searching for reflections that weren't her own.

But Miranda grew up. She no longer hoped to step over a secret threshold and leave Roanoke Island behind forever. Instead, she grabbed whatever escapes were in reach, no matter what they were. No matter that she stayed right here.

For three summers running, her best escape had been interning for *The Lost Colony* at Waterside Theater. She sanded wood, hammered nails, sewed seams, and did whatever else needed doing to make the show's version of history – complete with musical numbers – come alive for the tourists. In exchange for those hours of scutwork done without complaint, the stage manager, Polly, let Miranda join her at the side of the outdoor stage every night to watch the show's final scenes.

The set's faux oak tree, hollow boulders, and packed dirt floor passed for an abandoned settlement, except for the shining spotlights. While Miranda half-listened for her favorite part, she cocked her head back to take in the stars light years above. The view was as familiar to her as the small constellation of calluses dotting her palms, or as the lines of the play drawing to a close beside her. As familiar and set as everything in Miranda's life.

The season was almost over, and then she'd endure senior year. Everyone was talking about college, preparing for the next act in their lives. She wasn't going anywhere. She wouldn't even have this. After she graduated, it'd be time to get a year-round job that paid more bills.

"They've survived!"

The bullish voice of the actor playing Governor John White snapped her attention back to the stage. The line signaled his return to the site of the colony after his trip to England.

Surrounded by sailors, White gasped as he pointed at the oak on the far side of the stage, the simple cloak around his shoulders flying out with the gesture. Miranda couldn't see the word from where she stood, but the famous Croatoan was carved into the bark in desperate, crooked letters. White went on, overacting like crazy, "My granddaughter, I will see her beautiful face!"

Miranda and Polly exchanged a look. Polly shook her head, her prematurely gray ponytail bobbing. Director Jack, aka His Royal Majesty, would give the actor a scathing note on that later.

The governor froze, along with the sailors in the background, and the lights dimmed. This cued up the final reveal. Miranda could never help wondering where the colonists had gone. Disappearing was some trick to pull off, even hundreds of years ago when there were more wild places left. The standard theories involved bad endings and tragedy. Even on such a humid night, not knowing – knowing that no one would *ever* know the truth – was enough to give her a small shiver.

A single low spotlight fixed on a solemn young blonde girl as she wandered ghost-slow through the frozen men. Her face was chalk pale.

His Royal Majesty's biggest change to this year's show had been making Virginia Dare the show's deadpan narrator. The actress, Caroline, was a local kid, seven years-old and a mean-girl-in-training, and yet, the casting worked.

Miranda leaned over to see how the scene was playing for the crowd. The show wasn't sold out, but the curving rows of the amphitheater were nearly full. Probably about twelve hundred people, riveted and silent as Caroline haunted the stage.

The shadow appeared at the back of the audience. Miranda had no idea what it might be – it was definitely *not* part of the show – only that it was *there*. The large unformed shape was simply a growing darkness until it resolved into an immense, old-fashioned black ship. The kind of ship used long ago by colonists and pirates. Strange gray symbols bloomed on each of three billowing black sails, the shapes a mix of straight lines and arcs, a half-moon curving above a circle at the top. The sailcloth rippled in a wind that she didn't feel on her skin.

Miranda blinked. The ship was still there.

She put her hand up, and her hand was *in front of* an immense black ship with tall gray sails. And the ship was moving forward now, swallowing the audience row after curving row.

In a few seconds half the audience was gone beneath it, and Miranda's breath caught in her throat. The ship glided steadily closer. When she turned to Polly, the stage manager smiled at her with the normal relief of reaching the end of the night. She gave off no hint of concern.

But the ship was heading straight toward the actors, those odd symbols shifting on the sails in curving and slashing lines. The black monster gathered speed, moving faster and faster–

When Caroline hit her mark at center stage, only a dozen feet separated her from the black ship. She gave no sign of seeing it either. She might be a brat, but she was also seven.

"Look!" Miranda pointed and staggered forward onto the stage. Caroline opened her mouth to speak and Miranda threw herself at the girl, shielding her with her arms.

There were a few shocked cries. Miranda closed her eyes and waited for the impact.

And waited.

There were more murmurs and questions from the crowd. But nothing else.

Caroline squirmed in her grasp, struggling. Miranda

opened her eyes and the massive curving prow loomed above her unmoving, throwing a heavy shadow over her and Caroline and then – between one blink and the next – it vanished.

The spotlight blared into Miranda's face and she squinted, not used to the bright heat. She glanced over her shoulder, still holding the wriggling Caroline tight. Governor White stared murder at her, but none of the men broke character. They were supposed to remain frozen until the lights came down, and they were.

Caroline said, "Let me go, *Blackwood*." Miranda didn't understand right away, didn't understand anything that had just happened. Caroline yanked a handful of her hair.

"Ow." And Miranda realised: the spotlight was still on. That meant the show wasn't over.

She'd interrupted the performance because a giant ship had appeared. A giant ship no one else seemed to have seen. From the side of the stage, Polly said, "Miranda! Get. Over. Here."

The knowledge that she'd disappointed Polly finally got her moving. She released her hold on Caroline, and hurried off stage. Polly grabbed her arm. "What was that?"

Caroline looked like an angry ghost, her face pink instead of white. Polly brushed at the sleeve of Miranda's shirt where the girl's make-up had rubbed off.

"I'm so sorry," Miranda said.

Polly frowned, but stepped next to her to wait while rosy-cheeked Caroline managed her last lines.

"The one hundred and fourteen men, women, and children

of the Roanoke colony remain lost, their fate unknown. A mystery trapped in time."

At last, the spotlight died.

Walking out from backstage at the end of the night, Polly was trying her best to pull an explanation out of Miranda without passing judgment. Miranda nodded along and kept silent, barely absorbing Polly's chatter about how she knew Miranda loved the theater and would never sabotage the show, but she just couldn't understand what had caused her to interrupt...

At a hastily called post-show meeting, His Royal Majesty had informed cast and crew that he had never had anyone disrupt a performance while it was in progress before – let alone a member of the crew. And a lowly intern at that.

The handful of locals in the cast and crew were already muttering that having a Blackwood around was asking for bad luck. That anyone could have predicted Miranda would screw something up eventually. That she'd done it in such spectacular, inexplicable fashion didn't surprise them.

The director had finally ended with a caution that he'd be consulting with the stage manager about Miranda's future employment and praising the cast for not breaking character. Not finishing the show despite the interruption would have meant ticket exchanges. They couldn't have that.

Polly defended her, saying there must have been *some* explanation and she'd talk to Miranda. The problem was Miranda couldn't tell her the reason.

She had listened closely to everyone talking about what

she'd done. No one else said anything about a big black ship with billowing sails. No one said anything even close. She was the only one who had seen it. But she *had* seen it. Hadn't she?

"I hate for you to go straight home after that," Polly said. She stopped next to head of the trail that looped along the coast to the complex where the non-locals lived. "Come out to the Grove and I'll sneak you a margarita. We can talk more about it tomorrow, OK?"

Miranda bit her lip. She had to ask, to make sure. "You didn't notice anything…"

"Anything?" Polly prompted.

"I don't know… Odd?"

Polly frowned again. She'd never seen Polly frown this much. "You mean besides what you did?"

Yes. "Was there anything else?"

Polly's response was careful. "No. I didn't notice anything else odd. Did you?"

So Miranda really was the only person who'd seen the ship. "Probably not. I better go on home."

"Sure?" She waited, giving Miranda a chance to say more. Then, "OK. Be careful. We'll figure this out." Polly split off toward the trail with a wave, rushing to catch the people who'd left a few minutes earlier.

One of the reasons Miranda liked the theater so much was that the out-of-towners who worked summer stock didn't know much of anything about her or her family. They had always treated her like they treated each other. Normal. That was over.

She knew all too well how losing normal status felt. The kids at school hadn't truly decided to turn on her until she was thirteen. Her mother was dead, which was bad enough, but then the new police chief's kid – Phillips Rawling, radiating cool like all new kids did – had humiliated her in front of everyone. She didn't believe he'd done it on purpose, but that didn't matter. What mattered was he'd given the others the confirmation they needed that she'd never be like them.

And her night just kept getting worse. The instant Miranda hit the pavement of the mostly-deserted parking lot, her incredibly sad nemesis Bone's pickup truck roared alongside her. There were a dozen Tarheels stickers pasted on the bumper and back window. Basketball was the closest thing North Carolina had to a state religion. He was a devoted member of the faithful.

He rolled down the window and Miranda asked, "What?"

That his rich kook of a dad had to *force* him to work at the theater didn't usually get to her. Life wasn't fair. That she already knew. The fact she hallucinated a phantom ship *and* that she knew he was about to remind her yet again of her family's reputation, well, *that* got to her.

Bone's elbow jutted out the window. He was gawky, skin and bone, the source of his nickname.

"Sorry about your Blackwood luck," he said.

Grrrr. "Sorry you're a jerk."

"I'm going to hang out with some friends. Where are you going? To pick up your dad?"

Miranda raised her hand and made a shooing motion. "Leave, begone, scram."

He hesitated, stumped for a comeback. Finally he said, "I will," and roared away.

Miranda reached her beloved car, Pineapple, and patted the pale yellow hood. "Thank you for not roaring."

When she started working at the theater, she'd bought Pineapple for a few hundred bucks. The original make was impossible to determine, and she never had to figure it out. She'd never signed on the dotted lines of any insurance or registration papers. Her dad claimed that forms and laws were for other people. Respectable people.

Miranda drove out of Fort Raleigh, the plastic hula girl stuck to Pineapple's dash wobbling seductively with each turn. Downtown Manteo, the island's main drag, was packed with tourists on this warm summer Wednesday. The town center resembled a perfect model of itself, preserved Victorian houses and Colonial-style storefronts with the Sound's peaceful waters as scenic backdrop. Gelato shops and fancy restaurants were tucked next to pricey B&Bs that offered tickets for fishing expeditions and dolphin spotting.

Her street was off a more remote stretch of highway, a small pocket of cheap, mostly rental houses shoved where the tourists would never see. A different kind of lost colony.

Miranda pulled into her usual spot at the curb and got out. Maybe she'd hallucinated the ship, like when Gaius Baltar hung out with his not-really-there Cylon girlfriend on *BSG*. Maybe. She gripped her keys so their teeth stuck out through her fist. Her dad had shown a rare flash of concern when she started at the theater, forcing her to promise this little action whenever she was outside at night alone.

Walking quickly, she crossed the patchwork yard to the house. The white paint had been flaking for years. The porch light was off, and in the darkness she tested the front door. It was locked.

A golden retriever loped across the yard to join her. Miranda reached down to scruff the fur under his neck. "Hey, Sidekick, hey pretty boy." Sidekick had shown up a couple of years ago out of nowhere. He got his name because sidekicks were always the characters she liked most. TV binge-a-thons were her other main escape.

Miranda fished her keys from her messenger bag and fumbled at the lock. "The great provider must not be home, huh?"

She managed to drop both her bag and the keys with a clunk. With a sigh, she bent to pick them up. The low, angry sound of Sidekick's bark made her jump. His yellow head whipped toward the street. His body stretched tight from nose to tail as his throat rumbled.

He rarely barked. And never like this.

Then the others started.

Every dog in earshot bayed and howled in a riotous symphony devoid of any melody. Sidekick's neck craned to the sky, more wolf on a postcard than happy golden retriever.

Miranda refused to look up, afraid she'd see the ship again. She jammed the key into the door's lock and twisted it hard. The knob spun and the door gave. She kicked her bag inside. Hesitating halfway in, she held open the door, and said, "Come on, boy, come on."

Sidekick arched his head at her and whined. His eyes glinted in the dark.

"*Sidekick*," she said. She fought to keep the panic out of her voice. "*Now*!"

Sidekick came, galumphing through the door. His growling quieted once he hit the threshold. The howling outside continued without pause, without song.

Miranda slammed the door and slid the deadbolt into place. She pulled aside the faded blue curtain and checked outside.

No ship. Nothing but a cloud floating across the pale moon. The dogs' racket ended, just like that.

She settled down on the too-soft cushions of the old beige couch, and dragged in a breath. What a night. At least the room that surrounded her was normal – the easy chair covered by the red slipcover she'd made from an old blanket, the ancient floor model TV, and, above that, the grinning photo of her mom playing tourist beside the mast of the *Elizabeth II* at Festival Park. Sidekick panted at her with his usual mellow-dog grin.

"Honey?" A voice called from up the hall. "Is that you?"

Her father was home after all. He stumbled up the hall with the clumsy but somehow sure-footed steps of a professional alcoholic, weaving into the room. Sidekick leapt up next to her, pressing against her side.

"It's me," she said, when her dad paused and squinted at her.

His face was stained a red that meant nothing anymore. His skin stayed that way. The distinctive snake-shaped birthmark that crawled up his cheek toward his temple was nearly hidden by the permanent flush. Too many years of drinking for his angry pores to ever calm down.

"Of course it is, kiddo. I'm headed out…" His voice trailed off.

She could have traced a thought bubble and provided the caption showing the dot-dot-dots as his mind went blank. It broke her heart a little, every time.

"Do you need me to give you a ride somewhere?" She didn't want to go back out, but she had to offer.

"Nah," he said. "Fine… evening for a walk."

Miranda dropped her head back against the sofa, closed her eyes to a flash of the black ship behind them. She bolted upright to find him watching her.

He'd be safe out there, wouldn't he? Safe as he ever was? "Have a nice time," she said, "but call if you need me."

Usually that would have been his cue to stumble the rest of the way to their small kitchen for his keys, then out the door and to whichever bar in Manteo he was welcome at that week. Tonight he hesitated, wavering on his feet, focusing on her with an expression she didn't recognise.

"You're a good daughter," he said.

She ruffled Sidekick's fur, not sure what to say.

Wavering, wavering, and he said, "I want you to know," before completing the circuit to the kitchen and the front door, where he fought the deadbolt and won. He closed the door behind him well enough that she was able to stay put on the couch, half-waiting for the dogs outside to go crazy again. There was only quiet.

Miranda had a firm policy of never being the silly girl – the kind who went to see what noise that was, or who would believe she'd seen something no one else had. The kind who would call Polly and confess why she'd ruined the show. The kind who wanted someone she could talk to, period. There was no one for her to tell everything or anything, no matter what she wanted. She'd best stick with the policy.

Plumping the waiting pillow, she eased onto her side and let her eyes close with Sidekick's head on her hip. Her dad would wake her when he stumbled back in later.

But this way she'd know he made it home OK.

The Silence

A realtor wearing high heels and too much lipstick clicked her way across the gas station parking lot, returning to the pumps.

The fluorescents inside lit the building like a blaze, but no one had answered when she called out at the counter. She'd taken a pack of cinnamon chewing gum. She hadn't shoplifted anything since high school and stealing the gum was a thrill, a memory of what it felt like to get away with something.

She opened the door of her Prius, and then heard a baby crying. Nearby.

She considered ignoring it. Instead, she slid one acrylic fingernail around the edge of the gum to open the pack, took out a piece and chewed. She tossed the red sealing cord and wrapper onto the ground and walked toward the baby's cries, telling herself nothing was wrong. Rounding the pump, she could see that the gas nozzle was in the side of the minivan. But no one was watching it. The minivan's window was cracked and, as she neared, the baby's crying got louder. She looked back at her own car. She chewed her gum. She got closer, seeing the fat baby thrashing in a car seat inside. Still, no one came.

She eased open the car door, feeling more like a criminal than she ever had in her life. She'd stolen gum, but she wasn't going to steal a baby.

The smell wiped away her guilt. She cupped her hand over her mouth, replacing the foul odor with the warm sweet scent of the stolen gum. The fat little baby must have been alone for a while. She needed to call someone, needed to get the baby out of there.

Something wasn't right.

The man woke up and couldn't place what was wrong. He threw an arm over the other side of the bed and found it empty. Empty? He sat up.

"Honey?" he called. Her name wasn't Honey, but she didn't mind the endearment.

No answer.

He stood, waiting for a response. When none came, he wandered through the house. Checked the bathroom, the kitchen, the living room. Her fancy headphones were next to the doorway, so she wasn't out jogging. She'd worked late at the office the night before. He'd taken three round white melatonin tablets and turned in early. He hadn't wanted her to wake him when she came home.

He went back to the bedroom and looked at her pillow, covered in ivory Egyptian cotton, the high thread count she liked. The pillow's surface was plump, save the outline of where his hand had landed.

He walked outside to check for her car. The sedan sat in the driveway. He tore across the yard, wet grass soaking his bare feet.

The driver's side door hung open. Her purse lay on the ground next to the car. He made an awful sound...

The girl and her friends had stayed up late, first drinking margaritas, then moving on to tequila shots. One of them had eaten the worm. They'd laughed and passed out. She'd stayed on their couch because she didn't think she could make it to her own rental a few doors down.

Now she couldn't find them. Were they mad at her? Everything had been fine the night before. How could they have left without waking her? They'd have had to go right past the couch. She usually woke at any strange noise.

She screwed up her courage – they probably weren't mad at her, she hadn't done anything, right? – and called each of their cell phones. In turn, they chirped, sang, beeped.

She heard them. None of these girls would ever leave the house without their cell phones. She would never go anywhere without hers.

She'd spent her life watching too much TV. She wondered if they'd been kidnapped, were trussed up by some serial killer with a bloody dissection in mind. She'd have been taken, too, though. Wait. What if someone was still in the apartment? But, no, she'd checked. She was alone here. All alone.

A breeze blew in through the screen door. She'd left the door open when she checked outside. A tiny drink umbrella all pink and yellow and blue cheer spun off the edge of the sticky kitchen table.

It hit the floor and twirled away.

2

Breaking News

Miranda stretched and hit Sidekick with her feet. He was curled up on the other end of the squishy couch. Bright morning light stabbed around the sides of the blue curtain, a harsh wake-up call. Her dad must not have made it home last night. Or had he?

She got up and opened the door. She wouldn't have been that surprised to find him laid out, snoring, on the concrete porch. But he wasn't there. She let Sidekick slip past her into the yard, leaving the door open so he could come back inside.

Miranda shuffled down the hall and peeked into her dad's room, just in case. The room was empty of everything besides a rumpled bed and piles of clothes. She tried the bathroom next. He wasn't passed out at the foot of his porcelain master either, so she brushed her teeth and got cleaned up.

Her dad almost always made it home. The times he didn't were because some rookie hauled him to the drunk tank instead of bringing him here like Chief Rawling did.

In her room, Miranda dressed quickly. She paired a faded red T-shirt with a denim skirt she'd made herself out of a pair of old jeans, using the ancient sewing machine she inherited from her mom. She paused for a longing look at her little shelf of DVDs scored at yard sales and on eBay (or burned off torrents using free wireless). She wanted nothing more than to hole up for a few hours, visit a faraway galaxy or watch hot boys fight gross creatures on the hand-me-down netbook Polly had given her at the beginning of the summer. She wanted to forget about the drama at the theater the night before, about the ship no one but her had seen.

Instead she'd make a jail run. *This is your life, Miranda Blackwood.*

She gave Sidekick the option of outside or in, and he chose in and a bowl of kibble. As she headed toward Pineapple, she discovered the morning was full of unwanted developments.

Along the driver's side of Pineapple, thick black letters shouted the word FREAK.

Miranda closed her eyes and colors bloomed inside her lids. She wished for something to kick. *Like Bone and his friends.* Something clever, like maybe Croatoan, would've been too much to ask of them. She took a breath, walked over, and tested the words with a finger.

Shoe polish instead of spray paint. That was a small favor. She considered cleaning it off before retrieving her dad, but she didn't want to leave him sweating in a cell any longer than necessary. She'd just have to park so he didn't see it. Otherwise he'd ramble and rage.

Miranda's first hint that something was wrong – something bigger than her dad being MIA and Bone being a jerk – came when she turned onto the main highway toward town. The traffic made her wonder if there was a hurricane evacuation. The flow was too heavy for this early in the day, even for peak tourist season, which late summer wasn't. Big evacs didn't happen without a day or two's warning, though, and there weren't enough rental cars in the mix. Tourists took off when weather threatened, but plenty of locals, including Miranda and her dad, chose to ride out hurricanes the old-fashioned way, with sandbags, boarded-up windows, and peanut butter sandwiches.

By the time she reached the edge of town and Manteo's box of a police station – bizarrely painted bright blue – she was convinced something was really, *really* wrong. The jail's parking lot was across the street, and way bigger than it would ever need to be. Only, the lot was full.

At least a couple dozen people were milling around outside the jail. Slowing, she watched the woman who owned the town movie theater hug a bearded older man. They were both crying. A local TV van was parked half on the curb, a cameraman capturing the pair's worried embrace.

She managed to find a spot a street over, and hurried back toward the jail. The people spilled onto the sidewalks around the station gave off fear and worry like a force field. She was about to make her way inside the jail when Chief Rawling emerged from the glass doors.

A sleek-haired blonde reporter launched out of the van toward him, snapping her fingers for the cameraman to follow. She had giant blue eyes like an anime deer's. Miranda had seen her in person before, when she'd come to the theater to announce the winners of random prizes. But Miranda couldn't remember her name. Blondie would do for a nick-name. *Wait. Scratch that.* Blondie had been her mom's favorite band. *Blue Doe.* That was better.

Blue Doe approached Chief Rawling, leaning into her right hand to cradle her earpiece and signaling for him to stop walking. He looked like he was having a very bad day. He was as put together as usual – black hair clipped short, face clean-shaven, navy uniform pressed – but deep lines cut into his forehead and around his mouth.

The chief had always been nice to Miranda, one of the few people in town who didn't treat her or her dad like outcasts. He had that problem child of his own – so what if hers was her dad? – or at least Phillips had been a problem before his parents shipped him off to juvenile delinquent school. Miranda flushed thinking of Phillips. Her memory of him that day at school stayed sharp as a film she could replay at any time. So did the memory of how he'd looked at her later, like he understood how she felt. It wasn't fair he could look at her like that after what he'd done.

Behind Miranda, someone choked down a sob. She put away thoughts of the chief's trouble-making son and shifted a few steps closer to hear better. The crowd quieted when Blue Doe held up a finger, signaling the interview was about to begin.

"Live in three, two…" Blue Doe said. She put on an impor-tant voice, "Chief Rawling, what can you tell us about the events of this morning? Is this a mass kidnapping? Is it a ter-rorist action? A hoax?"

What in the world was Blue Doe talking about?

Chief Rawling rubbed his forehead then lowered his hand, visibly remembering he was on camera. "We're not sure at this point, beyond reports of a large number of missing people."

A large number of missing people.

"How many citizens of Roanoke Island are believed missing at this point?"

"We've had about a hundred missing persons call-ins this morning, but that number is extremely preliminary. Most of those people will probably turn up," Chief Rawling said.

Most of those people will probably turn up.

"Should people leave the island?"

"It's too early to recommend that people leave. What we need now is for people to let us know if a loved one is missing, and to report any unusual activity. I'm sorry, but I also need to ask everyone to please wait at the courthouse. We need to keep this building free for police work. Further updates as I have them. Thank you."

The crowd around Miranda erupted into conversation as Chief Rawling went back into the building. She couldn't move. Was her dad *missing*?

She didn't even see the microphone until after Blue Doe had thrust it in her face. "You're just a girl," the reporter said, "are you looking for someone? Is someone you love among the lost? What can you tell us?"

The reporter's tone held a hefty dose of false sympathy. Miranda, reeling, made a mistake. She spoke.

Phillips Rawling scooted along a wide stone ledge halfway up the outer wall of the four-story dorm. He pressed his fingertips into the space between fat red bricks above his head. His arms flexed as he lifted his lanky body, leaving the safety of the ledge. He fit the rubber tips of his all-stars into the wall, then repeated the whole process again – finger hold, then foot hold – making steady progress toward the open window of his room on the second floor.

He was cutting it close. The sun was already up, so scaling the wall made the most sense, even if it was crazy. This side of the dorm faced the woods, which made being spotted unlikely. And some kids would already be heading down to the lobby for the group hike over to the dining hall for breakfast. He'd be running a bigger risk of being seen walking in the front door and heading the wrong way up the stairs to his floor.

And Phillips never got caught. Not since he'd come to Jackson, anyway.

He jumped in the window, landing on the floor with a satisfying thump. He grinned, thinking of the principal's face at the end of the day when he went out to his car to drive home. The supplies for making the bumper sticker had taken a few months to collect. Adhesive, the right sort of paper, the letters to make the message, all ordered online and sent to the nearby house of a teacher who happened to be on sabbatical for a year. Grabbing them from the mailbox wasn't hard, given the power of delivery confirmation. The principal had put a uniforms-even-on-the-weekend policy into place six months before, followed with a ban on "personal decorations" – aka posters – in the dorms, and so the message practically decided itself: I Love Fascism.

The principal always arrived at least a half-hour before any of the faculty, probably so he could write up the ones who were five minutes late. That meant all Phillips had to do was sneak out and be waiting to smooth the sticker onto his sedan's bumper.

He was pulling his vintage Clash T-shirt over his head so he could change into his uniform when the knock on the door sounded. A man's voice called, "Phillips Rawling?"

That was not the voice of one of his charming Neanderthal fellow students. Too old, and he had a sinking feeling he recognised it.

"One sec," he called back. He should already be dressed, so he let the T-shirt fall and raced to get his standard-issue white button-down over it, leaving the shirt unbuttoned and the tie loose around the neck. He yanked on the jacket that went with it, scrubbed a hand through his chin-length black hair and opened the door.

Yep, it was the fascism-lover. The principal had a half-moon hairline and a thin mustache. He'd been trying to figure out Phillips' story since the day his parents dropped him off in Kentucky at semi-reform school and headed back home to Roanoke Island. Phillips had never imagined this guy capable of busting him. What if his parents tried to make him come home?

Phillips raised his eyebrows, not volunteering anything. He needed to see how bad it was.

The principal gave a disapproving glance at the T-shirt beneath Phillips' uniform but motioned him down the bland beige hall. "Your father's on the phone for you," he said.

The kids in the hall were openly curious as Phillips shut the door and followed the principal without speaking. Phillips didn't hang out with anyone here and as far as they knew, he was one of the good kids. He wasn't someone the principal gave a personal escort anywhere.

This couldn't be good. His dad never called him, and he'd just talked to his mom the night before.

Phillips stayed quiet on the way down the stairs to the first floor. When they reached the bottom, the man said, "Over here." He led the way into the dorm's front office, a part of the building Phillips rarely saw. The big room had a couple of desks and filing cabinets, along with a counter and a short row of chairs in a waiting area.

The principal pointed him to a small table next to a copier. A light flashed on the phone. "Line two," he said.

Phillips picked up the receiver, his finger poised over the button. "Can I have some privacy?"

"Of course." The principal deflated and scuttled across the room.

Phillips clicked the line, did his best to hide his nerves. "You rang, Father?"

His dad hated being called Father.

"Phillips, thank god," his dad said. "It's just... There's something..." He was talking too fast. He sounded out of breath.

"What's wrong? Is Mom OK?"

There was a long pause. His dad breathed heavy into the phone, but Phillips felt no urge to make a joke about it. Then his dad said: "Do you know where they are?"

"Where what are?"

His dad let out a sigh, maybe of relief. "Listen, son, I think I need you to come home. Something's happened…"

He could sense his dad searching for the right words.

"It's not Mom, is it? Tell me it's not Mom," Phillips said.

"No, no, your mom's fine. But it's bad." The line fuzzed with soft static as his dad paused. "Bad's understating it. Maybe you can help. Maybe I… the island needs you here."

Phillips longed for his iPod. He wanted to put his earbuds in and crank the volume loud enough to drown out what his father had just said, to drown out the world. Pretend this conversation wasn't happening. It was so quiet here. His sanctuary.

"I can't go back, Dad. I can't do anything there. Trust me."

Phillips reached out, pressed down the line to hang up the phone but kept the receiver at his ear while he thought over his next move.

He'd been thirteen when he first heard the spirits, the day his gram died. Unfamiliar voices chattering in his mind, so many and at such volume he could barely think. Once he decided he wasn't going crazy (yet), it wasn't that hard to figure out who the voices belonged to. The dead went everywhere on Roanoke Island that he did.

Pressing the voices to the back of his mind had taken constant effort. But they were always there. A hum, a buzz, and, sometimes, a riot. During the worst moments, it was like every person who'd ever lived and died on the island – and it had been occupied for a very long time – shouted to him. Their voices rushed him, a pack of bullies bringing chaos he couldn't begin to control. He'd felt frayed at the edges, like he was unraveling. When he confessed to his mom, she made an appointment with a neurologist in Norfolk. As they drove off the island, the voices faded. Not gone, but lower. A miracle.

So Phillips had made enough trouble that his parents had no choice but to send him away. His dad was the police chief. His reputation couldn't take the hits. Phillips gave the year-round boarding school pamphlet to his mom, and she agreed to go along. Leaving had been his last hope.

The further from the island they'd gotten, the more normal he had felt. The voices quieted, and then disappeared.

He'd been here three and a half years. Staying here was better for them all. He wasn't going back.

Decision made, he replaced the phone and rose. He ran a hand through his hair, and caught the principal watching him.

He thinks he's finally getting his chance to figure out my dark and stormy past.

The principal walked across the room and laid a hand on Phillips' arm. "Your father has asked me to put you on a plane home. I'm to stay with you while you pack and escort you to the airport in Lexington. You are not to leave my sight. Those were his instructions."

Of course they were. Phillips shrugged, already beginning to work on possible ways out. Maybe he could convince an airline staffer to put him on a flight somewhere else.

"He told you what's happened, I take it?" the principal asked.

Phillips shook his head. *Curious, even if I didn't involve his mother.*

The principal said, "You should see this."

His tone made it clear he was playing his trump card. He gripped a remote and pointed it toward the TV mounted in the corner of the office. He unmuted the set and raised the volume.

Some news network, with the standard Breaking News crawl, blared. Everything seemed to qualify as breaking news these days, but this time it was true:

Mass Disappearance in Outer Banks: Colonists Lost Again?

The network was broadcasting the Norfolk affiliate's coverage from Roanoke Island. According to the blonde holding the microphone, they'd just run a spot with his dad. But that wasn't who the face he saw belonged to. That wasn't the owner of the voice he heard. Phillips drifted toward the monitor, every ounce of attention he possessed locked on the screen.

Miranda Blackwood was being interviewed on national television. And what she said was, "Leave me the frak alone," before striding toward the camera and out of frame, while the reporter babbled something about "this distraught young woman" being an indication of the local mood.

He felt like someone had thrown cold water in his face. Miranda Blackwood – he hadn't seen her in almost four years, obviously, but she had the same too-serious eyes, long black hair curling around her pale, pretty features.

"I've seen enough," Phillips said. "Let's go."

If Miranda was involved in what was happening there, he had no choice. He should've known he couldn't escape dealing. When he shut his eyes, the memory of the voices was as clear as if he was already back there. And his dad wanting him home was a tip-off about just how bad this would be. His dad had never acted like he believed Phillips had any unusual abilities, even though he'd grown up in a family legendary for its gifted members.

Phillips should have known. The island always won.

3

MIA

Miranda shouldn't have lost it with Blue Doe. But the lens of the camera had stared at her judgmentally, and the reporter had been in her way to find out if her dad was missing. She needed to get inside the station, see if he was safe in a cell. She'd stalked off, hearing unsurprised murmurs from the crowd.

Behaving like a Blackwood... like father, like daughter... She didn't need to hear their whole commentary to fill in the details.

Her dad hadn't been in lock-up. A younger officer she remembered being on the football team a few years before had taken her information, promised to let her know as soon as there were any leads on the disappearances or if her father turned up.

There was nothing to do but wait and freak out, so she decided to check on the theater crew. She might be forgiven for the night before now, no questions asked thanks to the more important one of where all these people had gone to. Morrison Grove, the tree-hidden village of multiplex apartments that

40

housed the hundred and twenty or so out-of-town cast and crew during the summer, bustled with action every time Miranda had been there. People who were drawn to the theater lived life loudly, and for many players at *The Lost Colony* this summer of noisy glamour had to make up for an off-season of quieter cast calls and auditions. But the parking lot had only a smattering of cars in it, and as Miranda left the quiet forest path to walk among the Grove's cozy chocolate-brown houses, they appeared as deserted as they would be come winter. The entire place was sunk in the deep silence of abandonment. The gentle roar of the Sound in the background was the only thing close to normal.

Miranda found Polly's apartment and pulled open the scratchy screen door. It squealed under the pressure of her hand. She rapped on the door, but no one answered.

The knob turned easily, door releasing with a click. Unlocked.

Feeling like a silly girl – for going inside *and* for being nervous about going inside – she stepped into the common room, taking in the kitschy knitting projects and trashy magazines scattered around like normal. A tiny drink umbrella lay discarded on the floor.

"Polly?" she called. No one answered.

Miranda walked around the living room and stopped at the dry erase board on the wall where the girls left each other snarky messages or notes about errands. There were no messages to explain the desertion.

The screen door squealed open behind her, and she whirled. Costumes Leah stood in the door, her face blotchy and eyes shiny. She wasn't one of Polly's roommates, but she hung out with them.

"Where is everyone?" Miranda asked her. "Where's Polly?"

Leah walked the rest of the way inside, stopping to pick up the drink umbrella. Her red hair was wet, like she'd just gotten out of a shower. "I... I can't find her. She was here. Last night. We were all here. I slept on the couch. Now they're... They're missing."

"Polly's missing?" Miranda probed.

"Not just her – Kirsten and Gretchen too. Jack just took half *my* housemates to stay with relatives in Shenandoah for a couple of days until this is sorted out. I was going to stay, but... I'm going too. I can't take the quiet."

Miranda didn't understand. "How will they get back for the show?"

"The theater CEO's wife is missing. He's canceled the show until further notice," Leah said. "The first time ever Jack said and... even *he* seemed worried. You sure you're OK? Do you want to leave with me?"

Miranda could have sworn Leah's teeth were chattering. Of course, the idea of the director being worried about anything besides his precious reputation *was* almost as disconcerting as the rest of the morning's events.

"No," Miranda said, "No. I'm going to stay in town. Everyone will be back. It's probably all just some weird coincidence."

But what if it wasn't?

Leah started to giggle, though it didn't sound like a laugh. "I hope so," she said. Leah flung her arms around Miranda in a hug before she could dodge, squeezed tight. "Hope you're here when I get back," Leah said, still giggling.

The older girl left, but Miranda stayed behind in Polly's apartment for a few minutes. She kept hoping to look up and see Polly walk through the door.

Miranda had watched *The Lost Colony* be performed hundreds of times. She felt trapped in that final moment where young Virginia Dare tells the audience the settlers were never heard from again. How did more than a hundred people disappear without a trace? For it to happen four hundred years ago was almost unbelievable, but to happen now? And for her dad to be one of them?

It turned out Miranda couldn't take the quiet either.

Phillips flipped up the collar of his jacket and lowered his head, the better to fake invisibility. He navigated through the terminal at the Norfolk airport, skimming past people weighed down with carry-ons they were too paranoid to check. He'd expected the voices to start chattering as soon as his feet hit the ground, just from being so much closer to home. On the island, listening to music had been the only thing that helped. When the plane landed his iPod was ready in his pocket, his earbuds dangling around his neck. But so far, there was nothing. Not even the vaguest of whispers tickled the edges of his awareness.

The TV screens he passed were all Roanoke Island, all the time. Norfolk was close enough to pick up regional news. He didn't stop to watch.

Guilt did force him to a stop in front of an arrivals board.

The situation on the island would mean his dad had extra ammunition for special favors. He'd have done his best to get Phillips' mom clearance to wait at the actual gate, to make sure he didn't pull a runner.

Phillips found the flight number he was looking for and backtracked. Not far, a couple of gates. He stayed close to the wall.

There she was. She sat in a chair waiting for him. Her smooth brown hair was cut shorter than the last time he'd seen her, framing her face. She held an e-reader in her lap, but stared ahead at nothing instead of reading. She looked tired.

He walked to the bank of pay phones and dialed her cell. Remembering that his dad also had access to GPS tracking, he left his own cell off. "Mom?" he said when she answered.

"Yes, sweetie?"

She wasn't too happy about him having lied about his flight details. He'd called her from Lexington and told her he was switched to a slightly later flight on a different airline – the one she sat waiting for, not the one he'd actually been on. She was even less happy when he told her he'd see her at home later.

"Phillips, how will you get there? Do you know what will happen when you're back on the island? It's been almost four years." She always worried about him. He wished she wouldn't worry so much. He'd noticed a few new streaks of gray in her hair.

"There's something I've got to do. I'm sorry," he said. He didn't tell her about seeing Miranda on the news. He could still hardly believe *that*. He knew how hard it was to get her to react. He'd done his worst, hadn't he? And she'd just stood there.

He hadn't been able to forget that, to forget *her*. He needed to see her, and there wasn't time to make his mother understand why.

When he hung up the phone, he realised his mom was right. How was he going to get there?

He did the obvious thing.

His mom always parked on the third level in the thirteenth row in the parking garage. That way, she never forgot where the car was. He found their faithful maroon sedan and located the spare keys in the little magnetic box behind the rear right wheel. Then he stole the family car.

Once she made it home, Miranda sank onto the sofa. Her hands formed a tight ball in her lap. Sidekick sat on the floor beside her, big eyes full of worry.

The family legend ran that the Blackwood name was linked to the fate of the island. None of them had ever lived anywhere else. The knowledge lived deep in her bones: Blackwoods were doomed to Roanoke Island. She wouldn't have believed her dad could leave, let alone *disappear*.

But if all those other people had done just that, if her dad had, who was to say she wouldn't be next? Even if her life *was* going to be spent in a place that didn't want her, that didn't mean she was ready to vanish. And where had the missing people vanished *to*? She couldn't imagine that it was any place good. When she was young she might have hoped differently, but there were no waiting fantasy lands, no sudden entries to worlds where wizards and unicorns frolicked under glittering waterfalls and everything became magically perfect.

Wherever the people were, she bet they weren't any safer than she was.

Then she remembered the closet in her dad's room, which he'd stuffed full of boxes the day they moved in. He caught her going through it soon after, and pulled her aside, shaking her twelve year-old shoulders. "Don't ever go in there," he told her. "There's a gun in there." When she got older, she thought about going through the closet when he was out and getting rid of the gun. She worried about it, about her dad and his bad days. She'd never liked the idea of it waiting there, cold metal of some unknown shape and size. But he'd told her not to touch it and she hadn't. The idea of a gun in her hand had made her too uneasy.

But now she walked up the hall and into her dad's room, careful not to look too closely at the messy bed and discarded clothes. The stale smell of boozy sweat made it feel like he was home. Not missing. Not gone.

Holding the closet's contents with one hand to prevent an avalanche, she slowly opened the door wider. She reached up and pulled the string that lit the bare bulb, then began to carefully rummage. She moved out a box crammed with the button-down shirts her dad used to wear when he held a straight job, and another that proved empty. Three more boxes followed, filled with dust, old newspapers, and neckties.

She emptied about half the closet's contents, enough so she could lean inside and look around. Stretching to see behind the remaining cardboard boxes, she spotted a thin wooden box about the size of a briefcase, crammed in sideways behind the rest. She made a fist and rapped the edge. A hollow echo of the rap replied, like she'd knocked on a door.

Behind her, Sidekick whined. "I'm being careful," she said. "Shh."

Wedging herself into the closet, she perched on the unstable stack of boxes and reached down to pull the box up and out. The case was made of dark wood and had a brass catch.

She'd never seen it before. The clasp sprang open easily, and she lifted the lid.

It took her a moment to identify the object inside as a weapon.

The dull gleam of hammered metal, the surface as long as her forearm, wavering with the memory of the strikes that had created it. A thick base gave way to a thicker barrel, like a small cannon. Jewels encrusted the handle, and even she could tell they were the real thing.

Some sort of antique firearm, it had to be. Puzzling over the heavy object in her hand, she shut the closet. The bizarre weapon must be worth a small fortune. She couldn't believe her father had never pawned it for a bottle. Could this really be what he'd meant when he told her there was a gun in the closet?

Then she spotted the small strange symbol nestled between the gems, a sort of stick figure with a circle body that had curved legs and straight arms, and an open half-moon on top.

She'd seen it before. The same symbol had been stitched at the center of those three black sails, whipping in wind that didn't exist, flying above the decks of a black ship that didn't exist either.

Phillips had never been a good driver and – judging by the horn blows of skittish drivers on I-64 – his skills hadn't improved from taking several years off. He didn't even have a license. He'd taken his dad's car years before and been apprehended by one of the island's stalwart officers. His parents had told him he could have a license when he turned eighteen and became "responsible for his own actions."

The long bridge that cut across the Croatan Sound was dead ahead. Instead of going across at Manns Harbor, he'd decided to take the new bridge, since it bypassed downtown Manteo for the convenience of people headed to other islands. If his mom had already reported that he'd taken the car, his dad and the rest of the force would be on the lookout.

He hoped his mom would understand why he'd ditched her once he could explain – if that was even possible. Truth was Miranda's face – then, now – had transformed the flickering uncertainty inside him into a strong, sure flame. He was *certain* she was in danger. Which meant he had a chance at redeeming himself. A chance to help keep her safe.

If only you had a clue why you're so sure she's not safe.

He took a deep breath. Once he crossed the bridge, there was no going back. He'd be home. His mom was right. He had no idea what was going to happen.

Three and a half years of quiet. They'd been nice.

The bridge rose up in front of him, a green sign with white

letters telling him exactly where it would take him. The way to get back to the home he'd never missed.

He eased onto the bridge and floored the gas, letting the car surge forward and whip across the asphalt at dangerous speed. The other side of the highway crawled with cars like slow-moving bugs, but his side was nearly empty. The lanes went on for so long he didn't know how he'd stand the suspense. He suffered for five miles of wide road over the choppy blue Sound.

The highway finally leveled out onto land, tires separated from the earth by pavement alone. The familiar forest, thick treetops like green bubbles, came into view lining the highway. An idyllic glimpse of home. A lie.

The backed up traffic on the other side of the bridge continued onto the island – honking tourist rentals and retiree fancy cars mixed with a few older vehicles of long-time residents, all creeping toward the bridge. The mass disappearance was real. It was real enough to empty out a good portion of the Outer Banks at the end of tourist season.

Phillips braced for the spirits to sense his presence.

No whispers. No screeching. No voices.

Other than horns and road noise, Phillips didn't hear *anything*. Huh?

Phillips eased off to the side of the road as soon as he could find a wide spot and cranked down the window by hand. An insistent breeze swept through the car, ruffling his hair and T-shirt. It carried no voices to him.

He waited in case the sudden rush of noise made him unable to drive.

The breeze tugged at him. The sounds it brought were natural ones. Finally, he eased the car back onto the road, driving with more caution in case the voices showed without warning. There had never been any warning.

Welcome to Roanoke Island, said the sign he passed. No matter that it felt like someplace else, he was back. Had he changed that much, or had the island? The question was pushed aside by a more pressing one.

If he wasn't going to be sidelined by the dead, then he had an itinerary to keep. Where did Miranda Blackwood live?

4

The Call

When the knock at the door came, Miranda was on the couch examining the strange gun. She scooted forward, about to get up, before realising she had no clue who was outside.

Her father would never go with a simple knock if he couldn't get in. And they never had visitors. When she wasn't working, she'd sometimes hang at the Grove with Polly and the crew, but wouldn't dream of inviting anyone over. She preferred to keep what little privacy she had intact.

Miranda waited to see if the person went away. There was another knock instead.

Miranda slowly climbed to her feet, gripping the metal of the antique gun. Any weapon was better than nothing. She could use it as a threat or to hit someone with or–

A muffled male voice spoke: "Mr Blackwood? Or Miranda, Miranda Blackwood?"

There was something familiar about the voice, but she couldn't place it. The familiar made her fingers tighten around the gun. Whoever was out there, her instincts said they were somehow a danger to her.

Sidekick's body brushed the side of her knee as he stood beside her. His tail thumped a steady rhythm against the coffee table.

Could it be Bone or those idiots he hung out with? She'd never considered any of them dangerous, but she'd never been all alone like this either.

Breathe. You have a sort of weapon. You have to answer or this person won't leave. Just point the gun with the right amount of menace.

She opened the door in one quick motion, stepping back and raising the weapon as the door swung in. She attempted to imitate a movie stance, to radiate confidence. Her hands trembled.

"What do you want?" she said.

"Miranda?"

And – click – she placed the voice, matched it against the tall boy standing in her doorway. It was early evening and not anywhere near dark outside yet, but his face was in shadow. Still, she knew him. She took in his messy black hair, the glint of eyes that would be more black than brown. She'd never expected to see him again. Not after he managed to leave.

"Phillips Rawling?" She blinked in disbelief, but he didn't vanish. Her fingers loosened and the gun clattered to the ground between them.

He lunged forward, bending over the antique weapon.

"Careful," she said.

"You be careful. You're the one acting like a CIA assassin."

He *would* say something like that.

He didn't even look at her, instead leaning forward to check out the gun. "Anyway, I'm safe – at least I think I am," he paused. "Is that a matchlock? Awfully ornate. And it has a trigger. Hmm…" He shifted it with the toe of his shoe for a better look.

Miranda couldn't figure out what he was doing at her house. Or on the island, for that matter. He'd gotten *away* from here. He was supposed to be off at some reform school. And even if he *had* come home on purpose, that didn't explain what he was doing on *her* doorstep.

"What's a matchlock?" she asked, mostly to say something. Anything.

He glanced up at her, then immediately back to the gun. "Matchlocks were the precursors to modern guns, more or less. Ones like this – although not exactly like this, because this one is weird – were developed during the Elizabethan period, and they're not easy to use. You have to light the barrel, essentially."

Miranda was impressed. "How do you know all that?"

He straightened, and finally looked at her. There wasn't much distance between them, just the space of the threshold she hadn't invited him over yet. And there was just enough light to see that the years that he'd been gone had been kind… to his face, anyway. She resisted the urge to smooth her hair.

He shrugged. "My dad's really into antique firearms, and I grew up around the Outer Banks. Don't you still work at *The Lost Colony*?"

"I'm an intern, not the prop master," she said. "Wait. How

do you know where I work?" She put a hand up to stop him from answering. A couple more inches, and she'd have touched him. "And, um, why are you here?"

"Why are *you* answering your door wielding a valuable historical artifact?"

The gun *was* worth money, then. Miranda stooped to pick it up, dangling it by the barrel like someone might hold a dead rat by the tail. "I just found it looking for... Never mind."

"Can I come in?"

He didn't seem to be joking. She almost said no, but he looked so serious. She gestured with her gun hand for him to come inside, swinging the metal in a semi-welcoming fashion.

"I guess so."

"Thanks," he said.

She shut the door behind him, watching as Sidekick nosed Phillips' fingers. *Some guard dog.* He slumped onto the floor, tail thumping.

"Is your dad–" he started.

"No, he's not here. Which is good for you. He doesn't care too much for you."

At least, not if he remembers who you are.

"Understood," he said, and then, "Listen."

Which she did, but he didn't say anything else. She moved the heavy gun again, indicating the couch. They sat down on opposite ends of it. Unlike at the door, she carefully made sure she created as much distance between them as possible, fingering the gun that lay flat in her lap. Never in a million years would she have expected Phillips Rawling to be on their couch.

"So," she said. "Just get back?"

Phillips nodded. "Yeah. A couple of hours ago."

"So," she said.

He shifted to face her, erasing a fraction of the distance. "Yes?"

"Why're you here?"

"Look, I'm sorry. I know it's weird to drop in here out of nowhere and... surprise you. I'm sorry about that. But I had to see you."

Miranda listened hard. She let the gun slide onto the couch between them.

"Please put that thing on the table or something," Phillips said.

"What did you call it again?" she asked, keeping it in her hand.

"A matchlock – where did you get it?"

"I–" she stopped. "No, I don't think so. Not until we talk about why you *had* to see me, after all this time."

Phillips didn't rush to say anything.

Wait. "Have you heard about the missing people?" Even as she said it, she figured out why he'd come. Injury, insult, the whole enchilada. She'd been distracted by how he looked, by the surprise of him showing up. Too distracted to see the obvious. "You think *I* had something to do with it, don't you? Because I'm a Blackwood. Because of... everything. Are you going to call me a snake again? We can probably get it on CNN this time."

He still didn't say anything, only looked at her. It wasn't that different than the look he'd given her all those years ago, the one she'd never forgotten. She wanted to be wrong about why he was here. *Let me be wrong.*

He sighed. "You're sort of right – I am worried that you may be involved. Is your dad one of the missing?"

She hadn't been wrong. Miranda picked the supposedly useless gun up and pointed it at him. "Get out."

He held out his hands. "Wait–"

The phone rang, its high-pitched wail like a slap. Miranda squeezed the gun's trigger without meaning to.

Phillips cringed even though there was no noise. Not at first. The whoosh came a heartbeat later, as a curtain of black powder sprayed from the end of the barrel, coating him as completely as a shower. A faint burning scent filled the air.

Miranda struggled to breathe. "Are you OK?"

Phillips used a finger to sample the powdery film coating his skin, sniffed and tasted it. "Just coated in… sulphur and, maybe, charcoal?"

"I didn't mean to…" *Shoot you.* She couldn't say the words.

"I know. No big deal. I'm fine."

The wail of the still-ringing phone made it through her shock. "I should get that." She checked the handset before picking up. Manteo Police. Her stomach tightened. "Hello?"

While she listened, she watched Phillips attempt to get the worst of the dust off his eyelashes. Having sprayed him with the powder should feel satisfying. He deserved the payback. Especially since he'd come here to accuse her of – well, she still didn't know what exactly.

"Be right there," she said, and clicked the phone off.

"Who was that?" Phillips asked. His curiosity seemed to transcend the thick powder still clinging to his skin.

Miranda considered lying, but told the truth. "Your dad."

Phillips jolted to his feet. Black dust flew in the air around him. "What? Why?"

"He needs me to come to the courthouse. They found mine."

"Found your what?"

"Dad," she said. "They found my dad."

Reality crashed down around her, settling into place like the walls of their ramshackle house. Ramshackle, but inescapable. She placed the gun on the table, being more careful. She frowned. "I thought you said it couldn't fire without being lit."

Phillips looked like he wore Halloween make-up gone wrong. Sidekick nosed his fingers, testing them with a lick and shuddering.

He said, "It couldn't. But this is gunpowder. I can smell the sulphur. So it has a trigger mechanism even though it shouldn't. Where did you find it?"

The box she'd unearthed from the closet was a few feet away, and she was taken aback by how much she wanted to show it to him and see what theory he'd have. But she didn't have any reason to trust him, not after eighth grade, not after he'd rushed here to say she was "involved" with the disappearances. An answer would only provide more ammunition. So to speak.

"You better get cleaned up. I have to go get Dad."

5

Found

There wasn't anywhere for Phillips to park his mom's sedan around the courthouse. There might not be that many permanent residents in town, but every single one left must have converged on downtown. Cars crammed all the spots that the media's satellite trucks hadn't occupied. Every major network was represented, along with the local cable station's van. Phillips had let Miranda out a block away and was searching the side streets for a gap.

Miranda. Up close, he'd been able to see the changes the years had made in her. She was taller, and her curly hair was wilder. He could tell that she was still the same girl, with too much weight on her shoulders, trapped by the island and what being from her family meant. He related. She hadn't wanted to let him drive her to the courthouse, but she'd flagged him down before he could leave. Her own wreck of a car wouldn't start.

He couldn't have screwed up the conversation at her house worse. She believed he'd come to embarrass her again, to hurt her. She hadn't said an unnecessary word to him on the drive.

He had to find a way to make it right. He was even more worried about her after the appearance of the weird old gun. Not being able to explain why he was worried didn't change what he knew.

Miranda Blackwood wasn't safe.

That wasn't the only thing worrying him. Where were the voices? He wasn't willing to risk trying to call them. Not yet. He'd summoned the voices intentionally just once, and the response had left him muttering in bed for two days, struggling to mute the overwhelming chaos chorus.

But he couldn't help wondering if he'd been gone for three years for no reason. The voices had *felt* real. That they started the day his gram died and stopped when he left seemed to confirm they were – and that they were tied to the island, somehow. Maybe not, though. Maybe he had some brain disorder and the timing had been a coincidence.

Phillips found a spot in front of the Pioneer Theater. The box office was dark, despite the fact the movie theater prided itself on always being open. He needed to get back to Miranda.

The courthouse square consisted of a wide lawn with a fountain and a gazebo, shaded by the white courthouse with grand two-story columns and a wide front porch. Phillips kept his head down as he waded through the lunatic fringe clogging the square, hoping no one would recognise him and flag him down. Unfortunately, the reputation he had to earn in order to leave made him memorable.

He passed uninterrupted through the crowd and stopped near the bottom of the broad set of steps that led to the courthouse entrance. He hesitated, not eager to face his dad.

So when the professor type coming off the steps barreled into Phillips, he knew it was partly his fault. Still, he said, "Watch out–" before he realised who the klutzy professor was.

The man in front of him hadn't changed a tweed fiber. He was wearing the same fussy style suit he always did, no matter the weather, and had a familiar leather binder clasped under his arm. He was known around town as Dr Roswell, so christened because about the only theory on the lost colonists he hadn't held at some point was alien abduction. He really was an M.D., and to Phillips he was also Dr Whitson, the shrink he'd seen to keep his parents happy. Better, he was the shrink who'd spent most of their time together talking history and ephemera while Phillips poked through his personal library.

Phillips smiled despite the hold-up. "Doc."

Dr Roswell's beard and mustache took on a friendly walrus shape when he grinned back in recognition. "You magically appear in front of me and now I know I'm officially going mad," he said.

Phillips gestured at the mob scene. "What do you think all this is?"

"CNN got my name from Bitty Reynolds, and they thought I'd know." Dr Roswell leaned in, growing serious. "But, Phillips, I don't think what this is can be easily explained. All I know is that it happened once before."

CNN might not be so far off base. Dr Roswell did know a lot of things that regular history buffs ignored. "I have to go, Doc. There's a girl I have to…" Phillips swallowed, unsure how to finish. "Is it OK if I drop by later? Talk over some explanations that aren't easy?"

Dr Roswell nodded, "You're always welcome. And good luck."

"Good luck with–?"

But Dr Roswell continued on, waving off the calls of the locals now all too eager for his theories. Phillips watched him parting the sea of townspeople, and then walked up the broad limestone steps that would take him to his father.

At the top, Phillips met the nod of the beefy cop on security, and the guy recognised him instantly. "Your dad's been wondering when you'd turn up. And your mom's pissed. Get in there."

Great. He headed to the courthouse's revolving door, deciding how best to handle his dad. He was out of practice at being in trouble.

Despite the sweep of the building's exterior, inside no grand vista waited. The lobby's scuffed marble floor was filled with a crowd of people who weren't usually there. A few tables had been set up, outfitted with phones for a call bank. Phillips' dad had an office on the first floor, up one of the hallways branching off the lobby. He preferred not to work in the jail when he could avoid it.

Phillips spotted Miranda hovering off to the side of the entrance. He hung back for a second, watching her watch his dad. She must be waiting for his dad to notice her, and all the buzzing activity meant that hadn't happened yet.

Phillips wasn't sure why his dad had summoned Miranda here, but it bothered him. There was no reason for him to have called her personally.

His dad stopped to talk to a state trooper and a pasty guy

in a black suit. He looked even more tired than he had in the glimpse Phillips got on TV in the airport. Dark circles hung under his eyes like he'd gone weeks instead of less than twenty-four hours without sleep. He responded to something the guy in the suit said, body language dismissive. His dad's mouth fell open mid-sentence as he stared at Miranda.

Make that *past* Miranda. Phillips waved.

Miranda turned her head, frowning when she spotted him. "Thanks for the ride. But you didn't have to come in."

"I wanted to." He shrugged in his dad's direction. Phillips could tell from El Jefe's scowl as he shot across the lobby that he hadn't even noticed Miranda. Phillips talked fast, "I'm sorry. I don't think any of this is your fault. I'm just worried for you. I did a crap job of explaining before, but you can trust me. I promise."

"I should…" Miranda hesitated, tilted her head to give him a closer look. Then she stepped between him and his father. Phillips didn't know why she'd decided to delay his moment of reckoning, but he was grateful anyway. She said, "Hey, Chief Rawling. You called me?"

His dad looked from Miranda to Phillips and back again, finally seeing her. "Yes, I did. You better step into my office." He motioned for her to follow him before he spoke to Phillips, "*You* wait here." Then he added, "Until I come back."

Miranda looked puzzled. "Where's my dad? Is he in your office?"

His dad said, "You'd better come with me." He touched Miranda's arm, extended his other one to indicate which direction for her to go.

Miranda dealt Phillips another surprise, when she hesitated and said, "If it's OK, can Phillips come with us?"

His dad's forehead wrinkled in confusion, but he said, "I guess."

Phillips trailed Miranda across the lobby and along the hallway into his dad's office. The space hadn't changed much. His dad closed the blinds on the tall, narrow windows to the outside, turning the room into a cave. He peered at Phillips from the other side of his desk. "How are you holding up? Any... problems?"

"Good, actually," Phillips said. "Fine."

"When we finish here, call your mother. You can drive the car home to her. She'll bring you back here."

Phillips ignored the part where his dad was allowing him to drive the car, and instead bristled at the command. "What am I supposed to do here?"

His father lowered his voice. "You know. What you do."

"There's nothing," Phillips said. "Not since I got back."

That wasn't what his dad wanted to hear.

Miranda coughed to interrupt. "Where is he?" she asked, the question small in the high-ceilinged room.

Phillips didn't fully understand why he wanted to protect Miranda, but he did. It just didn't make sense that his dad would want to see her in person with everything that was happening, not to release her father on a drunk and disorderly or a public intoxication charge.

"You might want to..." Phillips' father trailed off as he sat, and Miranda and Phillips slid into the chairs in front of the desk. Phillips tried to catch Miranda's eye, but she was staring straight ahead.

"I have some news," he went on.

"Where is he?" Miranda asked.

"I understand this is hard–"

"What's hard? You found him, right? He wasn't missing."

Phillips touched her arm. She flinched. He said, "Miranda, you have to let him tell you."

Miranda gulped in air, and said, "No, you don't understand. I promised to take care of him."

Father and son exchanged a glance.

"Well," his dad said. "You've had a tough time of it, Miranda. You have been a devoted daughter, and this news will not be easy. I'm glad that my son is here with you." He paused. Phillips figured he wanted to know why the two of them *had* come together. "I hadn't wanted to tell you alone, but there's no one to call... Our social worker's among the missing and I know you wouldn't want that anyway. You've been running your household for a while now and you deserve to know, especially with everything going on. There's no easy way to say this."

Miranda remained motionless. Phillips wasn't even sure she kept breathing.

"Your father was murdered."

Phillips had expected injured, maybe even dead, but not... "Murdered?"

"His body was discovered in an alley downtown this afternoon. He's the only one of the missing we've recovered so far. But he brings the reported number down to one hundred and fourteen. Meaning his death is probably *not* related to the missing persons."

Miranda put her head down, her hair falling forward. Phillips wanted to do something, to comfort her. He didn't know how. So he sat there in shock, fixating on the number, teasing out his father's logic. Miranda's dad was probably unrelated *because* now it was a hundred and fourteen people gone. The same number John White had left behind in 1587.

"The coroner is having some difficulty determining what happened to him, but it's not anything that could be considered accidental or self-inflicted. We've ordered an autopsy, and we'll know more once that's finished. If you want to see the body, we can arrange that. I'm sorry, Miranda."

"I'm sorry, too," Phillips said, the only words that made sense. He had questions for his father, but they'd wait.

Miranda lifted her face.

"I understand," she said, steady as a flatline on a hospital monitor.

Phillips had heard his dad talk to his mom about notifications before. How most people fell apart before you even got through the facts. How the ones who didn't were the ones that took it hardest.

Miranda rose, then seemed to think better of it and dropped back into the chair. "Do you need me to sign anything?"

6

Mothers

While Phillips drove her home, Miranda stared out the car window feeling lost. As lost as the missing people, maybe. Chief Rawling had agreed to let Phillips take her, but he was supposed to end up back at the courthouse. Phillips had told his dad again that there was nothing he could do to help there. For some reason, he seemed reluctant to leave her.

She didn't know what she should feel, or what she should say.

But Phillips didn't have much to say either. He kept his eyes on the road, his knuckles tight in a death grip on the steering wheel.

"What your dad was asking you before… you hear voices still?" she asked.

He didn't as much as glance over. "You remember."

The grass blurred to a soft green outside the car window. "Yeah."

Of course, she remembered. He'd heard the voices talking about *her*. She'd been in eighth grade, thirteen years old. It was the first day of school, not long after the Rawling family moved in from Nags Head. They took possession of the house belonging to the chief's mother – aka the Witch of Roanoke Island – after she died of cancer. To Miranda, it seemed like everyone eventually died of cancer. Phillips had possessed the glow of celebrity all new kids have in a small town. She'd been standing against the section of lobby wall that belonged to loner misfits. He walked toward her like he was in a trance. The other kids in the lobby laughed as he reached out a hand and touched her hair. He said things to her, about her. Things that didn't make any sense, but that scared her. He called her a bad thing. He called her a liar. A traitor. A carrier. A snake.

The other kids loved that – a snake. They thought he was being funny. The funny new kid, picking on the Blackwood girl, something most of them had wanted to do for a long time.

The principal had stepped in to pull Phillips away, and called her dad to pick her up. What people whispered about their family was bad enough, and had gotten worse since her mom died. Their curse had been confirmed. Her dad ripped through a half-case of beer when they got home, getting angry. He loaded her in the car at midnight and drove to the Rawlings' house. Two months later and he wouldn't have been able to – that was when his license got grabbed for good, and he sold the car for drinking money.

Chief Rawling tolerated her dad yelling and taking a swing at him, though he didn't let it connect. Phillips came downstairs and stood at the screen door. When he saw Miranda, he ran outside and whispered to her, "There were voices talking in my head. They said things about you. But they're just *voices*." And then he gave her that look. She could tell he was sorry. Even then, she didn't believe he'd done it on purpose.

Chief Rawling sent Phillips back inside. Then he drove her and her dad home in their Oldsmobile. His pretty wife with the black hair followed them in his police cruiser. Miranda had been surprised that Phillips didn't turn up at school the next day. His mother home-schooled him for half the year, rumors of his escapades around the island traveling the halls anyway.

She studied his profile, just inches away. She'd always wanted to ask him if his voices had said anything else about her. She wanted to know. Maybe. But she didn't ask that. Instead she asked, "Do you mind if we stop by there?"

A thick black fence thrust from the ground like jagged teeth, a forbidding boundary made of painted iron. The evening light made shadow spears that thrust toward the gentle slope of ground the fence protected.

"I can't believe I'm about to say this," he said. "But, why not?"

He turned up the dirt drive and drove them into the graveyard, dust ghosts trailing the car.

Miranda got out first and wandered through the chalky white tombstones, some carved with angels or winged skulls. There weren't many recent burials in this part of the cemetery. Phillips didn't follow her. He stayed in the car. She figured he'd join her if he felt like it.

She was alone now. Alone in the world.

She walked up the slope, grass that could have used

mowing tickling her ankles. She turned back and saw Phillips still inside the car. She started down the other side of the small hill, leaving his sight. The markers changed to reddish marble and gleaming black. There were plain gray stones mixed in, but not many of the oldest pale ones.

Miranda didn't care for modern headstones. When her mom died, they'd only been able to afford a smallish marble rectangle to mark her grave. She had wished for something large and sweeping that captured her mother's spirit. Or at least something small and noble, like those old ones. She was pretty sure the guy at the Outer Banks Monument Company who sold them their stone had already cut them a deal though. There hadn't been any way to ask for something more.

She reached the not-so-special gray stone. Kneeling, she traced the letters of her mother's name with her fingertips. Anna-Marie Blackwood. Miranda leaned against the stone, and said, "I didn't forget my promise, but I wasn't able to keep it."

Miranda didn't ask for her mom's forgiveness, but she wanted it all the same. She eased down on the hillside next to the headstone and pulled up a yellow dandelion growing on the top of the grave. She shivered at the idea of her mom down there in the cold, damp dark.

The tombstones on either side were close. There'd be no room for her dad's marker to go next to her mom's. Not that they – not that she – could afford one.

She heard Phillips climbing down the hill to join her. He must have been stomping as loud as he could through the grass, to give her fair warning to compose herself. He wasn't turning out to be anything like she expected.

She patted the ground beside her. He kicked at the grass, then sat down.

"Phillips Rawling, meet Anna-Marie," Miranda said.

Phillips didn't say anything.

"She was great," Miranda said.

"I'm sorry."

"You say that a lot."

"Sorry," he said, then, "Last one, promise."

They stayed like that for a few minutes, not talking. Low, gray clouds passed overhead. The rolling hills of the cemetery grounds were dotted with purple-flowering bushes and a few trees. This was a peaceful place, even with the highway so nearby.

"I can't believe he's gone," she said. "I still can't believe she is."

"What was he like?"

Miranda shrugged. Before her mom had gotten sick, he'd been different. Quieter, not so much of a crazy talker or drinker. Able to hold a steady job. Her mom could make him smile with such little effort. She read Miranda book after book, Narnia and Alice and the first couple of Spiderwicks, while he drank a beer or two, no more, content to listen.

She plucked another dandelion, this one already transformed to a head of white cotton spokes. "He wasn't able to be himself anymore. Not after she died… Losing someone, sometimes it's too much. He felt it too much. He couldn't shut out the dark."

She blew on the dandelion, scattering the white particles all over Phillips' shirt.

"Thanks," he said, brushing them off. "You have a thing for coating me with random substances you want to tell me about?"

Miranda laid back instead of answering, grass brushing her ears, and watched the clouds. "I don't know what's going to happen to me. I never really thought beyond taking care of him. Never made any plans." She thought. "Never figured there was any point making them."

Phillips took a moment to respond. "That part is a good thing though. Right?"

Miranda didn't answer. Was it?

Phillips hauled himself up on his knees and reached over her. He touched the headstone. "Nice to meet you, Anna-Marie," he said.

Miranda smiled up at him, without meaning to. This was a boy who lent himself to wondering about. Especially when he jolted up, a sudden uneasiness overtaking his whole body – she wondered why.

He gave her a stricken look. "I don't think you should go home…" he hesitated. "You shouldn't be alone. Come to my house? You can meet my mom."

She agreed, despite the fact he was wrong. She *was* alone. But she'd be that way for the rest of her life. There was no reason to rush home and embrace it.

Phillips heard the words the moment after he touched her mother's headstone, the moment he looked down and found her smiling at him with the first genuine approval he'd seen cross her face. One voice, low and right in his ear, glass clear: *Curse-bearer. Curse-bearer, she is a curse-born child.*

He couldn't figure out how to tell her.

So, he didn't. Not yet, at least. He angled the car up the driveway toward the white two-story house that had originally belonged to his "gifted" grandmother. It was the kind of house that should feel comfortable to anybody – the sort of place pictured in Webster's next to the word home. Maybe that was why he felt nothing when he saw it. The normal white and normal wood and normal shape were too normal to be connected to him.

"Like something straight out of house and beach garden, huh? My mom should be cool, but if she's not, I'll just drop my stuff, and then we'll get you home," Phillips said, aware he was rambling. Now that he was about to see his mom again, he worried he'd underestimated how ticked she'd be about the whole 'stealing her car and leaving her at the airport' thing. "OK?"

Miranda straightened. "Oh, frak, it's after nine. I missed curtain."

He turned off the car. Where did the fake-curse frak come from? He couldn't remember. He'd have to look it up later. "They'll cancel, won't they?"

Her shoulders slumped. "Right. They already did. I forgot. Everyone's left town. No show to go on. But Sidekick will need food at some point soon."

Her disappointment about the cancellation was clear and he wished he'd kept his mouth shut. He had never seen *The*

Lost Colony and vaguely wondered what it was like: he pictured cartoon savages wampuming around a set, overdone Elizabethan stuff. He managed to keep these ideas quiet as they left the car, since the show was clearly important to her.

There was one interesting thing about the house besides its history. His mother. She swung back in the porch swing and then rose from her perch in a smooth motion. She waited at the top of the steps, arms crossed, as they dragged lead feet across the lawn.

"Phillips Rawling," she said. "I should kill you right now."

He ducked his head. "You probably should. This is Miranda."

Miranda directed a shy wave at his mom.

Whose arms did not uncross in welcome. "And she is?"

"Miranda Blackwood. You remember her."

"Of course," his mother said, nodding after she got a better look at Miranda. She stuck out her hand, but Miranda didn't take it. Unbothered, she took Miranda's arm and squeezed. "I'm Sara Rawling."

"I know. Small town," Miranda said.

"Please come in and pretend not to listen while I yell at my son."

Miranda blinked. She probably hadn't expected his mother to be funny.

"Sounds like fun," Miranda said.

"It will be," his mom said. She steered Miranda across the porch toward the door, leaving him behind.

"Don't worry, I'm here for my entertainment value," Phillips said.

His mom hung back to hold the door for him after Miranda went inside. She caught Phillips' arm, and said, "Why is she with you?"

He wished he knew. "Be nice to her. Please? I'm... helping her with something."

"I'll need more than that later. But for now, OK." His mother squeezed his arm, with affection rather than any intent to harm. "It's good to see you. How are you doing?"

"Quiet," he lied. Sure, there had only been the one voice so far, but where there was one whisper, more would follow. So much for brain disorders. He didn't understand what curse-bearer meant yet. He didn't want to.

But he'd have to puzzle it out anyway, and talking to his mom about how quiet it was wouldn't help there. "I bet Miranda's starving," he said. "I am."

One, two... His mother processed his meaning in less than the five seconds he'd guessed it would take. "Oh!" she said. "I'm the world's worst hostess." She dragged Phillips through the door with her. "Let me fix you guys something. Go clean up, wayward son. Leave us girls to it."

His mother's voice was far easier to read than most of the ones he heard in his head. He had no choice but to leave them "to it." He couldn't believe that with everything going on – a hundred and change missing people, most of the voices missing too, and Miranda's murdered father – he was nervous that "it" would involve baby pictures, embarrassing anecdotes, and cutesy nicknames being spilled. Moms were psychic *and* evil.

But relief beat his nerves about that into submission. He had a few more minutes to figure out how to tell Miranda about the curse-bearer thing. The thing he didn't understand yet.

An explosion of laughter shattered the silence behind him.

"That should drive him nuts," Sara said, grinning as she pulled a loaf of bread down from a shelf. "Turkey OK?"

Miranda nodded. "Perfect," she said.

The Rawling family kitchen wasn't small, but it was cozy. Evening light streamed in through a windowed back door and a picture window over the sink, further warming the honeyed tones everything was designed in.

Sara started removing items from the fridge. She asked, "How do you guys know each other?"

That didn't take long.

"We don't really. Phillips just–" *happened to come by so I shot him with an ancient gun* "–gave me a ride to the court-house."

Sara laid several slices of bread across the sparkling clean counter. "I take it he didn't tell you that he took the car with-out permission and left me abandoned at the Norfolk airport?"

Miranda shook her head, slowly.

"He has a way of leaving out these things. You said the courthouse. Did you guys go by the office?"

"You mean, did Phillips see his dad?"

Sara nodded, waiting for the answer.

"What's the deal with them?" Miranda asked.

"You saw them in action?" Sara slathered some Dijon mus-tard across a slice of bread. "They think they're polar opposites. Really, though, they're not so different. Neither of them likes doing what they're told."

Miranda accepted the sandwich from Sara. She took a bite, talked while chewing. Delicate graces weren't her forte. "Who does?" she countered.

Sara considered her and Miranda squirmed, feeling sized up.

"Is your dad one of the missing?" Sara asked the question quietly.

"No," Miranda said.

Sara had obviously been expecting a different answer. "Then why'd you go by there?"

The turkey sandwich congealed in Miranda's stomach. She'd have to say the words at some point. The first time might as well be to someone being nice to her.

"He's dead," she said. "My dad's dead. That's why we went to the courthouse. The chief wanted to tell me in person."

Sara was instantly at her side, rubbing a hand across her back. Miranda felt a stab of loss, sharp and mean in her chest. She put down the sandwich.

"Oh, honey," Sara said, her hand tracing a circle across Miranda's shoulders.

"I'm eighteen in a few months," Miranda said. She needed to lighten the moment, keep the tears away. Her dad had felt too much, and look what happened to him. She needed to stay strong. "The orphan card will get me a lot of sympathy at school. Hello, homework extensions."

Sara smoothed Miranda's hair back, and Miranda knew she wasn't fooled. Sara said, "You deserve better than sympathy."

Miranda didn't have anything to say to that. She picked up the sandwich.

Sara considered her for a long moment, traced another circle on her back. But then she left Miranda's side to finish making Phillips' turkey on wheat, apparently getting that Miranda wasn't comfortable talking about any of this yet.

"Phillips is special," Sara said, not looking up. "His dad knows that, but he doesn't understand it. Even though he grew up with a mother who was also... special. It's why he lived away all those years. We met out in New Mexico. I dragged him back here because he missed it too much, even if he wouldn't admit it. He doesn't know what to make of things that aren't easily explained. That you just have to take them for what they are, sometimes. He doesn't understand what it's like for Phillips. He loves him, but he doesn't understand."

Miranda chewed the chalky bread, taking in what she'd said. "He worries about him, right? That counts for something," she said.

Sara watched her. "It's hard not to worry about Phillips."

"Special how?" Miranda asked.

Phillips' footsteps clopped on the stairs, coming down fast. Sara raised her voice, "Just let me get those pictures. He's dressed like a little cowboy. So cute."

Miranda laughed, despite the tightness in her chest, waiting for Phillips' mock protest. But her laugh faded as she realised why this felt so strange.

This must be what normal families were like.

7

Marked

Phillips slid into the sedan's passenger seat, his mom taking over the driving duties. He was happy to have a few more minutes away from Miranda – not that he wanted to leave her, but it was hard to think with her around. Deciding what to do next was proving difficult enough.

Convincing Miranda to spend the night at his house hadn't been easy, but his mom wasn't taking no for an answer. First Phillips had proposed that he run over to get Sidekick and pack her a few things. Miranda's eyes had gone wide in horror at the prospect of him rummaging through her stuff, and she said she'd just go on her own. His mom stepped in and suggested it'd be better if Miranda stayed put, instead of pushing herself to go home so soon. She settled Miranda into the guest room with an old robe and a bunch of bath products. Then she seized the opportunity to take Phillips along with her on the errand.

At least Miranda's house wasn't that far a drive. Still, Phillips was shocked that his mom was able to contain her curiosity until they reached the end of their cul-de-sac. Her first question came along with the turn onto the highway, one of the main drags that more or less ran the length of the island.

"So, now you're going to tell me what's going on?" She rummaged a pack of cigarettes from her purse and tapped it on the top of the steering wheel. She glanced over and caught Phillips' frown.

"You kept smoking?"

"No," she said, sighing, "this would be my first one since we dropped you off in Jackson." With that, she rolled down the window and chucked the white and red package out.

It wasn't an environmentally sound disposal method, but it was better than her smoking. Besides, no one would ticket the police chief's wife for littering. "I hope a wild animal doesn't eat those," he said.

"It won't – they're disgusting." She reached over to brush his shoulder. "It's good to have you home, no matter what the circumstances."

The circumstances. No matter how hard he tried he couldn't get the missing people and Miranda's dad's murder to fit together.

"Phillips," his mom prompted, "it's not optional. You have to tell me what's going on. Why the sudden interest in Miranda Blackwood?"

"You have a problem with her? You seemed to like her."

"She's delightful, but that doesn't explain why you felt the need to steal my car to go see her. Or why you brought her home with you." She kept going before he could cut in. "Bringing her was absolutely the right thing. But I want to know what the deal is. It's really quiet in there?"

She meant in his head.

"I wouldn't go that far. But no voices, if that's what you mean…"

"Phillips."

"OK, one voice. I heard one voice – we stopped at the cemetery and we were at Miranda's mom's headstone and…"

"And?"

"And there was this one voice and it said she was the curse-bearer or something."

The one eye he could see of hers widened. "You didn't tell her?"

"Not yet."

"Good. That's the last thing that poor girl needs right now." She drummed her fingers on the wheel. "Where do you think the missing people are? You think it has something to do with the Blackwoods, don't you?"

He shook his head. "No, not exactly. That's what I need to explain to her. I feel – I can't explain it. She's in danger. Her dad's murder seals it." And that weird gun. He'd bring that home too.

"He was *murdered*? Here?"

"I know." Tourist drownings and drunken accidents, sure. Murder? Not unheard of, but rare, and almost always due to family crap gone wrong.

"But where are all the people? Our neighbors are missing. Half my rook club is missing."

The question sent a chill deep into his bones. Out the car window a few lights were visible through the trees along the roadside. He'd forgotten how dark the interior got at night, away from the town's bright center. The branches were like fingers, reaching into the sky.

"They're gone, just like the voices," he said.

She slowed at the stop sign, signaling to turn onto Miranda's street. "They had to go somewhere. People don't vanish, not all at one time. Not unless they're cult members – and my rook club is not full of cult members. People don't vanish," she said, again. "They turn up dead or move elsewhere and start over. None of us believe the original colonists went away forever in a blink. And this isn't hundreds of years ago. People have cell phones with GPS – nice work turning yours off, by the way. I should lock you in a–"

Phillips interrupted before she could go further down that path. "What if they did?"

"Did what?"

"Went away forever in a blink." *And what if the spirits had gone too?*

His mother's expression told him she longed for the cigarettes that had flown out the window. He didn't blame her.

No matter how welcome Sara and Phillips had attempted to make Miranda, she became uncomfortable the second they left.

It wasn't the Rawlings' house. Like the kitchen, the rest of it had proved cozy, full of worn-in things and warm-glow lamps. Miranda stood in the decent-sized guest room Sara had shown her to, taking in walls covered by shelves full of books with cracked spines, and colorful pieces of art that hadn't come with the frames. She tried hard not to think, and harder still not to feel, but being alone was wearing down her defenses.

If she stayed in here – thinking, feeling – then she'd break. She needed to *do* something.

An idea hit her. Well, not so much an idea as a fact: Phillips' room was somewhere on this floor, and there was no one else in the house but her.

Miranda had always believed she and Sydney Bristow would hit it right off. Spying, it was.

So what if Phillips hadn't lived here for years? He was a mystery to her. At the courthouse when he'd told her she could trust him, she'd believed him without understanding why. She'd stepped between him and his dad because of it. Had she been right to believe?

Miranda padded out into the hall. The first room she went into housed a nice sewing machine, scraps of fabric surrounding the workstation. A patchwork quilt that appeared to be made entirely of old Bruce Springsteen T-shirts lay folded on the floor.

Sara must be a crafty type. Like Miranda's mom had been. Part of her wanted to pretend it *was* her mom who worked at this sewing machine, wanted to pretend that this was the life her dad and her mom and she had together.

But it wasn't. None of this coziness belonged to her. She nearly stopped exploring, then.

Instead she left the sewing room and hurried down the hall. The door at the end of it called out to her, mainly because of the Jolly Roger emblazoned across the center. The skull-and-crossbones sported a tacked on set of Groucho

Marx glasses. Taking a breath, listening for any noises, reassuring herself they couldn't come back this soon, she turned the knob and entered.

Jackpot.

The room even smelled like Phillips. A peppery clean scent. Wait – since when did she know what Phillips *smelled* like? She refocused on the task before her, fighting off a blush.

Phillips' room was shockingly messy for a room that hadn't been lived in for three years. CD cases, books, and laundry were strewn across the space. A big duffel bag lay across the unmade bed, a vintage Ramones poster hanging over it. She picked her way around the mess and peered into the bag's open top.

An iPod rested inside, earbuds still connected. There were also a couple of slim paperbacks and a bunch of clothes. That was it.

She snared the iPod – it would give her something to listen to in the bath. She should have time to sneak back in here and put it away. Besides, Miranda's mom had taught her that while eyes were important, music was the real window to someone's soul. Phillips had heard voices talk about her. She deserved some intel of her own.

Miranda hurried back to the guest room, crossing into the bathroom and starting the tap. She changed into the robe, dumped in the bath salts, and leaned against the sink to wait for the tub to fill.

She thumbed through the music, putting in the earbuds. There were a lot of artists she'd never heard of, but several that she liked. The Black Keys, Neko Case, the Dead Weather.

She sorted by favorites and turned up a playlist called North Carolina Stuff – the Rosebuds, the Bowerbirds, Ryan Adams. Maybe listening to it had been like a connection to home for him.

No Blondie, but she approved of the bands she knew. She hit shuffle mode and play and learned something else about Phillips. He kept the volume cranked way too loud. Jumping at the blare, she dropped the iPod on the vanity. Retrieving it, she looked up into the mirror, expecting to see nothing of note. Just her own tired face. Frazzled hair. Dark circles. Et cetera.

The strawberry-colored snake crawled along the top of her cheek toward her temple. Unmistakable. A birthmark, but not hers. Her father's.

No one heard Miranda's scream.

8

Dead Man

Phillips shimmied inside carrying a plastic clothes basket filled with Miranda's things, while his mom held the door for him. The house was dark and quiet. Had Miranda gone to bed already? It was getting late, and she must be exhausted. A twinge of disappointment spiked through him. He dismissed it.

You're just helping her. You don't need to say goodnight to her.

But his mother must have read his mind – she was way too good at that – and she clucked, closing the door. "We have to take her things up regardless, just be quiet."

The thought of seeing Miranda asleep made Phillips uneasy in a different way, but he followed his mom to the staircase. No more voices yet, but they could return at any moment. The sound of running water met them halfway up the steps. At the top, his mom looked over and said, "You wait out here."

"What? Oh." Phillips stood in the hallway outside the guest room, balancing the basket. Waiting.

He heard his mother say, "Oh, honey." The water turned off and an awful gasping keening sound like death rose up in its place. *Miranda.*

He dropped the basket, rushing through the guest room to the bathroom. The water surged at the lip of the tub, sloshing onto the floor. Not full enough to completely overflow, so *this* hadn't been going on that long.

This was Miranda in tears. He took one look at Miranda in a fuzzy blue robe big enough to swallow her, rocking back and forth on the floor, heaving like waves in the ocean, while his mother ineffectually patted her back and tried to lift her face, and he knew.

This was heartbreak. Miranda, heartbroken right in front of him.

He went down on his knees in front of her and joined his mother's tentative chorus of coos with words. "Miranda? We're here, what happened?" His mom shot him a confused expression, and he clarified, "Is this about your dad or... did something else happen?"

His mom mouthed "oh," understanding, and getting more worried. She stood. "Phillips, you stay with her. I'll be right back. I'm going to get a glass of water and call your father to make sure nothing has... changed."

Phillips put his hand on Miranda's shoulder and tried her name again, "Miranda? What is it? You can trust me."

But if she heard a word he said she gave no sign of it.

He shifted his hand and his fingers tangled in the cord of his earbuds. "Are those mine?" he asked. "Did you go in my room?"

She rocked for another moment, then stopped and tipped her face up at him. Her green eyes were wide and bloodshot. In the years he'd been away, Miranda had become, well, beautiful.

"Are you mad?" she said, through ragged breaths. "I just borrowed them."

He needed to keep her talking. "Did you find anything interesting in my room?"

She scowled.

Definitely beautiful.

She said, "Of course not. I was looking for some music. To listen to in the bath…"

"And my taste in music made you completely wig out?"

He thought he'd messed up and she was going to start howling again as a flash of pain crossed her features. She put her hand up to smooth the hair back off her cheek, and he did it for her.

"So, I get most of them," he said, "*Battlestar Galactica*, those Whedon shows, *Supernatural*, but… why do you own season one of *The Vampire Diaries*?"

She blinked, but he couldn't tell if it had worked until she said, "You snooped in my room?"

He had her.

"I had to help pack your stuff." He wrinkled his nose. "You have a thing for brooding vampire brothers?"

"You've seen it?"

Keep her talking. He shrugged. "Study lounge has a TV. Doppelgangers are hot. I'm not proud."

She sniffed. "The town reminds me of this one. Repressed

and… full of secrets. Everybody in everybody else's business."
Her eyes widened. She was still scared. "Wait, where's Sidekick?"

"He's in the car – I'll go get him."

But Phillips sat down across from her, and they stayed that
way, silently, until he heard his mom's footsteps start up the
stairs. She'd be back any second. "What happened?" he asked.

Miranda blinked at him again, hesitating, and he saw the
exact moment when she made the decision to tell him.

"This," she said. She pointed to the top of her cheek.

It wasn't that Phillips had memorised Miranda's face or
anything like that, but he knew in an instant the birthmark
didn't belong. *And* that it was the snake he yelled at her
about all those years ago. The flurry of voices had been so
intense he didn't really remember what they'd said and barely
what he'd repeated. The main reason he left school was
because he couldn't stand the idea of listening to the jerks
there taunt her with ammunition *he* had provided.

"Where did that come from?" he asked.

"I think it's my dad's. I need to see the body."

His mom called out, "Here's the water coming right up."

Phillips considered the options. "Pretend you were sad
about your dad and go to bed. I'll come get you later."

"To go where?"

"To see the body." He reached out as his mom crossed the
threshold, and plucked the glass of water from her hand.
"Now drink this," he said, holding it to Miranda's lips to
make sure she did.

• • • •

Miranda was convinced she'd never be able to get to sleep, not while she expected Phillips to come in and wake her. Visions of drooling on her pillow danced in her head. She didn't know if she snored or talked in her sleep or anything else embarrassing. No one had ever told her, but who would have? Her dad? Sidekick?

She patted the dog's head where he lay sprawled next to her on top of the covers. Sara was nice enough to let him sleep with her, even though they didn't have any pets that lived in the house. Miranda rubbed Kicks' belly, glad to have him with her while she tried not to obsess over the *thing* on her skin…

When Phillips shook her shoulder an hour later, Miranda could tell by the reluctance on his face he'd been trying to wake her for a while. "We can do this tomorrow," he said, the whisper apologetic, "if you need the sleep more. I just figured you'd want some privacy. If we go now no one else will be there."

Miranda rubbed her eyes and yawned, which sent Phillips to his feet and scrambling a few steps back.

Oh-kay, so I do look scary when I wake up.

She matched his whisper. "You're right. I don't want anyone else there. But…" She climbed out of the bed, already dressed in a T-shirt and jeans. "This means we're breaking in?"

"Don't worry about it," Phillips said. "I've got experience."

The more she learned about Phillips, the more of a mystery he became. "Why'd you start doing all that crime stuff?"

"Later. We'll wake up mom," he said. "We'd better go, sleeptalker."

Miranda thanked the low light in the room for concealing the way her cheeks flamed traitorously. *Don't ask what you said, don't ask what you said...* "What'd I say?"

"Later," he said.

She slipped on her sneakers. "What about Sidekick?"

Whispering with Phillips like this in the middle of the night was kind of fun, like a secret mission or a conspiracy. Then she remembered why they were doing it, chasing the fun away.

Phillips must have seen the change. "He'll be quiet if he stays here?"

She leaned in to pat his head. "Stay," she told him, half-wishing she could crawl back into bed beside him and forget about doing this.

She didn't expect it when Phillips reached over and touched her cheek. "It'll be OK," he said.

"Good lie."

He motioned for her to tiptoe out of the room in front of him, and once they were both through he pulled the door closed. He took the lead on the steps, signaling her to follow his path exactly. Not a creak sounded on their way down. And then came the discovery that he'd moved his mom's car already, so the noise of it starting would be a distant cough from the house. Once they were settled in and heading downtown, a song she'd never heard playing from a custom mix CD in the stereo, she said, "You're good at this, 007. Why?"

He didn't answer, just tapped his fingers along to the song. The lyrics were something about a guy being handcuffed to a fence in Mississippi. Finally, he said, "I wanted to get sent away."

"Oh. Why?"

"Because I couldn't stand it here."

She got it. "Repressed town. Everybody in everybody else's business."

He said, "In that show the whole town isn't the problem – it's the supernaturals killing people and screwing things up."

They were passing a spot where the Sound became visible, the water sparkling in the moonlight. "You don't think the townspeople would be nosy without vampires?" *Stop talking.* "And I kind of envy the vampires. A secret life where you can tell everyone exactly what you think of them and then make them forget? Not caring what people think because you never have to deal with them unless you want to? It appeals."

"But then you miss everything," he said, though he didn't sound like he believed it. "You miss getting to know who the people around you are. A lonely way to live." That he sounded like he believed.

"Well, I don't want to drink anybody's blood," she said. "Hey, why do you know so much random stuff like matchlocks and music and *The*, ahem, *Vampire Diaries*?" *I never met anyone like you.*

He didn't answer for a long moment, pulling the sedan up to the curb so the weepy hanging branches of a big tree offered cover. Not that there was anyone else on the street to see them. He turned off the car, and looked over at her.

"I had too much I didn't want in my head. I thought maybe if I…"

"Filled it with other stuff it would crowd out the bad," Miranda supplied. It made sense. "Did it work?"

He flashed a smile. She pretended not to notice the way it made her feel fluttery, like a silly girl. This was probably how Blue Doe felt all the time, light and airy, like her head was a bubble and might float away.

"I don't know yet," he said. "Let's go."

"Where?"

"Next street over."

He hopped out, walking around behind the car to open her door before she could, as she calculated where he meant. She planted her feet on the pavement. "But that's the funeral home. I can't afford a funeral. And who would come?"

"I'd come, but no, they won't have one unless you want it. This isn't New York – we don't have a real morgue here, just the funeral home our county medical examiner runs. They'll be storing the... your dad's body in the cold room here until they can get it schlepped off to one of the universities for the autopsy."

"How do you know this?"

"Police chief's son, remember?"

That hardly explained it, but she nodded. "Let's go then," but her stomach hardened into a small, heavy stone. The funeral home. She stayed quiet while they walked there, and he didn't push her to talk, so quiet must have been required anyway. The night lacked the humidity of the day, the streets empty like so many people's lives on the island were right now.

The funeral home's front porch came into view, the place the men and the smokers hung out during the big town social events that occurred whenever someone died. Funeral visitations were like church – a chance to see and be seen, and without all the pressure to be godly that came along with sermons. A flood of images rushed over Miranda from her mother's funeral, the people who'd shown up with whispers and fake sympathy for her and her father. People who'd done nothing but gossip for years about why that nice Anna-Marie Johnson – even if she *was* an out-of-towner, with no family of her own to speak of – had to go and marry a Blackwood. And how her girl, that Miranda, she wasn't ever going to amount to anything now.

"Miranda?" Phillips whispered, turning to see why she'd stopped. "You OK?"

Miranda drew in a shaky breath, and caught up with him. "How do we get in?"

"Around back," he said, frowning at her in concern.

"I'm fine," she said.

He led them to the rear entrance without another word, but when they stopped, she could see the wrinkles of that frown still on his forehead. They vanished as he took out a long skinny piece of metal. "Where do you get something like that?" she asked.

"This?" He raised his eyebrows. "eBay."

Miranda trusted him, she did, but… "What if someone's here? Maybe I should just wait until tomorrow."

He stepped back, off the sidewalk into the parking lot so the whole back of the funeral home was visible. She went along, curious. He pointed to the upstairs. "When Marlon is here, the TV in that room is always on. See how dark it is?"

She nodded, and he hesitated. "What else?" she prodded.

"Marlon's wife is one of the missing. There's no one in the

funeral home for embalming or viewing, just your dad. I checked the obits for the last week online. So he's at their house. Not here."

"OK," she said.

"But we don't have to do this." He watched her. "Not if you don't want to."

If she balked at this point, she'd have to explain the reason – that she was afraid. She'd rather get this over with than that. She touched her cheek. "No, I need to see him."

Phillips had the door open within a minute, saying simply, "Old lock."

He pulled a flashlight out of his pocket and shined it up the hallway in front of them. Powder blue walls, worn navy carpet, framed seascapes lining the walls. Another wave of memories threatened to overwhelm Miranda as she walked inside and smelled that too-clean smell, the smell of terrible things being covered up, a smell meant to pretend this was somewhere besides the house where death lived. Somewhere besides a place that would ruin your life.

She drew in another shaky breath, glad that Phillips couldn't see her in the dark.

They made their way up the hall and through a small kitchenette where unfortunate scuttling met them, then Phillips "unlocked" another door. They passed into a hallway, the beam from the flashlight tunneling through absolute darkness, and she imagined they were traveling to the underworld. With each step, the floor creaked. Miranda was comforted by the fact that Phillips didn't know this place well enough to avoid the noisy ones.

At the end of the dark hall, he opened a heavier door and let her go in first. He joined her and flipped on a light. The suddenly bright room was cold and reeked of formaldehyde.

The flat black sheen of a body bag dominated the center of a metal table. Miranda approached it like she was levitating, unable to feel her feet moving, but getting closer just the same.

"It's freezing down here," she said.

"Actually, it's 39.2 degrees. Not freezing."

She stopped at the side of the table. "Shouldn't it be freezing?"

"Freezing would be ideal, but this is a funeral home, not *CSI*. The cold still majorly slows decomp." Phillips swung around the table's other side and checked the surfaces nearby for something, then held up a thin file folder and flipped through it.

Miranda stared at the black plastic, preparing herself for what was inside. *Dad.*

Phillips made a noise of interest, and said, "You want to know what the preliminary ME report says?"

She managed to look away from the shape of her father's body beneath that plastic and at Phillips. The kindness in his face startled her. "What does it say?" she choked out.

"It says that it appears…" He paused, took a look at her and went on. "That all the visually observable bones in your father's body were broken at the time of death, but that he had no outward signs of struggle or harm. No bruising or cuts. And his blood alcohol level was nearly .18."

"That's a baseline." She didn't understand the broken bones. How was that possible?

"The bones must be why Dad said they couldn't determine cause of death."

Miranda concentrated on breathing. Her attention settled on the body bag.

"Do you want me to look for you?" Phillips asked. "I can describe him."

"No."

Phillips held out a small pot of something. "You should at least put some of this under your nose…"

Miranda reached forward and opened the bag with fingers that fumbled the zipper. She stopped when the metal teeth hung up at his waist and pulled back the sides to reveal his head. She forgot to try to breathe. The air left her body.

Her father looked better dead than he had alive. The broken bones mentioned in the report weren't visible, not even in his face, which struck her as odd given the description. His eyes were closed, a mercy she thanked Marlon James for, and so all she had to do was lean over and check.

She put her hand up to her mouth, even though she saw what she expected to. The snake on her face? Definitely her father's. The skin of his upper cheek gleamed at her, clear as polished glass, as smooth stone, as bleached bone.

Her feet thumped the floor as she ran, back through the door and into the hall, her body hitting the walls as she kept running, blood roaring in her ears, getting out of there, getting away from the smell and the body and the house where death lived. The warm night air hit her skin like an electric shock.

You *have* *nowhere* *to* *run*, she thought, and stopped. *Nowhere to go.*

9

Curses

Phillips wanted to go after her, but first he had to put back the file and seal up the body bag. Marlon James might not be there, but he wasn't a sloppy man. He'd notice if things in his cold room were disturbed, and given how freaked everyone was about the disappearances even the most harmless change risked being misinterpreted.

He reached over Mr Blackwood's chest to close the bag, holding his breath against what was surely a god-awful smell. The zipper fought him, and he had to release his breath while he worked it. He waited for the stench to invade.

But there wasn't any, only the sickly smell of formaldehyde's chemical perfume. That was strange. So was how pale and perfect the body looked, despite all those supposed-to-be broken bones and the lack of embalming fluid to keep the skin from bloating and puffing and discoloring. Phillips removed a handkerchief from his pocket – one of his dad's, a handy tool for breaking and entering – and pressed his hand across the dead man's cheek.

Phillips had never touched a dead body before; had only ever been in the room with three, two of them relatives. He would rather have done just about anything else.

The cheekbone was *not* broken. He checked the right collarbone next.

It was perfectly straight and intact. Huh.

He considered doing a more thorough exam, but he'd lingered too long already and the thought of it made him shiver. Or maybe the room's chilled air did. He took the zipper and began to reseal the body bag, pausing when he got to the neck. "You should have been better for her," he told Mr Blackwood's body, and finished the job.

He tossed the white cloth into a step trashcan with a biohazard symbol on top and turned out the lights. He hoped Miranda hadn't gone far.

Luck was with him, for once. She sat next to the back door, staring out at the parking lot. *She's not crying, that's good*. He slid down the wall to join her, and, without thinking, laid his hand on top of hers, where it rested on her thigh. She didn't move, so he left it there.

"Miranda, I'm sorry."

"What do you have to be sorry about?" Before he could answer, she said, "Nothing. You've been nothing but nice to me. It's not your fault I'm cursed."

Curse-bearer, curse-born child. "You're *not* cursed."

Miranda lifted her free hand and brushed her hair back to reveal the angry snake crawling up her cheek. "Then what's this? What else makes a birthmark leap bodies?"

"I don't know, but we'll figure it out. I'm sorry about...

bringing you here. I didn't even think of your mom. Her funeral was here, wasn't it?"

"That was a long time ago." Her words slipped out softly. "That's not even the worst part."

He raised his eyebrows, drawing a circle on the back of her hand with his thumb. "I'm almost afraid to ask."

She turned to face him. She was so close he could see the green of her eyes even in the dark. "I was supposed to take care of him," she said.

"You keep saying that, but it's not true."

"Yes, it is. My mom wanted me to – it was like I could feel her over my shoulder in there, disapproving. I was the one left to look out for him. And I... I didn't. Maybe I deserve this."

"Look. He was supposed to take care of you. And–" he beat her protest "–your mother wasn't in there."

Her eyelashes fluttered shadows on her pale cheeks. "How do you know?"

Phillips closed his eyes for a moment, finding it hard to believe he was about to talk about this with someone besides his mom.

"I would have heard her. There aren't *any* spirits on Roanoke Island that I can hear right now. Another weird thing. Because usually, I can't *not* hear spirits here. Usually, they're everywhere, saying everything. All the time."

He watched her reaction, his doubt telling him she'd think he was crazy.

"The voices you hear – they're the voices of dead people?" She gave him a suspicious look. "How did you know about the funeral home stuff? About Marlon's TV?"

"You think that was…" He squinted at her. "Not a bad guess. But no, the spirits aren't helpful at crime that I can tell. Don't you remember the Bela prank?"

She shook her head, curious instead of looking so lost, which made him feel better. He released her hand to put his over his heart as if she'd mortally wounded him. "You weren't a fan? Not even a little bit?"

"Of what?" A slight smile edged her lips up on one side.

"My masterpieces – the things that got me sent away? During my brief Bauhaus-wannabe goth phase at thirteen I broke in here and then lettered the sign with the viewing times for Bela Lugosi."

"You are the weirdest person I've ever met."

He made a little bow. "Finally, you're beginning to appreciate my genius."

She laughed, but then the weight sank down on her again. Her shoulders actually fell with it. He was done with that.

"No," he said.

"What?"

He picked up a stray gravel off the sidewalk and tossed it toward the parking lot. "This isn't you, this defeatist 'oh, I'm so cursed' stuff."

"How would you know?"

He didn't care if he'd gone too far. He was right. "I just know. The girl I met in eighth grade was stronger than this. She wouldn't let some birthmark break her."

"I'm not broken…" But she let it trail off. She got up, and he worried she might run away again… until her hands balled into fists.

"You're right," she said. "I'm being one of those frakking girls in distress. Frak."

He got up, loving her *Battlestar Galactica* cursing. He'd looked up the reference while he was waiting to wake her. "What are you going to do?" he asked.

"I'm going to find out what happened to my dad. And get this stupid snake off my face. It's ruining my looks."

"No, it's not."

"What?" She grinned.

He almost took the last step toward her, but the sound of a siren in the distance stopped him. Time to go.

"We'd better get out of here."

"Does that mean you'll help me?" she asked.

"I already am," he said.

Back in his yard, Phillips held Miranda's hand as she stayed close at his side. The shadows thrown by the trees in the security light – thankfully not motion-activated, or he'd have had to climb it and take care of that – poked around them like the long fingers of invisible people. The house remained dark and quiet, and Phillips relaxed. He'd been concerned about leaving her dog behind. Even an obedient dog, happy to be somewhere soft and warm, was capable of whining and waking parents.

Miranda whispered, "Did we make it?"

They climbed the steps onto the porch, and he stopped in front of the door to look at her one last time before getting some sleep.

"We did." He smiled. "I never get caught."

She rolled her eyes. "You mean you always get caught."

"I was trying to back then."

She rolled them again.

He decided to press his luck. "Goodnight," he said, leaning forward–

The porch light flared to life, sending them both stumbling back like vampires at daybreak.

"Oh god," Miranda said, miserable.

"Don't worry, I'll take the blame," Phillips said.

"But I like your mom and now–"

"I'll handle it." Phillips put a hand on her arm, and opened the screen door. "It's not my mom. She doesn't do dramatic."

Her expression said which parent it was made little difference, but when he held the door open she walked through it.

His dad loomed in the front hallway next to the light switch, the night-black circles ringing his eyes giving Phillips a second's pause. But Miranda's head was tilted down in the universal posture of shame, her feet rooted to the floral carpet. Given what she told him earlier about having to look out for her dad, he bet she'd never had to deal with being in trouble.

Thanks for murdering the mood, Dad.

"Miranda, I need to speak with my son."

Miranda said, "It's my fault–"

"It's OK, Miranda," Phillips interrupted. "You don't have to take the blame. It was my idea. Go get some sleep."

She flew up the steps. He heard twin clicks as the guestroom door opened and then closed.

"Where were you?" his dad asked.

Phillips shrugged. "Out."

"Do we have to do this, son?" His tone was close to exasperation, the dark circles like a lost fight.

Phillips walked closer to his dad. They were the same height. That was new. Phillips asked, "Do you have to be such a drama king? You couldn't have waited five minutes?"

Without a word, his dad made his way to the darkened living room, where he sank into the couch. Phillips followed, and noted the bottle of whiskey and short – empty – glass on the table. His dad was drinking. That was also new.

Phillips eased into a chair opposite his dad. The only light was filtered through the curtains and came from the security pole outside. Phillips imagined this as a dim Turkish prison, with his father playing interrogator.

"Have the feds showed yet?" Phillips asked.

His dad's head came up. "A few hours ago. To assist, not to take over. Yet."

"It *is* a missing person's case."

"Is it? I don't know, Phillips." His dad sighed. "Listen, I know I haven't ever wanted to talk about this before, but–"

"I know about the birds and the bees, Dad. Also, about sex. I've been at boarding school in Kentucky, not a monastery."

"I don't care about that – not right now." His dad paused. "Except you don't hurt that girl any more than she's already been hurt."

He waited for a response, and Phillips nodded. "She needs my help."

"That's fine, but we need to talk about you – your gifts. I know my mother had them too. I tried like hell to pretend she didn't, but it wasn't hard to miss the stream of women who showed up at our back door so she could talk to their dead or help their daughters. I didn't want that for you."

The curtain behind his father had a sheen to it. Turkish prison with artful drapes.

"But you want it now?" Phillips asked.

"I want to find these people and get them home. This whole town – an emptiness like the one that's here, it will kill us all. It'll kill this island."

Phillips didn't have any love for the town. Or any hate for it, really. Except for the way they'd treated Miranda, and she was in this up to her temple.

"I can't hear anything right now, but I'll work on it tomorrow. I'm going to be helping Miranda–" Phillips held up a hand to cover his father's protest "–find some answers. Those answers are the same ones you need. I think."

"Do you have any idea what's going on here?"

"No clue. But I'm going to find out, because if I don't Miranda's the next to go. Or something bad will happen to her. I don't know what exactly, but something."

His dad leaned forward and poured a drink, downed it in one shot. He had on his cop face, thoughtful.

"But her old man didn't vanish, he died. He was killed. A mystery in itself, since he was a sad drunk. Harmless. But he didn't vanish."

Not harmless to Miranda. "I told you I don't know how, but it's connected. Get the autopsy done on him as fast as you can."

"The university can't do it until Monday."

"Use the feds, then. Convince them somehow. You need to know what killed him."

Phillips waited to see if his dad would believe him for once. Trust him. The drapes swayed as the air conditioning kicked in.

His dad nodded. "There's one more thing. Mom... your gram... when she died, she left a letter for you. I was supposed to give it to you. But I kept it."

He held something out to Phillips. A cream envelope, gram's stationery with her initials on the front. The envelope was wrinkled, like it had been worried over.

He didn't want to take it. His dad held it closer.

"Your mom doesn't know about this, but I guess now I'll have to tell her. I didn't want this for you, but I don't think it's up to me anymore."

Phillips didn't have a choice. He took it, halfway expecting a lightning strike. But the earth didn't move, the voices didn't clamor at his ears. His name was written across the back in his gram's small neat handwriting. He put the envelope in his pocket.

His dad said, "You'll let me know anything important?"

"Of course."

"Go get some sleep."

Phillips practically leapt to his feet. His father had never talked to him like this, like they were almost equals. Like he didn't blame Phillips for hearing spirits.

Then he ruined it. "Don't think I'm not going to tell your mother what you were doing out there. Don't hurt that girl, Phillips. I mean it. She's been through enough."

● ● ● ●

Miranda bolted back to the guest room, pressing the door quietly closed before Phillips busted her on his way upstairs. She'd known Phillips thought her family was connected to the disappearances, but hearing him tell his dad was different.

He really did want to help her. And he thought she was next. Where were the vanished people?

Miranda closed her eyes. She didn't want to go anywhere besides the one place she couldn't – off the island. Blackness waited inside her eyelids. The snake crawling toward her temple throbbed.

She was so tired.

Miranda pulled off her jeans and slid into bed next to Sidekick, blushing when she considered the porch. Phillips had been about to kiss her. And then the porch light, and his dad...

She groaned and pulled the covers over her head. How would she face Sara? Who had let her stay in this nice house, who offered her turkey sandwiches and bubble bath?

When she closed her eyes, her father's too-pale face swam before her. So instead she studied the ceiling, painted the pale blue of a spring sky. She remembered Phillips' reassurance that her mom wasn't watching, but the truth was: she wanted her watching.

Miranda rolled onto her side and closed her eyes, waiting until her father's face faded and left only darkness.

The Island

The waves heaved against the shore in muted attack. Sand refused to shift and trees held still and inland streams flowed slow, soft. The island listened for the crash and roar of the coming storm. Craved the sound, the fury.

The island did not care for its spirits being held quiet.

Spirits that clamored, desperate to speak, more desperate to be heard. The boy had finally come home after too many years away. But the devil's hands have hushed and smothered them. Only those preparing to cross the border speak, and only to each other. The living cannot hear those awaiting resurrection. The living never have.

The dead hear every twisted syllable.

The waves and the sand and the trees listened. The island listened, and waited.

He has fashioned his will into a reality intricate as blood and iron and words. Soon, he will unlock the passage.

Soon, the spirits will not be silent.

10

Biscuits and Roses

Despite the need to get moving and find a way out of the whole "being doomed" situation, Miranda lingered as long as she possibly could in the guest room the next morning.

She let Sidekick out the door, knowing someone would give him backyard access, and finally managed that bath. Pacing around the guest room afterward, she picked a random book out from the shelf in the corner and started reading. The book was titled *The Haunting of Hill House* and unsurprisingly involved an old house that was supposed to be full of angry ghosts. When the sense of dread in the book began to mix with the one already hovering around her like an aura, she tossed it aside and checked the clock.

10am.

Sigh. She straightened her T-shirt, and left the room.

She almost missed the single flower waiting on the floor out-side the bedroom door – a perfectly formed rose made of... duct tape. Intricate silver folds shot up in a spray of triangular points to form the bloom, tear-shaped leaves dropping from the thick stem.

Picking the unreal flower up, she twirled it, feeling a lot better about facing Sara's disapproval if Phillips wasn't going to be guy-like and ignore the night before's *almost*. That was what she'd feared, mainly because the only guys she knew were jerks (witness Bone).

She slipped the rose stem through a loop on her jeans. The motion reminded her of sliding a hammer into place on her tool-belt. Concern spiked through her for the people at the show – even His Royal Majesty and demon Caroline. And, of course, Polly. Missing Polly.

The smell of frying food tempted Miranda the rest of the way down the stairs and to the kitchen. Sara stood at the stove, transferring crisp slices of bacon onto a plate covered with a paper towel. Sidekick waited next to her, tail thudding against the cabinet, observing her every move with great hope. A heap of scrambled eggs waited on another plate.

Miranda hovered at the entry. "Should I set the table?"

Sara's head whipped toward her, startled, and Miranda couldn't stop a cringe as she waited to see whether she was in for cold distance or a heated talking-to.

Instead Sara gave her a non-angry mother smile. "Why doesn't my son ever make that offer? That'd be great." She waved her spatula, "Plates are right up there, silverware in that drawer."

Miranda took several plates and picked out some silver-ware. They came from matching sets. A novelty.

Sara craned her neck and yelled, "Phillips, breakfast!" No response, until she added, "Phillips – I know you can hear me. Oh, and Miranda is already down here."

Feet battered the steps in a fast drumbeat, and Phillips swung around the edge of the arch. Miranda finished the last place setting and slid into a chair. She held up the rose, giving him a nod, then placing it awkwardly on the table next to her plate. *I'm a moron.*

But the weirdest thing happened. Miranda could've sworn Phillips looked slightly embarrassed.

He moved in close enough to the counter to grab a piece of bacon, handing her half as he sat in the chair next to hers. *He gave me bacon.*

Sara joined them, setting the plates of food in the center of the table. She raised her eyebrows at the fake rose, but didn't ask about it. Snapping her fingers, she said, "Biscuits," before turning and attending to the oven.

Phillips lowered his voice so he spoke only to Miranda. "It's a steampunk rose – I didn't make it, bought it from another delinquent at school."

She had to say something. "It's beautiful. And, um, it'll last forever."

He smiled at her, and she wished with everything inside her that the snake would disappear and she could live in a normal world with this strange boy who – for some reason – had decided he liked her.

Miranda crunched her bacon, taking in the fluffy golden tops of the biscuits on the plate Sara carried to the table. They looked like someone who grew up around there made them. As Sara slid into her chair, Miranda reached over and took one.

"Where'd you learn to make actual biscuits?" Miranda asked.

Miranda fully expected to discover that New Mexico was a hotbed of biscuit activity and her impressions gathered from an inadequate education were wrong. When you'd never been anywhere, it was impossible to know what other places were *really* like.

Sara gave Phillips a look before answering, and Miranda wondered why the question had brought a strange stillness over the sunny kitchen. "The recipe is Phillips' grandmother's," she said. "She taught me before she passed away."

The Witch of Roanoke Island. Miranda was desperate to ask about her, given what Phillips had told her about the voices he heard and his conversation with his father.

"I never met her," Miranda said. She'd sometimes fantasised about the Witch of Roanoke Island becoming her defender, after her mom died. Giving the jerks at school boils if they taunted her, or giving her a magical potion that made her normal. Broke the curse. She reached up and touched her father's birthmark.

"She was a strong woman," Sara said, again watching Phillips. He didn't react except to keep chewing his eggs. "She couldn't stand the thought of someone living here who couldn't make her son and grandson the right kind of biscuits. The house has been in the family for generations, but it's always passed down to the daughters before. Biscuits are part of its legacy."

Miranda tried to remember if the chief had any sisters or brothers. "Why not this time?"

"She only had a son – there'd always been a girl child in the family line, as far back as anyone remembered. And they'd always lived well into their nineties, active right up to the end."

Phillips stopped eating, but he didn't interrupt.

"Technically," Sara said, "the house belongs to Phillips. His grandmother felt strongly it should be his. That this was the place he was meant to be. We don't really know why though. We only know the island's not good for him."

Phillips said, "Mom."

Miranda realised Sara was fishing. *She wants to know what the letter said.*

She went on, "He and his father are both tied to this place, in different ways. I don't think I can fully understand. I never had that. My roots moved when I did. My roots are my family."

Phillips' hands landed on the table on either side of his plate and he stood. "We really should get going." He cast a pleading glance at Miranda, added, "Unless you aren't finished with breakfast?"

Miranda's plate was still half full... but she was staving off awkward. "Sure, let's go." She grabbed a biscuit. "Thank you for breakfast." *And for the bits of info.* "Should we take Kicks? Is he trouble?"

Sidekick gazed at Sara as if she might drop a crumb or a piece of bacon on his head. She scratched behind his ear and he leaned into her fingers. Sara said, "You guys go on, do your investigation. We'll make do. But you be careful. Phillips, we'll talk later."

Miranda didn't realise until Phillips steered her through the front door with his hand on her back that he hadn't given any hint of where they were headed in such a hurry.

"Where are we going?" she asked. "Your dad's work?"

"Dr Whitson's place."

The name meant nothing to her. "Who?"

"Oh. You know, Dr Roswell."

Miranda stopped on the steps down to the yard. The day was cooler than the one before, a promise of fall wrapped in late summer colors, and a strong breeze wrapped around her. The breeze wasn't unusual – there was always a breeze, whirling in from the outer islands and the ocean, flying across the salt-free Sound. But this wind didn't come from the ocean. It had begun somewhere else and now danced around them, the whole island in its cooler embrace.

Of course, it comes from the ocean. Where else would it come from?

An image flickered in her mind of that enormous black ship on the horizon, moving fast toward the island, sails filled with uncanny billowing speed on a windless day.

She chose her next words carefully. "I need help, not a kook."

"He was my shrink." Phillips took her hand and tugged, and she knew she'd go anywhere he suggested. "He knows more about the island's history than anyone around and we're *in* kooksville here. We need a kook's perspective."

Miranda had no feelings about Roswell one way or the other, another colorful local character she mostly avoided. But he was Bone's dad.

"Do you mind if we swing by and pick up my car?" Miranda said. "I miss her."

Phillips' eyebrows rose. "Sure."

Her hand warmed in his as they walked to the car. What did the day have in store? What would wreck the fragile connection between them?

Sure as the ghosts in Hill House, something was coming. The breeze told her that.

Pineapple had done Miranda the favor of starting. Phillips had frowned at the word scrawled on the yellow car's side, suggesting they hit a car wash on the way, but she told him not to worry about it. *Part of the price of being me*, she told him, and he let it go. Being behind the wheel made her feel more in control of their destination and what they'd find there.

"Why does he live all the way out in Wanchese? Do you know?" Miranda asked, cutting Phillips a look.

Phillips hadn't been watching the scenery. He leaned against the door, angled in toward her. The weight of his gaze on her profile made it difficult not to blush. She was grateful the snake was on the other side of her face, hidden for the moment.

"I never asked him. It's probably cheaper out here?" Phillips reached a hand over to brush a hair off her cheek and Miranda hiccuped Pineapple's wheel. He laughed. "Am I making you nervous?"

The car windows were down to make up for the lack of a/c. The day was a joke of perfect. The mystery breeze, the bright blue sky, the too-green trees and grass. Why had she remembered the black ship?

"It's not just you," she said, truthfully.

"Good," he said, then, "Not good that you're nervous, but good that I'm not why. Roswell's OK, I swear."

"If you vouch." She considered warning him about Bone, but that would ruin the main point of driving Pineapple. She didn't expect to get anything useful out of Mr Crackpot Theories, so the best she could hope was to find out if her status on the island would spook Phillips now that he was back.

Now that he's back and you want him to be yours.

Her fingers tightened on the wheel. It was as if a spirit or a demon had invaded her mind and body.

"Did you know your grandmother that well, Mr Home-owner?" Why was she prodding him? Because she wanted him to tell *her* about the letter – the letter she shouldn't even know about. She couldn't explain it, even to herself.

He slipped around a fraction in the passenger seat, looking out at the scenery. "Not that much. My dad always made sure we had limited time together. He didn't want her teaching me stuff."

Leave it alone. "Did you want her to… teach you stuff?"

Phillips exhaled. "No, I only wanted it to go away. To go somewhere so I could be normal."

"That would be nice," Miranda said.

"That's not what I–" Phillips tapped his fingers against the door, a repetitive pattern. "You are normal."

Leave it alone. "Just what every girl wants to hear."

Miranda wished the silence that followed didn't strike her as familiar, but it did. *You have to know how easy he is to push away.*

Wanchese was on the far side of the island, which still wasn't that long a drive. May as well have been a world away. Far from the tourist haven of Manteo, Wanchese possessed a wilder feel, despite having a couple of bed and breakfasts and boat rental places, and a harbor packed with commercial fishing vessels. This wasn't where the big money was – it was where the fishing village was.

There was no picture-prettified downtown to echo Manteo's, not even a Main Street. Most of its locals hoped to remain lost to the tourist flood by keeping a firm hold on this tip of the island. This was the perfect place to live if you didn't want to be bothered.

"Turn here," Phillips prompted. He pointed to a road ahead that shot through trees.

A short way into the woods, they came to a small rise with a nice cottage on top. The house must have been originally intended for a timeshare, by the looks of it. The sandy paint had faded over time, though, and now the place looked more like a home than a getaway. Bone's truck occupied the driveway.

She put Pineapple in park and Phillips climbed out of the car. He poked his head back in after a moment. "You coming?" he asked.

"Against my better judgment," she muttered. Pineapple's motor died with a rattle of agreement.

11

Crackpot Theories

Miranda examined the cottage from the yard. This was definitely a house designed as a vacation home. The bedrooms would be farther apart than normal, a large common room and kitchen separating the parents' room from the children's. A deck at the back stretched into the woods, the edge of the railing just visible.

Phillips turned from the front door. "Miranda?"

So he knew she was stalling. *Why am I trying to scare him off?* She didn't have an answer. And she'd have sworn the snake crawling up her cheek heated under his questioning look. Burning, glowing, flashing "not normal". Wait until Bone saw her.

Miranda tromped up the steps to join Phillips, the house too simple to justify further lingering to study it. The door swung open as she reached his side.

Bone appeared in the doorway, wearing a light blue Tarheels T-shirt. His cheeks hollowed even more than usual as he exhaled in surprise, mouth dropping open into a black hole.

She suddenly regretted her plan. What if Phillips *did* get spooked? Miranda angled her head so her hair hid the mark on her face.

"If you're here to try to get me in trouble, I didn't have anything to do with your car," Bone said. "So forget it."

Phillips' eyebrows shot up – *he practically talks with those things* – as he gave her a questioning look. He said, "Did he–"

"Forgotten," Miranda said, not to Phillips but to Bone. "I know it was you, but we're here to see your dad." Bone's mouth opened to say something, and she sighed. "Not about you, Bone. About something else."

She looked over and discovered Phillips hadn't taken his eyes off her yet. His eyebrows finally dropped, and he said, "You must be the Boner."

"Just Bone," Bone gritted.

Miranda bit back a smile. "Where's your dad?"

"In the library," Bone said, suspicious.

Phillips said, "You could wash the car while we're talking to him."

Bone snorted, stepping out onto the porch. "I didn't have anything to do with it. I already told you."

Was Miranda imagining it or was Bone actually nervous? They were far out in the woods, but, come on, Phillips wasn't a bruiser, and neither was she. And his dad was home.

She let her own eyebrows shoot up in an imitation of Phillips. "Are you scared?"

Bone straightened. "Scared that bad luck just showed up at my doorstep." *This* was the Bone she knew and loathed. "Bad," he added for good measure, "luck."

Phillips nudged Miranda through the door with his shoulder. She had to get way too close to Bone to enter, but she did it. Phillips moved fast behind her, lightly pushing her the rest of the way inside. His hand shot back to slam the door and lock it. With Bone still standing outside on the porch.

"I don't want to be in the same house as the broken Bone," Phillips said.

Miranda idly worried that Bone would do something else to poor Pineapple. She hadn't imagined his fear though, and he wasn't banging on the door. *Good enough*. She tipped her head to Phillips in thanks.

Phillips called, "Dr Whitson? It's Phillips."

Miranda tried to figure out where a library might be inside the neat house with the exact floor plan she'd predicted from the yard. Who'd have guessed Bone would live in such tidy digs – or his eccentric dad, for that matter? Clean hardwood, modern furniture, and no TV in sight. It could have still been a timeshare waiting for the next guests to arrive.

The floor shifted under her feet, and Miranda stumbled into Phillips. He caught her, seemingly not bothered by the door opening *below* them.

The square section of the wood floor that had tossed her slowly rose. It was a trapdoor hatch into a level below. Basements were so unheard of on the island that Miranda had never seen one before. Sure, the house was on a little hill, but what about the water table? Was this guy truly insane?

"Down here." Dr Roswell's hand reached over the lip of the opening to wave them down, his feet thumping on the rungs of a ladder painted a pristine white as he descended back into what appeared to be a well-lit if snug underground space.

"It's safe – I promise," Phillips said. He released her elbow and started down the ladder. He paused, the opening a frame around his face. The moment was like a strange photograph. *My whole life is like a strange photograph.* "It's OK," he said again, lower.

He continued down, the top of his head disappearing, leaving the ladder clear for Miranda. She'd be safer down there than upstairs where Bone might decide to reappear. She took a deep breath and did her best not to think about being trapped under the earth, about worms and dirt and the things she sometimes had nightmares about crawling over her mother's body in the cold, cold ground. She pressed from her mind the steps down to the coroner's room, her dad laid out on the table, clear skin mocking her.

She reached the last rung.

The library was a little smaller than the living room. Three walls were lined floor to ceiling with books, some in glass-fronted cases. Framed area maps and prints she recognised as John White's drawings covered the fourth wall. Tables held high stacks of yellowed documents with frayed edges. All of it was probably arranged in some system only Roswell could comprehend. Frankly, the crackpot's library reminded her of *The Lost Colony* gift shop.

"Do you mind getting the door?" Dr Roswell asked.

Phillips must have suspected the effort it took for her to stay down here, because he hurried back up the ladder. The door thunked into place, deepening the hard shadows thrown by the lamps in the corners. Tight spaces didn't usually bother Miranda, but she was already off her game. Her hand went to her cheek automatically.

Roswell extended his hand to her. "I don't believe I've had the pleasure of making your acquaintance."

That his bearded face was familiar didn't make him any less of a stranger.

"Miranda Blackwood." She shook his hand, ducking her head when it seemed like his eyes gravitated to her cheek.

"She's a friend," Phillips said. "Her father was murdered the night of the disappearance and we're trying to figure out if there's a connection."

Roswell was interested. "How do you think they're connected?"

"I know you have theories about the lost colonists," Phillips said. "I bet you have theories about this disappearance too. I want to know what they are."

"Sit, sit," Dr Roswell said, taking a seat.

That left only one small wooden chair at the nearest table. Miranda chose to take the carpet and let Phillips do the talking.

"Where should I start?" His question wasn't for them, since he didn't wait for an answer. "At the beginning."

Miranda exchanged a look with Phillips. *This better help.*

"These are my theories, understand, but they are based on years of research. I am not a crackpot."

Miranda studied the loops of the carpet beneath her. "Of course not," she said.

"Go on, Doc," Phillips said. He was comfortable with this man in a way that Miranda didn't get. "Tell us."

Roswell leaned forward in his chair. "The first colony was actually a joint project of Sir Walter Raleigh and John Dee. Everyone here knows Raleigh – are you familiar with Dee?"

Phillips made a sort-of sign with his hand. Miranda scanned the show's character list in her mind and came up empty.

"Dee was a philosopher, a physician, and an alchemist. His power is difficult for us to understand today, so it may help if you also think of him as something else. A sorcerer. A holy man, even."

An involuntary cough escaped Miranda's lips.

Phillips reached down with an open palm and she scooted forward to let him take her hand. He held it on his knee. "Go on," he said.

"Believe me, I know how all this can sound to someone who hasn't sifted through the documents in this room. Someone who has grown up believing the local version of events," said Dr Roswell, peering at her with way too much intensity. "But haven't you ever thought to yourself that parts of the story about the colonists are awfully vague? Why on earth would they have traveled across the ocean to live in such an inhospitable environment? If you think about it, you'll discover I'm right. That, in truth, you know little about the colonists themselves, even less about why they came here, and nothing about where they disappeared to."

What he was saying wasn't *totally* cracked. Miranda thought about *The Lost Colony*'s script, knowing it stretched the truth anyway, and could find little except the colonists doing the stuff of daily colony life and fearing starvation and attack. Still… "The colonists were absorbed into the local tribes, weren't they? We're sure of that now."

He tapped a finger against his lips. "Are we? It's a very convenient theory that one. No one has to die in that configuration. Here's another little known fact about the colonists – not long before John White left for England to try and summon help and provisions, there was a murder."

"A colonist was murdered?" Phillips asked.

The word murder rang in Miranda's ears. *My father was murdered.* Somehow it hadn't sunk in fully until that moment. Murdered meant someone killed him. He was so helpless. Why?

Dr Roswell switched his focus to Phillips. Miranda welcomed the chance to listen without his eyes burning into her.

"Yes, one of the local tribes killed a man named George Howe. They had their reasons for doing so, undoubtedly, having witnessed what the colonists were doing on the island."

Did that mean someone from here killed her father? What had the tribe witnessed?

"What does this have to do with Dee?" Phillips rubbed his thumb across the top of her hand. She wished they were alone. She wished them being together had nothing to do with the ancient history pouring out of Roswell's mouth.

"I'm sure you've heard some of the legends about witches during the period we're discussing. They were thought to be people who signed a contract with the devil himself, to do his bidding. But," Dr Roswell paused, "according to what I've found, in England witches didn't make a deal with the devil. They made a deal with Dr John Dee. And witch meant something besides black cats and flying broomsticks."

"I don't see how the murder's connected," Phillips said.

"Of course, I'm being obtuse," Dr Roswell laughed. "I have found not a little support for my pet theory, which seems borne out by recent events."

"The theory, Doc," Phillips prompted.

"The colonists weren't witches, but alchemists, under the rule of John Dee. They came here to build him an empire, starting with a New London."

Miranda's mouth opened and closed like a perplexed fish's. "The colonists were alchemists," she said.

"In those times, witch was as likely a term as alchemist in certain quarters. These were people dedicated to unlocking the secrets of nature, of life and death itself. The discoveries alchemists made during this period are the foundation of modern chemistry. Dee may not have been known as a kind man, but he *was* known for his power and intellect. He wanted to rule, believed his achievements meant he deserved to. The colony was part of his plan to do just that. Men like these, they wish to live forever. Dee invented some sort of device that would allow him and his followers to do so, when combined with the right sorcery. Or, more accurately, the right manipulation of the natural world."

"Doc–" Phillips started, but the older man had warmed to his topic.

He's treating this like a CNN appearance. He waved Phillips silent, grabbing a book from the table and flipping through the pages until he came to a painting of a man with a thin face and long beard. And black, black eyes.

Below the haunting face was a symbol. It was *identical* to the one on the phantom ship's sails, the one repeated on the grip of the gun. The circle, the curved arms and legs, the half-moon on top... She sat up straighter.

"This man secured the land rights to our coast, much of what was known of North America at the time. He arranged for Raleigh to be in charge of transporting his colonists here, along with their sacred artifacts. I believe Governor White left not to request help, but to fetch Dee back. Dee's great experiment was set to begin. He had forged this device and the colonists awaited his arrival. I haven't been able to identify precisely what the device *was*. But the coded information hidden in the documents left by those involved make clear that it existed." He paused for effect. "And what I do know is that on the shore of Roanoke Island, they planned to use the device to become the first immortals."

Miranda didn't risk looking at Phillips. The man's explanation was crazy – except for the antique gun she'd found in the closet, handmade strikes showing in its metal. Phillips would be thinking the same thing.

Lucky I didn't immortal him with it.

She'd lost track of the gun. Was it still at her house?

"What stopped them?" Phillips asked.

"I don't believe they were stopped. I believe they were delayed," said Dr Roswell, closing the book on that thin face at last.

Phillips reached out across the small table like he meant to take the book, but just laid his hand across the surface. "You can tell all this from examining old documents?"

Not at all the question Miranda wanted to ask. Hers was more along the lines of: *Are you nuts or not?*

"Yes," Dr Roswell said. "The code they used is a fairly simple cipher of the time. Finding the documents that contain the concealed information has been the harder part. Some of Governor White's personal papers and drawings, a few of Raleigh's, a handful of Dee's own letters from the period. It's been a painstaking process and I'm still missing key pieces, but I'm convinced of one thing."

Again with the pausing, until Miranda sighed, caught up in the story despite questioning their host's sanity, and said, "Which is?"

Dr Roswell's chin tilted down and he regarded her over the top of his glasses. His beard didn't seem as neat as it usually did. Stray hairs flicked out from his cheeks. As if he'd gone a few days without trimming it. And there were dark circles smudged around his eyes. *I bet he's been staying up all night poring over these papers – all these years haven't been enough, not when it finally matters.*

"I'm convinced that the messages were meant to be found. To continue the project," he said. "The plan was disrupted, but it's been set in motion. That's the only explanation for the mass disappearance."

Miranda climbed to her feet, bracing against Phillips. "I don't get it," she said.

"It's a pattern. This is what happened last time, everyone gone. Or, rather, a certain number of people gone. I can't say yet what's next in the pattern," Dr Roswell said. "And there is one other thing."

Dr Roswell had such a flare for the dramatic that Miranda wondered why he'd never come down to audition for the show. He obviously wanted to climb back inside history and live there. Discover its secrets. She waited for his next words, and so did Phillips – eyebrows rising to prompt Roswell with a silent question.

"There was a name removed from the colony manifests that have been passed down through history. It belonged to an ancestor of yours, Miranda – at least, that's a logical assumption."

"What?" she asked. The snake pounded like her heart had moved to her cheek.

"There was a Blackwood in the party of colonists," he said. "Mary Blackwood, an alchemist."

12

Miranda

Phillips wished he could read minds instead of hear spirits chatter as he watched Miranda's back. She hadn't looked at him since climbing out of the library and rushing outside to leave. Of course she was wigged by what Dr Roswell had told them – anyone would be – but he didn't know her well enough to know how bad. He didn't know the right thing to say. And he definitely didn't want to make the situation worse.

Turned out Roswell's loser son had already done that.

Miranda had parked her faded yellow car with the driver's side facing the doc's house. Phillips hadn't known what to say at her house that morning when he first caught sight of the moronic graffiti. Now, instead of washing off FREAK, Bone had decided to add to the message so it included Phillips. It read: FREAKS IN LOVE.

"And tools doing graffiti," Phillips called, hoping Bone was near enough to hear.

Without slowing her pace, Miranda held up her hand for him to stop. She levered open the car door and climbed in, the set of her features not promising.

Phillips jogged across the lawn, curious if she'd actually leave him behind. But she waited until he got in before she started the car. "Miranda, it's not a big deal – what an idiot. *He's* probably in love with you."

Miranda shook off the hand he tried to lay on her arm, and put the car in drive. Phillips was still watching her when she finally looked over – past him, out the window.

Phillips should have expected the loser to put in a final showing. Bone lounged on the front porch where Phillips had left him before, the door open behind him. His whole head was flushed pink, and by Phillips' estimation not from the sun. Bone raised a hand and saluted them with a tight grin, and Phillips decided that he was *absolutely* burning some kind of torch for Miranda. Why else would he go to so much trouble to torment her?

Miranda flipped Bone off and jammed her foot on the gas, throwing up dust and sand behind them as she angled onto the narrow road.

The thing that worried him most was that Miranda hadn't seemed bothered by the graffiti earlier. She'd told him matter-of-factly that it was part of being her, giving no indication she was the least upset. In fact, he was convinced bringing her car had been a test. She wanted to see how he reacted to the stupid word. How he reacted to Bone's treatment of her.

The graffiti pissed him off, because as pranks went it was stupid and inelegant. It pissed him off because it was directed at Miranda.

"I know that was a lot to take in..." Phillips said, "But I need some help figuring out what's upsetting you the most?"

"Witches," she said, teeth gritted. "Alchemists."

She was forced to slow behind a pick-up truck hauling a fishing boat called *The Lucky Strike*.

"I know it all sounds crazy, but the gun – it's got to be Dee's missing object, right?" If he could get her talking everything would be OK. "Did you see that symbol? The caption said that's Dee's personal mark. The *monas heiroglyphica*."

Her eyes flicked over to him, and then she veered around the fishing boat. "It does sound crazy, that's for sure. Did you leave that thing at my house? Maybe we should throw it in the Sound."

"No," Phillips said, qualifying when that earned a scowl. "What if we need it to… save the people? Or you? We don't know enough yet."

"Where is it?"

He hadn't told her what he did with it. She hadn't asked. Maybe that would help calm her. "I left it in the trunk of my mom's car. I didn't want Mom or especially Dad to see it. He's an antique firearms nerd, remember? But I didn't figure it'd be smart to leave it at your house."

A nod. "Of course. The long lost alchemists – of which my frakking ancestor was one – could come to retrieve it at any time."

Miranda turned at the next major intersection, heading back toward Manteo. Phillips made another attempt. "Where are we going next?"

Her mouth opened as if she meant to speak, to answer him, but she didn't say anything. She sped up, the hula girl on the dash shimmying hard with the force of the pressure. "Where are we going?" he asked again.

"I'm going to see," she said, "whether I can get off this island."

Phillips let her drive on in silence for a while before he chanced speaking. "We're just going to abandon everyone?"

She laughed, but without humor. *You don't really know this girl.* He knew her well enough to know *this* wasn't her.

"Why wouldn't I? What have they ever done for me?" she asked.

"I can't just go." He hadn't wanted to come back, hadn't wanted to get involved. But he couldn't leave without seeing this through.

She gave that little laugh again. "You believe what he said?"

Phillips didn't want to answer Miranda's question yet. She'd breezed through town way over the speed limit, and now headed on past the turn-off to Fort Raleigh. He wanted to understand what switch had flipped inside her to send her running.

He opened his mouth to say something innocuous and she shocked him into keeping quiet with her next words. "You know I've never been off the island? That's part of the family 'curse' supposedly. Our feet 'are bound to walk this patch of earth.'"

She was quoting something, but not anything he'd ever heard. There were plenty of whispers and rumors about the Blackwoods. He'd heard a good share of them in his short time on the island, after he went raving psycho on her in the lobby. Nothing like this though – just that they never amounted to much, that her dad was a drunk, that her mother had been soft-hearted, that Miranda was bad luck just because she was born a Blackwood. The stories had always struck him as local legend, the kind of reputation that accrued to families who made the mistake of hanging around Roanoke Island too long.

Like the Rawling family "gifts." But this... was it possible?

He struggled to keep his voice level, to betray no skepticism. "You're saying that you've *literally* never been off the island?"

Her head bobbed in a fierce nod and she looked over at him, engaging with him fully for the first time since they'd left Roswell's. "That's exactly what I'm saying. I grew up–" she slowed Pineapple a little, the dashboard dancer weaving to a more peaceful melody "–being told I could never leave. Being told stories that gave me nightmares... that *were* nightmares. If I ever left, my feet would burst into flame. My body would disappear and I'd become a ghost. Stories about how my grandmother walked off the island toward the mainland once and lost her mind at the tenth step exactly. She sat in a rocking chair for the rest of her life picking grains of sand off beach glass."

What kind of lunatic had her dad been? "This island is eight miles long. About two miles across. You've *never* left it?"

"I tried when I was a kid. I waded out to my waist in the Sound and nothing happened, so I started to swim and then... then, I've never been so sick. My whole body hurt. It was enough to convince me. After that... until my mom died I stopped trying to even *want* to leave."

"Maybe it was psychosomatic? Maybe you freaked your-self out. You said your dad told you that you couldn't leave."

"He told me those stories, and I don't know if I believed them. I told myself I didn't. But I guess I believed them enough not to chance trying to do it for real. Not after that one time." She shook her head, black curls jostling. "You must think I'm crazy."

"I hear the voices of dead people," he reminded her. Had he ever heard the voice of her cracked grandmother? Not that he'd been able to distinguish individual voices. He pictured the cream envelope that held his gram's letter – he hadn't been brave enough to open it yet. He'd planned on asking Miranda to read it with him later.

The Manns Harbor Bridge and the waters of the Sound were coming up fast in the distance. Perfect rows of tall trees flanked the highway, the sign that bid visitors farewell just ahead. It was a postcard view.

Miranda angled the car off before they reached the bridge. She pulled into a parking lot bordered by sand. There were some rocks, a bench, and a tree prettily arranged beside the snatch of beach, and then the bridge itself, launching over the greenish blue water. A cluster of purple birds on the beach took off at their arrival, rising from the sand in a shuddering wave of wings.

"What are you planning to do?" he asked.

"Stay here. I don't want you to get hurt."

She left the car. He jumped out to follow her, catching her on the sand. The wind tossed her hair in a storm as he grabbed her shoulder and spun her to face him.

"You never went on a field trip?" he asked.

She whispered the answer so low the breeze almost stole it. "Never. He wouldn't sign the slips."

She wasn't crazy. She was just *acting* crazy. He understood the things in your own mind that could make you push the world away, flailing.

"I support your crazy plan," he said. "I think you *should* try."

Her eyes narrowed. "You do?"

"We need to know exactly what we're dealing with. Roswell helped – at least I think he did – but he admitted he doesn't know everything yet. It'll be an experiment. And if you can leave, then you'll feel better, right? Having an escape route?"

She was still wary, still waiting for him to disappoint her. But she nodded.

He said, "We should just take the car across the bridge. Together."

"No, I'm not risking you getting hurt. I'm going on foot."

Miranda whirled and crossed the small slice of beach that remained, continuing without pause over the grassy patch next to the bridge. He stayed right behind her.

She didn't hesitate so much as brace herself when she reached the white line at the edge of the actual highway. Her shoulders rose and fell with a deep breath, and then she stepped onto the road. One deliberate step, followed by another...

He checked her progress over the side. The next step would be the one that took her off the mainland, over the water of the Sound. How precise were curses anyway?

A sob ripped from her throat.

He trotted to her side. "What's wrong?"

"Oh god…" Fear etched her features, but she moved forward. A baby step. She trembled in the wind breaking across the bridge.

Seven steps, then eight. What if the story about her grandmother was true?

"Phillips, it hurts. It *hurts*," she said. Misery and pain filled her voice. Then, she howled. The scream was like knives stabbed her.

She stumbled, lifted her foot…

Before she could complete the tenth step, Phillips grabbed her and hauled her back to the edge of the bridge.

She barely fought. Miranda was breathing so hard he worried that her heart would burst, worried that it already had. What if the curse could do anything it decided to?

"Miranda, talk to me."

"It stopped when you put me back here." She wailed, "I can't leave."

He was desperate to do something to help her. A yellow SUV drove by with its horn blaring and Phillips flipped it off, which made him feel marginally better. He steered Miranda over the barrier, afraid she'd dash back onto the bridge if they stayed near the highway.

"I can't leave," she said again, tearing loose and kicking the sand. "I can't fucking leave this place."

No frak. This is bad. "Miranda, I'm sorry…" He reached out to her.

"You're sorry," she said, laughing that crazy laugh from the car.

But she shuffled closer to him. He caught her, hands on her shoulders, steadying her.

She went on, "Do you believe Roswell? Witchcraft plans, immortality, my family cursed since the start of the colony?"

"I wasn't sure before, but... Yes. Now I believe it. We have to do something – and leaving is off the list."

She pushed against his chest, leaving her palms flat against it. There were noises in the background: a few cars, birds flapping and calling overhead, trees rustling in echo of the water. Phillips barely heard them. The sadness in her face was too much.

She said, "I can't leave. You can. You made it off. Why would you ever come back here? What if Mary Blackwood *was* evil, and I am too? And that's why I'm cursed? What if our family deserved everything we got?"

He slid his hands down her arms and back up them. He was desperate to stop the pain, to bring her back to being Miranda. The fighter. He tugged her closer by her shirtsleeves, meaning to kiss her.

She let him bring her in close.

He was winning her. For a moment, he was winning her, until she shoved him away.

He fell to his knees, hitting the sand hard. A keening sound came from his throat that he couldn't stop. But Miranda wasn't the reason he fell. What pushed him down and down and down was far worse.

The voices had returned with hurricane force and ripped his senses apart.

13

Criminal Grace

Miranda couldn't believe what she'd just done.

Phillips had stayed with her even though she was acting balls-out crazy, and she'd paid him back by shoving him to the ground. Full-on rejection when she didn't *want* to reject him.

Her flare into anger in Roswell's library, the way she drove here, the – god, frak – *true* stories she confessed to about not being able to leave the island, insisting on walking out onto the bridge... She'd come *this* close to telling him about seeking fantasy escape routes after her mom died. But all that paled next to what had flooded from her mouth after the childhood stories were proved right. It was nothing next to pushing him away.

One thing she knew: none of those actions or words belonged to her. Or maybe they poured from some small part of her, but it was a part she'd never willingly let take control.

Sand swallowed her feet and she had to pull them free to kneel before him. *What if he never tries to kiss me again?* She wouldn't blame him.

Only after her initial horror passed did she see Phillips was in pain. Only then did she hear the low noises from his throat.

Oh, frak.

His head slumped into his chest. She gently shook his shoulder. His face lifted a fraction, enough to show that his eyes were squeezed shut. The wrinkles at their edges were wounds slashed into his face. He cried out with the anguish of a torture victim.

"Phillips?" She did her best to tamp down her panic.

He tipped forward and rolled onto his side, forming an untidy ball on the sand. His eyes stayed closed as he rocked into the grainy embrace of the ground beneath him, hands rising to shield his ears from sounds she couldn't hear.

"It's the voices," she said. "The voices came back, didn't they?"

Miranda had no clue what to do. This was the kind of thing she should have brought up in polite conversation with Sara earlier. *What do I do if your son suddenly goes spirit tuning fork again?*

She petted his shoulder with a tentative hand and he grabbed it. She detected a slight tug, or thought she did, and – despite how strange it felt – lay down beside him, pressing her body against his in the sand. The hand gripping hers moved to re-cover his ear. His body trembled against hers. She held on, afraid that if she let go he'd be gone forever.

"Home," he said, after a while.

And so she had to let go, to get up so she could help him off the sand. She stumbled then froze, gazing out at the water.

The tall black ship sailed toward her. Three black sails of

varying sizes swelled in the wind. The ornate symbols stitched on them in gray clearly bore Dee's mark. What had Phillips called it? Right, the *monas hieroglyphica*.

The immense shadow the ship threw across the water nearly tricked her into thinking it was real. Real in the way she was real, the sand was real, Phillips was real.

The shadow shifted and billowed like the black sails. They needed to get out of here.

Turning away from the phantom ship's menacing glide, she bent and pulled at Phillips' arms until she got one over her shoulder. "We have to get up now," she said, and he managed to climb to his feet.

He leaned heavily on her. A low moan escaped his lips. "Home," he breathed.

She rotated them in a slow circle, not comfortable leaving the black ship and its shadow unobserved. "Do you see it?" she asked, searching the horizon.

But there was nothing to see. A bridge, calm waters, a brilliant blue sky.

No wonder old John White always seemed so cranky by the end of the play, looking for something and finding nothing.

Crossing the ten feet to Pineapple took an age with their clumsy tandem footsteps. "We're never going to be in an Olympic team for anything that requires synchronization," she told him. He was unresponsive, but she talked at him to ease her nerves, like he was in a coma and the doctor had said it might help. Sand coated them both in a fine, scratchy second skin.

"We could be in the freak Olympics," she said, depositing

him against the rear passenger door. "Well, I don't have any actual skills. No, no, that's not what I mean. I have skills, but not like you have skills."

Sand clung to his eyelashes, his eyes still closed. He looked like he was asleep standing up.

"If there *was* a freak Olympics," and she got the door open and slipped her arm around his side to help him ease into the seat. She clumped his feet over the edge so he was in the car, "maybe we could get training so we didn't suck so much at this."

On impulse, she reached out and brushed sand from his cheek, softly from his eyelashes. They fluttered against the pressure and he opened one eye. Bloodshot ringed the brown iris. "Miranda," he said.

"That's me," she agreed, glad he was in there somewhere. "I'm taking you home."

Careful not to get some limb of his caught, she shut the door and scurried around to her own side and into the driver's seat. "Not that you're going to change the subject that easily. We really need more practice. If we're going to medal."

"Music," the word a moan.

"I see how it is," she said, "trying to shut me up."

But she turned on the used CD player she'd installed in Pineapple's dash – one of her prouder moments – and cranked the volume. Neko Case howled about red bells. Deep red bells. Polly had given her the album.

Miranda drove, grateful she could stop talking. She needed to think.

What Roswell had shared with them was on the crazy

side, but she couldn't deny how much being on the bridge had hurt. She'd counted her own steps until the pain forced the numbers out of her head. Her feet had burned like she'd walked into a furnace – like she was a girl forced to dance in hot iron shoes, a mermaid forced to split her tail and walk on land. Fairy-tale level was the only description that captured it.

Which meant magic wasn't so crazy. Not when you factored in the leaping birthmark, the missing people, and John Dee's symbol.

How her father had died was important. Phillips had said so, and maybe his dad would have learned more. Roswell's theory might explain some things, but it didn't explain everything. They knew more than he did now.

She looked over at Phillips. His neck crooked back, eyes shut, mouth moving in silent accord with the lyrics or the voices in his head. The intensity of the pain had faded from his expression, at least.

He's in no shape to help you though.

"My turn," she said.

When she reached Phillips' driveway, the first thing she noticed was the unfamiliar vehicle parked beside Chief Rawling's cruiser. The hulking black SUV gleamed like invisible hands polished it constantly to remove any speck of sand or dust. Miranda watched too much TV not to know what it meant. There were federal agents inside the house.

Maybe they already knew who'd murdered her father – the rush autopsy might be complete. She turned off the car, the swell of Neko's voice dying so abruptly that the silence made Phillips moan.

"You stay here," she said, making a split second decision. She wouldn't subject him to the prying eyes of strangers when he was like this.

Smoothing her hair and T-shirt, she walked to the front door. Sure, she wanted to know if the missing pieces of the puzzle had been found, but first she needed Phillips' mom to help get him inside. The door opened before her second knock.

Chief Rawling looked around, and without asking for Phillips said, "Come inside, Miranda."

"Chief, I… Is Sara…" Miranda tried to banish the memory of him interrupting them the night before.

"She's in here."

He left Miranda no choice except to follow him across the creaking planks of the floor. The footfalls of his heavy-soled work shoes echoed. Sara sat on the floral couch in the living room, an unusual primness in her posture.

Across from Sara, on the love seat, were the expected agents. A man and a woman in nearly identical dark suits – he was young but already bald, her graying hair was slicked back into a knot at her neck. The tight quarters of the love seat forced them to sit close together, and their spines were stick-straight to compensate for the lack of room. Miranda decided that TV got feds half-right, based on these two. They were serious and intimidating, but neither was attractive enough to inspire fanfic anytime soon.

"Um, hello…" Miranda lingered in the doorway as Chief

Rawling pulled out a spare wooden chair near the wall for her to sit in, then returned to the sofa beside his wife. The feds watched her with interest. She asked, "Sara, could I talk to you alone for a minute?"

Sidekick bounded in from the kitchen at that precise moment, crashing into her with oblivious happiness.

"You'd better sit down first," Sara said.

The warning in her flat tone would have been undetectable to anyone who hadn't been around her before. Miranda thought of Phillips waiting outside in the car, but sank onto the chair. She ruffled Sidekick's fur in reassurance that she hadn't abandoned *him*.

"This is Agent Malone and Agent Walker from the FBI," said Chief Rawling. "They're the new heads of this case until it's resolved. We're cooperating fully. This is Miranda Black-wood, the murder victim's daughter."

The woman leaned forward, "I'm Agent Malone," she said. A tiny piece of lint clung to the lapel of her black jacket and Miranda focused on that.

"OK," Miranda said.

She couldn't stop thinking about Phillips. What if he tried to make it inside on his own? But Chief Rawling and Sara's tense expressions kept her pinned to the chair.

"I'm sorry about your father," Agent Malone said. She waited as if taking notes on Miranda's reaction to the statement.

"Thank you?" Miranda offered.

"Do you know anyone who would have wanted to kill your father?" Agent Malone asked. The light streaming through the pale curtains on the window behind the agent gave her a halo that didn't go with her business suit.

Miranda caught the chief laying his hand over Sara's. *What am I missing here?*

"Honestly, no," Miranda said. "You probably already know he wasn't the citizen of the year, but no... I can't imagine why anyone would kill him. No one else would have loaned him money, so he didn't owe any, except to me. He didn't have a job. His disability check covered his bar tab and most of our bills. He almost never got in fights. He was harmless. I'm sure the chief has told you all this."

A glance at the chief told her she'd said way more than she should have.

Agent Malone leaned back, spine a board. The other agent – Agent Walker – shifted forward. *Bad cop time.*

"What are you doing here now?" Agent Walker asked. "At the Rawlings?"

Miranda stilled. She didn't know what game this was, but honesty suddenly seemed like the wrong tactic. "I came to get Sidekick. Sara was nice enough to babysit him while I did some things today. She let me stay here last night."

"Is that because you're dating her son?" Agent Walker let one side of his mouth tick up.

The chief opened his mouth to protest, then closed it. "Wise decision," Agent Walker said to him, "since that fact came from you."

"This will all be cleared up," Chief Rawling said. "You're making the wrong leaps."

"You see, Miss Blackwood," Agent Walker said, eyes not

leaving the chief, "it's interesting to us that you and Phillips Rawling are so close, since he's been away for the last few years."

Miranda stared at him.

"We've gotten a warrant to search his belongings, his computer – we have agents up at his school. If you're colluding on this, we will find the evidence."

"Colluding on *what*?" Miranda didn't know if they were playing a game anymore.

"On your father's murder," Agent Malone said. "Which you don't seem too upset about."

Chief Rawling stood up. "That's enough," he said, turning to her. "Miranda, don't say anything else. Your father's body… It's missing."

"What do you mean missing? Like the people?"

"When Marlon got to the funeral home this morning to let in the federal expert for the autopsy, he was gone." Chief Rawling shook his head. "They think Phillips took the body – had something to do with it disappearing."

Her chair clattered to the floor as she leapt to her feet, Sidekick dancing out of its way.

"But that's insane," she said. "He wasn't even *here* when the murder happened. He's the one who told the chief to get the autopsy done. Last night. Chief, tell them."

Chief Rawling frowned at her. *Right*, she'd been eavesdropping. That hardly mattered now.

"He already has," Agent Walker said, "but Phillips Rawling *was* in the body storage room. We found his prints on a handkerchief discarded in the biohazard receptacle. He almost got away with taking your father's body, Miss Black-wood."

Miranda head was shaking, and so were her hands. *No.* "No…"

"Where is the boy now?" Agent Malone said, standing up, which prompted her partner to do the same. "We know you left together this morning."

She walked around the living room table and put a hand on Miranda's arm. The muscles of Miranda's arm twitched under the woman's touch. How could she stop this purpose-less witch-hunt? *Witch-hunt, very funny.* Maybe the spirits would warn Phillips to bolt. Maybe…

Agent Malone's tone softened to silk. "Miranda, I under-stand your dad may have deserved whatever he got. If you're just honest with us, we can make this a lot easier on every-one. We know you couldn't have gotten rid of one hundred and fourteen people. We're mainly interested in crossing your father's murder off the list of leads."

And the Emmy for most transparent attempt at manipula-tion goes to… "Do you think I'm that stupid? Don't *you guys* watch TV anymore, because I'm not–"

The sound of the front door opening interrupted her vow to get an attorney before saying another word. Not that she could afford one or knew anyone who would represent her for free. A heavy thump and breaking glass came next – the family portrait on the wall next to the door, Miranda guessed, willing time to stop – and then the noise of a body sliding to the floor.

She wasn't the first one out of the room. She was the last.

When Miranda turned the corner, she saw that they had Phillips. Sara bent beside him, fingers lifting his eyelids to check his pupils, shattered glass surrounding them on the floor. Agent Malone let handcuffs dangle from long fingers, glanced over her shoulder at Miranda with something that looked like pity.

They had Phillips. They weren't going to get her, too.

14

Caught

Phillips' parents and the agents were distracted. Sara was warning Agent Malone away from her son, while Agent Walker argued with Chief Rawling. Phillips' cheek pressed into his mother's hand, his eyelids fluttering like he was having a bad dream. The agents wouldn't understand what was wrong with him. They would want to ask Miranda more questions.

And she had too many questions of her own that still needed answers. She considered her options. Hard as it was to run out on Phillips, she knew it was the smartest thing to do. If they were both held at the station that helped nobody. Sidekick padded toward the cluster, no doubt to gift Phillips with a reviving face lick.

The snap of her fingers was so quiet she almost expected Sidekick to miss it. But he came to her side, and let her lead him through the kitchen by his collar. She held her breath as she eased the screen door open just enough for her dog to slip through, then herself.

Thank you, she silently directed gratitude to Phillips for being the kind of rule-breaker who would tighten and oil hinges, who would never live in a house with random squeaks. He'd probably checked every door and the step of each route out the night before, just in case. Where could her father's body be?

The backyard had sandy dirt and clumps of brown-fingered grass mixed with its short ragged blades. The grass was damp from the efforts of a green garden hose nearby, and brightly colored flowerpots were arrayed alongside the house. Sara must have watered not long before.

Heading around the side of the house to Pineapple, Miranda realised there was no way to take her car *and* make a getaway. Pineapple didn't start quietly at the best of times, and given her luck – nonexistent – the car would sputter and be stubborn. So she simply eased the passenger door open, crouching, holding Sidekick's collar so he wouldn't jump in for a ride.

The keys to Phillips' mom's sedan weren't in the passenger side seat. *Frak.*

Someone at the back door called her name, "Miranda!" The chief, she decided, followed by the non-dulcet tones of Agent Walker: "Miss Blackwood, you're making this worse for everyone!"

OK, she'd deal with not having the keys later. She'd get the strange gun from the trunk of Phillips' mom's car where he'd stashed it… somehow. At least the car was at her house where they left it when they traded for Pineapple. That was something.

She released Sidekick's collar and streaked toward the woods that began past the Rawlings' driveway, making it to them just as the front door opened. The tree she'd selected wasn't overly wide, so she stood sideways to maximise its cover. She tried to think like Phillips would in the situation, remembering Sidekick in that moment. He shifted on uncertain feet beside her, unconcealed. She bent and eased to her belly, pulling him down with her. His tail wagged and she reached back to stop it.

Proof that he was the best dog in the world? He didn't whine.

Sara and Agent Malone stepped out on the porch. Chief Rawling and Agent Walker joined them, body language revealing how much the two men were hating each other. Phillips must still be inside, suffering.

Miranda waited without much patience during their examination of her car and a clipped discussion about where she might have gone. She strained to hear, caught the gist. Phillips was the greater priority, they'd pick her up later. They needed to get back to the station, see if they could get him lucid enough for an interview, check in on the status of locating the missing people and her father's body. These weren't agents from the Fringe division. They were *not* looking for supernatural causes. Aliens hadn't abducted the people of Roanoke, perpetrators had. Or maybe this was a cult thing or a tourism stunt gone wrong. Something understandable.

And the police chief's son had murdered his girlfriend's father, which might be connected.

She should have known better than to expect outsiders to decode the island's mysteries. No, they were just here to get in the way.

"Secret alchemists," she whispered as they went back inside, presumably to collect Phillips. "There's your lead."

Her house was a couple of miles walk, if she cut through the woods and along less visible roadways than the main drag. She set out at a fast clip, praying to beat any searchers there. Praying for the spirits to talk to *her* and tell her how to jimmy open a locked trunk.

Praying that Phillips would be OK.

The voices had never been this bad for Phillips, not even the time he'd summoned them on purpose and spent days in bed when they'd answered. Back then getting enough distance from the voices to interact with the real world had been a challenge. But he'd been able to do it. He'd been able to slowly explain to his mother that the voices had descended with such fury and babble that he couldn't make them leave. He'd had to wait a day for them to fade, but he could answer questions.

He had no control of sense or clear thought now. Snatches of knowing fought to the surface, but not at his command. Nothing was at his command.

The hiss and howl of the voices was all that truly existed for him.

Coming coming – No, they are here – They have always been here – Under the bed – Stealing us – We want to live – Liar liars – The red streaks will be blood will run like – Coming back for you – Water running over us all – Death is here – You won't know them – You'll be too late – She's the cause of it – The ship – They'll use her – Listen to me, my boy, listen – Bluebell, blue sea, blue waves, I'm going mad – You saw the snake – We're all mad – Coming coming –

One of the few things Phillips knew was that he wasn't at home any longer. He had no idea where he'd been taken. But he knew Miranda wasn't with him anymore, though he didn't know how he knew that. He dimly remembered his weight against her, a ghost of a memory. He'd tried to reach her when he fell. He understood in a vague way, deep in his mind, that she'd taken him home. He also knew strangers had taken him from his mother, and that he hadn't managed one word to her first. He remembered slapping something cool away that had bound his wrists, something he no longer felt there. Unfamiliar voices, breaking glass. The past and the present became syrup he swam through, heavy against his limbs.

Weighing him down. Down. *Down.*

His cheek pressed against cool wood grain. The desire to see his surroundings developed over several minutes, the will to open his eyes building until he finally managed it.

The black bars of a cell greeted him. On the other side of them Dr Roswell stood, shaking his head. Then the bars were opening and his father was behind the doctor and there were strangers in suits and...

The snake inside her – The things they'll do – Can't be stopped any longer – Stolen life – COMING COMING COMING –

Phillips eyes closed as hands forced open his mouth and deposited a few pills inside. The gel casings gummed on his tongue and he sputtered as they poured water down his throat. But he swallowed.

Swallowed, without any real belief the drugs they fed him would do a thing to dam up the flood.

COMING COMING COMING–

Miranda tore through the woods like a chupacabra chased her.

She knew the dead didn't walk... the same way she knew witches and alchemists didn't exist. She felt silly for worrying that her dad was traipsing around zombielike on the island, that he'd come after her. That even now he was in the forest with her, watching as she ran.

She didn't feel silly enough to stop running. Marshy mud coated her sneakers, creeping up to the pink skin of her ankles.

Getting home took longer than she expected. Once she and Sidekick reached their neighborhood, they had to navigate an obstacle course of backyards. Zigzagging borders filled with broken down lawnmowers and refrigerators, toys and chained dogs with anger management issues (they hated Kicks on sight). Finally, the back edge of their unfenced, not-recently-mown yard appeared, then the back door of their house.

Just my *house now*, she corrected, closing her eyes against a sudden image of her father sitting at their sticky kitchen table. His pale, birthmark-free face grinned at her over a cup of stale coffee, his eyes and mouth gaping black as open graves.

No. There wasn't time to be weak. If those federal agents caught up to her, they'd be more convinced than ever she and Phillips had murdered her father, more inclined than they had been before to lock her up. No one would save her, either.

Her key slid into the flimsy back door lock, then the sturdier dead-bolt above it. She forced herself over the threshold. *Your father is dead,* not *sitting at the kitchen table.*

Still. Even if he wasn't a dead man walking, someone could have taken the body and brought it here to mess with her. Someone could...

She inhaled deeply. No *eau de* dead body met her.

"Right." She walked into the kitchen – *no zombie father, thank you* – and stuck a quarter-full sack of dog kibble in her messenger bag. "Sorry," she answered Sidekick's mournful silent plea. "No time for chow." Sara would have fed him a few hours ago.

The smaller toolbox she kept at home was stashed in her room. She'd locked herself out of Pineapple a couple of times before. The same principles she used to break in then should work on the trunk lock of Sara's sedan.

Miranda found her room lightly picked over by Phillips and Sara. Her *Vampire Diaries* boxed set sat on top of her pillow – Elena's reclining body upside-down and come hither.

Phillips was a funny boy.

Miranda retrieved the small toolbox and carried it outside. Up the street, Mrs Figgins was on her front porch with her nose in a paperback, her hair forming an astronaut-suit bubble around her head. Her long-range vision was shot, and she wouldn't see Miranda. She could barely see the book, held it cupped an inch from her face. Miranda liked to see what Mrs Figgins was up to when she drove by, whether it was a Sudoku or a cat-mystery kind of day.

Popping her toolbox open at the back of Sara's car,

Miranda rummaged and selected a specialty screwdriver. She slid a length of steel wire into an opening below the head. The tool was perfect for dislodging stray sequins or costume beading in cracks on set – and for this kind of job, which was why she kept one at home.

She inserted the metal into the trunk's lock and worked it around, searching for the release. With no immediate luck, she shifted her leg to change the angle of approach.

There was nothing for her to trip over but she did anyway, abandoning the tool to keep from falling. She stood and pulled on the tool. When it didn't come free, she wriggled it harder.

The wire was lodged in the lock. And the release didn't give a millimeter.

"Frak," she said.

She kicked the ground, then a tire on her way around the side of the car. There'd been *nothing* to cause her to trip.

She touched her face, just below her temple. Of course. The snake.

"Frak." She thought of her father and how he always was… Not always, though. He hadn't *always* been that way. First, he'd stumbled into things more. She remembered his hand gripping the frame around the photo of her mother in the living room to keep it from falling because he'd touched the glass too hard. Then, the drinking became a problem, bringing more stumbling with it, making him fight his own limbs.

She could see how his behavior changed over the years, and she understood the reason. The snake was mind-controlling her somehow. Not all the time, more like a radio frequency that tuned in and out.

She eyed the sedan, and purposefully thought like herself. Not like Phillips, not like whatever had invaded her body randomly earlier and spewed all that garbage. Not like whatever had caused her to trip over nothing. Like *herself*.

There'd be another way into the trunk, an emergency method to open it. Or a way aimed at convenience.

Mrs Figgins wasn't deaf, but Miranda took the chance anyway. Selecting a hammer from the toolbox, she went around to the other side of the car – checked the street one last time for anyone else, saw no one – and smashed in the smaller of the rear windows, reaching inside to pull up the lock. Mrs Figgins lifted her head, but she couldn't see anything this far away. She went back to her book.

Miranda opened the door, feeling around the top of the back seat until she found the plastic release lever and yanked it down. The back seat fell into her hand, flattening to provide trunk access.

The box that held what was apparently alchemist extraordinaire Dr John Dee's greatest invention sat inside, waiting like it had in her dad's closet all those years.

"Frak," she said, pleased. And also terrified.

15

Black Sails

Miranda wasn't sure what to do after retrieving the box, but staying at home seemed like a spectacularly bad idea. She couldn't go back to Phillips' house – Sara being there didn't change the chief's obligation to cooperate with the FBI. So Morrison Grove it was.

She'd set out on foot, the only choice available. A couple of federal tank-style SUVs spotted in the distance later, she and Sidekick left the roadside to hike through less visible terrain. The messenger bag was heavy with the gun box and dog food, and she was at war with her own legs. They protested every plodding, uneven step.

Adrenaline vs. Exhaustion: Which will be the ultimate victor?

Poor Sidekick trudged alongside her, no longer bothering to gallop ahead like he had on their earlier trek. "This is the only time you will ever hear me say it's a good thing we live on an island this small, dog," Miranda muttered. If the island had been any bigger, not having a car would have sunk them.

What Miranda knew and the larger shadows of what she

didn't swirled around her as she focused on putting one sneakered foot in front of the other. None of it seemed random. John Dee's hieroglyph was too much of a coincidence to be a coincidence.

Deep in thought, she didn't notice the enormous shadow that fell over her. Not until she stumbled over a rock cloaked in the sudden darkness it cast. Sidekick growled at whatever was behind them.

She didn't want to turn. She turned anyway.

The ship sailed across the land, cutting across the earth as if nothing inhabited it. The sails stretched a hundred feet in the air, the elaborate gray symbols pulling taut in gusts of phantom wind, the gleaming hull below polished black. People stood on the deck. She couldn't make them out in detail, not through the shadow. They were a line of still silhouettes, a wall of stone statues staring out over the island.

She knew that shadows didn't fall forward at this time of day, with this position of the sun, and that they never fell this far in front of an object. That hardly mattered since the ship's appearance nearly broke the rational part of her mind.

Morrison Grove wasn't far, the tree line and roofs of the first buildings visible ahead. Miranda picked up her pace, but Kicks barked his head off behind her. He wasn't following.

"Sidekick!"

She couldn't leave him, even if it meant the shadow ate her whole. She doubled back and pulled at his collar.

The ship glided slowly, steadily forward. They had to get out of its path.

Every dog within earshot struck up a chorus of barks to

match Sidekick's. His body thrashed against the pressure of her hand.

Just like the night my dad died.

Miranda had never leashed Sidekick before, but there was nothing else to do. She dropped her messenger bag and removed the strap, clicking one end into his collar as he growled. She caught up the other end and hefted the bag with her free arm. She put all her weight into heaving him forward.

"Come on!"

He fought, desperate to face the threat. But she refused to give in. She moved forward as quickly as possible with the bag clutched awkwardly against her. She didn't stop to look back until they reached Polly's door.

The ship was a dozen feet away…

It was going to sail right over them…

Miranda gave one last jerk to get Sidekick inside with her, then slammed the door and slung the bag aside. The box inside it clunked against the floor, the kibble rattling.

She waited for the impact of the black ship. She waited to feel all her bones breaking as the phantom ship crushed her whole, understanding suddenly that this was probably what had happened to her father.

The impact never came.

When she opened the door, the shadow had vanished. The ship, too.

Oh, it was out there, sailing through the night. The line of dark forms on its deck watching and waiting for an arrival point. *Something* was coming.

She needed to get to Phillips, get through to him that they didn't have much time left. That with the big black ship sailing toward her, maybe *she* didn't have much time.

The thought of going back into the night defeated her.

Adrenaline never had a chance. Exhaustion won.

The voices roared.

The noise woke Phillips from the fitful, sweaty sleep the pills had thrown him into. He rocked against the hard wood bench until he achieved the momentum to sit up. He pressed his head back against cool cinderblock. All the physical sensations were muted, as if they were happening to someone else. Someone far, far away. On a movie screen, or in the past. Someone barely real.

The voices overlapped in chaotic fragments, but then they began to sync, melding to a single word loud and clear as shattering glass. The chorus repeated again and again and again:

COMING COMING COMING COMING COMING COMING COMING COMING COMING

He fell onto his knees on concrete, an image of Miranda in his mind...

Miranda on the beach, thinking she'd pushed him down...

Thinking that he didn't understand...

Silence. There was a single moment of perfect silence.

Phillips was alone inside his head.

The Return

In the first moment there was no one, but in the next there was her.

The painfully ordinary woman straightened from a crouch, frowning at the asphalt surrounding her. She stood next to gas pumps with bright yellow heads topped by small video screens, unlit at this time of night. Dawn would come soon enough, and with it customers, blaring advertisements, flashing numbers below, the snick of nozzles being used and replaced. The song of motors coming to life. The fluorescent lights inside the store would shine like unflattering spotlights on all who dared enter.

She found her hands looking for something – someone – and smoothed them against the skirt of her long, flowing sundress. Her eyes possessed a wildness that didn't match the garment's modest lines, the conservative gather of her plain brown ponytail, the muted understatement of neutral brown swiped across her eyelids. The ordinary woman thought of nothing at first, her hands again reaching, searching for someone in unconscious reflex, wild eyes sweeping the parking lot, confirming its desertion.

She inhaled the night, throwing her arms out wide. Her sedate maroon skirt danced in the wind and she permitted her plain lips to curve.

The night was silent, but, eventually, she knew where home was from this spot.

She knew she could walk it.

Across town, another woman walked toward the front door of a big yellow house, her easy strides broken when she made an abrupt turn. She stopped in the night grass, holding the gaze that she'd felt on her back.

The man was on the other side of the street, and unlike her – she traced her attention over her own body, took in the sleek cut of a business suit – he wore a bathrobe over pajama bottoms. But his stiff posture would have told, if the timing hadn't.

They raised no hands in greeting, exchanged no words. She inclined her head and he sent her a slow smile, not of joy, but of knowing. He sat down, posture stiff, to wait on the curb, and a bolt of envy shocked her. She had to get inside, and so she went with deliberate steps.

Her hand remembered how to open the door quietly enough that he wouldn't hear. Her feet knew how to be clever and silent when coming in late, to pad up the hall so as not to disturb him. She let them lead her to the kitchen first, unable to resist the lure of taste. The mess surprised her, distantly. The refrigerator door was cool in her palm as she opened it, light sneaking out. She examined the contents. Too many boxes, unfamiliar items, the letters a blur that finally *resolved into words she could understand. Removing a carton of orange juice, she leaned against the counter and drank deep.*

She left the carton out, knowing it would never be noticed. Not in the mess.

She noted the man asleep on the couch, but he didn't wake and she didn't wake him. Instead her clever feet went up the hall. The softness of the sheets – high thread count, the words skated through her mind – was an embrace, and she relaxed into it, closing her eyes and waiting to be discovered.

The girl sat up in a bed that had never been that comfortable, even when it was new. But the sheets and blanket were soft and pink. They didn't belong to the house, but to her. The bedclothes were the only thing that truly belonged to her of the objects around her. Bed, nightstand, and chair had come with the room. This was rental housing. Looking around, she confirmed she was right, and the knowledge edged her to her feet.

She sensed that she wasn't alone in the house.

The other two young women waited in the front room, a landscape dominated by a coffee table littered with junk. Tabloids and dirty margarita glasses. The taller of the others – her hair a silvery gray despite her young age – raised her finger to her lips, and inclined a head at the door to the bedroom behind her.

Someone else had already been in the house, but not one of them. The girl gave a short nod, and they took seats on the couch in wordless agreement.

They didn't speak. There was no point. They needed more time to know enough to have anything to say.

A whine sang to them from inside the room that held the uninvited guest, followed by a low voice soothing the troubled dog. Then, the silence returned.

16

Missed

The silence didn't last, inside or outside Phillips' head. When morning came, he laid on the bench listening to the first clues that something big had taken place overnight. The staccato din of ringing phones, shouted queries, and fast footsteps reached his cell.

Chattering voices also buzzed in the background of his mind, but they weren't anything like the screaming horde that had smashed into him and taken over without so much as a *do you mind?* or a *thank you.* This was the rain without the storm, the never-alone sensation he associated with the island – only dialed up a notch because the voices bore a disturbed edge, sharper than usual. The voices were upset.

Not the only ones.

He must have freaked everyone out in the most major of ways yesterday – including Miranda. Trapped Miranda, who truly couldn't leave.

He stood and confirmed that he still wore his jeans and T-shirt, instead of a terrible jumpsuit. At least they'd left him in his own clothes. He had to get out of here.

He gripped the cell bars in either hand, pressing his forehead onto the metal. Wasn't he supposed to have a tin cup he could drag back and forth over the bars until someone came to shout at him? The one time Phillips had broken out of jail he'd still had the force's amused graces on his side and been able to talk his way out. Now that everyone knew his reputation, that wouldn't work.

Why *was* he even in here? All he remembered were his parents and Roswell and... frowning strangers in dark suits, barking questions he wasn't able to respond to. Who were they?

His mother rounded the corner and padded down the hallway, a styrofoam cup of coffee in one hand. The dark smudges around her eyes nearly matched the depressing gray cement wall behind her. She almost dropped the steaming cup, clearly surprised to see him standing.

"Mom," he said, "good morning."

She straightened. "Is it?"

He tried to ignore the buzz and hum raining through his head. "Better than yesterday."

"Anything would be better than yesterday." She must not have slept more than a few hours, if that. She took a sip from the coffee.

"Why am I in here?" he asked.

Her head snapped up. "You don't remember."

Given the busy noises coming from the station floor, he doubted anyone was snooping on their conversation. He spoke softly anyway. "It wasn't like anything that ever happened to me before – all of a sudden the voices just... overpowered me."

He paused, attempting to make space away from the buzzing chatter inside. "Is Miranda OK? How freaked out was she?"

His mother shifted so she rested against the bars beside him. She didn't want them to be overheard either, he realised. "Phillips, you're in here because the FBI think you and Miranda worked together to murder her father."

"But I wasn't even here when he died! I was a million miles from here. Well, several hundred." Their theory was as far off as the moon.

She gripped her cup with one hand and reached out with the other to touch his. "I know, hon. But they don't understand where the body could be."

Something in his memory clicked and a snatch of the shouted questions directed at him drifted through his mind. *"What did you do with the body?"* one of them had asked, a man. *An FBI guy.*

"Someone took Miranda's dad's body," he said, not a question.

She said, "And you guys were in the funeral home. Why exactly were you in the funeral home?"

So he was in trouble with his mom, too. "Miranda needed to see him and–"

"And you couldn't just ask your dad to arrange it." She sighed. "Phillips, what happened to you yesterday? You were gone. Unreachable. Do you know why it was so bad?"

His forehead touched the bars. "I don't understand it either."

"And the voices are back, aren't they? The regular ones you hear?"

He nodded. "How did you–"

"Your eyes," she said, waving her hand next to her own. "I can tell when you aren't alone in there."

She checked her watch, looked over her shoulder. Was it possible there was more gray in her hair from one night? "The agents will be coming in soon. Maybe we should ask them to transfer you to the mainland. I don't want to ever see that happen again."

Phillips frowned. His mother was on his side, always. "I'm not leaving. Where's Miranda?"

His mother's eyes landed on the wall behind him. "She took off – she's currently evading federal custody. Any idea where she is?"

Miranda Blackwood, federal fugitive. *I'm a bad influence.* Phillips couldn't stop his grin.

"I don't know," he said, and the truth of that sank in. He didn't know her well enough to know where she'd go, but he knew she was stuck here. "She's still on the island. Mom, you have to get me out of here – I'll find her."

There was a renewed force to the clamor in the front room, and someone broke out in a cheer. It wasn't like they were watching basketball out there. They might have, even in the middle of the apocalypse. But this was the wrong season, the wrong time of day.

His mom's coffee cup vibrated. Her hand was shaking.

"Mom, what's going on?"

The question rested between them for a moment.

She set the coffee cup on the cement floor. Then she rose and put both hands over his.

"They're back," she said.

"Who are?"

"The missing people. Your dad's scheduling a... group cattle call at the courthouse, to do a head count and make sure. But I wouldn't be surprised if it's all of them." She let him process the news, but went on before he could ask anything else. "So why don't I feel like the danger has passed? The danger to you."

The missing had come back to Roanoke Island. He allowed the brittle edge of the voices to bite into him, sure the dead's return was linked.

"Because this isn't over. But you don't need to worry about me – I need to get to Miranda. *She's* the one in danger."

His mom removed her hands from his, refusing to meet his eyes. She never refused to meet his eyes.

"Then maybe this is the safest place for you," she said, tapping her fingers on the bars.

"No," he said. "No."

"I'm... I'm sorry. I think it is, and I'm your mother."

"Mom, you have to trust me."

"This is new territory and... I can't let you go wandering around in it. My job is to protect you. This is the only way I have to do that. You can go back to being bad boy genius when this is over."

She didn't bother to pick up her coffee cup. She just turned and walked up the hall, leaving him there.

Miranda thrashed in her sleep. Sidekick's periodic low whining had made for a restless night. She'd been tired enough to get some sleep despite that, but not at ease enough to do it soundly. Instead she watched her dreams play, like movies she hadn't bought tickets for.

At first, the images had been of the sinister black ship, sailing ever forward. But this dream, the one that would finally wake her, took place in a beachside clearing that she recognised as the settlement that the theater mimicked. There was no ship, but there were people.

The dream settlers stood in rows facing the Sound, packed sand beneath their feet. They wore clothes that resembled costumes from the show, with one change. Long gray cloaks hung from their shoulders like so many pairs of broken wings. A storm had soaked the beach, and thick thunderheads above threatened its return. The settlers chanted words Miranda couldn't make out. As they raised their arms, their cloaks floated in the air, broken wings straining to fly, and always, always, the settlers passed between them some object hidden from her by their bodies.

She woke as the last of them began to turn, the secret about to be revealed.

Polly sat on the edge of the bed, looking at her.

Miranda scrambled from beneath the covers, questioning whether she was still asleep.

"Your face is a welcome sight," Polly said.

Her expression was oddly serious, but other than that she appeared normal. Premature gray hair, T-shirt with paint spatters, familiar brown eyes. A copy of a John White nature sketch hung on the wall behind her like a floral crown.

"When... Where... What happened to you?" Miranda forced out.

Sidekick wasn't growling or whining, but he edged closer to lay his head flat on top of Miranda's feet. His furry eyebrows twitched up and down with worry.

Polly said, "I'm not sure I can explain to you."

"But you're OK?"

Polly inclined her chin. "Why are you here?"

Miranda searched for a place to start. Her father dead, a cute boy swooping in from the past, Roswell's revelation about her ancestor... "I'm sorry about taking your bed. It's a long story. We didn't know if you'd be back or when–"

"We?"

Phillips. Miranda hoped he wasn't still being eaten by wild voices. But that didn't matter to Polly. Polly, whose expression had yet to change. *Solemn as fake Virginia Dare telling the audience the settlers will never return.* Weird.

"Is it just you who's back?" Miranda asked.

"No," Polly said, her features shifting into a frown. "I believe everyone managed to return."

"Return from where?" Even if it was negative, Polly's showing any emotion was a small comfort. What had she been through?

Polly rose. "The others have breakfast."

Miranda glimpsed herself in a small round mirror hanging on the wall. The snake crawled up her cheek, and she had to fight the urge to touch it. At least Polly didn't seem to have noticed. She glanced over to check the position of her bag against the wall, without really understanding why the idea of leaving it made her uncomfortable. Other than the fact it held the possibly sacred, possibly evil, almost certainly magical gun inside.

"Come on," Polly said from the doorway. "Breakfast."

Miranda had no choice but to go with her or make a scene. Sidekick moseyed along behind her. In the main room, she found two more familiar faces at the small table in the kitchen – she felt guilty that she hadn't really worried about Polly's missing roommates. Kirsten and Gretch were the type who stayed out late and picked up tourist boys on vacation. Miranda didn't know them that well.

All three of the others were dressed in real clothes, while Miranda fingered fuzzy pajama bottoms printed with penguins in top hats.

"Hi," Miranda said, uncertain.

Polly grabbed a seat at the table, smiling toward the other girls in a way that didn't reach her eyes. Miranda pulled out the chair next to her and sat, trying not to be so obvious in observing her friend. Which left her the other girls to watch.

They had the same serious expression as Polly – more disconcerting on them than on her. Miranda's memories of them not at work involved giggling and downing fire-red shots at after-parties.

The redhead, Kirsten, gripped a donut in one hand. She took an enormous bite of it, chewing with an energy that said she was either starving or the world's biggest donut fan.

Gretchen said, "Good morning… Miranda…"

The way she trailed off left Miranda waiting for more, but Gretchen said nothing else.

"Have some donuts." Polly filled the silence, tapped the box. "Kirsten would talk of nothing else."

Having finished her previous, the girl with red hair selected an enormous cruller shaped like a curled hand from the box and bit into it, using her other hand to shove the box toward Miranda.

"Um, OK," Miranda said, taking the smallest donut in the box, though she was more of a chocolate than a glazed girl. The box, soggy with icing, proclaimed its origin at the Stop and Gas less than a mile away. "When did you guys get these?"

"I walked for them." Kirsten spoke around a mouthful of cheap pastry. "The man at the gas station showed me a picture of us." Her eyes flicked to Gretchen, who tilted her head in curiosity.

"You didn't say before," Gretchen said.

"No, you didn't," said Polly.

Kirsten chewed, and said, "They were not good pictures." She paused, "Photocopies. He knew we were missing. The picture said so."

Miranda managed to swallow the one bite she'd taken. "Everyone knew you were missing. There were a lot of you."

"We know," Polly said.

"He gave me the donuts," Kirsten said.

Maybe they'd been taken by a cult after all, if this was what people who'd been brainwashed acted like – not like themselves, but not entirely different. "That was nice," Miranda said. "So, what happened to you guys?"

Kirsten hadn't lowered the donut, and the three of them

gazed openly at one another, having a private conference without speaking. "We can't tell you," she said. And Polly added, "Yet. We are not ready to tell you yet." Polly attempted to soften the words with a smile, which made Miranda even more uneasy. She needed to talk to Phillips.

Unfortunately, he was in jail.

"Have you checked in with the police?" Miranda asked. "They've been looking for you guys. You should probably go over there."

"I called," Polly said, "and after breakfast we will go to the courthouse. That is where they want us to go."

Relief nearly made Miranda fall off her chair. To get out of this house, away from these stiff, donut-scarfing girls, she'd take her chances at being caught.

"Great," Miranda said. "I can drive you, if you want–" Polly was frowning at her, so she came up with a reason "–you know, if you don't feel up to operating heavy machinery."

"Heavy machinery," Polly echoed. "That sounds like a good idea."

17

Connections

The minutes crept by with Phillips wishing he could make them pass more quickly. He drummed on the legs of his jeans, struggling to subdue the brittle voices in his head while he waited.

His mom might be scared, but that just left him to sort this out on his own. So he waited (and waited) for the noise in the station to die down. They'd take everyone they could spare to manage the crowd and check the identities of the returned at the "cattle call." There'd probably be just one or two guys left behind at the jail.

By the time it finally got quiet, he was more than ready to put his plan into action.

He stood, took a deep breath, and then launched his body forward. His knees hit the cell floor near the bars, and he shouted in real pain. He banged his fists on the floor, hard enough to bruise his knuckles. He raised his hands and tore at his hair.

He dove so deep into the performance that he barely noticed when the officer appeared outside the cell.

"Are you OK, son? Your father's not here."

He turned his head toward the voice. He didn't know this particular officer, some younger guy who couldn't have been on the force that long.

Phillips shouted again, his cry fading when he heard the officer curse and start to walk away. "Wait..." Phillips choked out the word. The choking part came easy, given how little he'd had to drink and the fact he really had spent the night moaning in agony. "Meds," Phillips said. "Need Roswell meds. Call doctor."

"I don't know," the officer said. "I can call your father and ask–"

Phillips cut him off with another roar of pain. "Meds," he said, "call Roswell."

He doubled over in what he hoped was a realistic imitation of pain. At the corner of his vision, he saw the guy nod quickly. "Hang on," the officer said. He was talking to himself as he walked away, "Sure, Chief, I'm the one who let your son go crazy. Sorry about that. Maybe you should just never promote me in return... Crap!"

Phillips moaned some more, settling in to a pattern of pitiful cries, lowering onto his back on the bench. He kept the pitiful low enough that if he strained to block out the voices – they seemed less agitated at the moment, or was he imagining that? – he could hear the officer's return. It didn't take nearly as long as he expected.

"Uh, Phillips," the officer said, "your dad actually had the doctor leave these."

I bet he did.

Phillips moaned louder and fought his limbs into an elaborate sit. He jerked to his feet. The officer had a small cup of water and a handful of several pills. This would be the hard part. The part he had to pull off or be stuck in here while whatever bad thing had come to town went after Miranda.

"Thank you, officer." Phillips forced out the words like a sleeptalker, tone loud and broken. He stumbled to the bars, then bounced off them and fell down onto the floor. He watched through slitted eyes as the officer realised he didn't have a free hand to unlock the cell door with and then maneuvered the styrofoam cup between two fingers of the hand that held the pills, angling the key smoothly with his left hand.

Not a fumbler then.

Phillips waited for him to get close, and reached up for the pills and the water. Looking skeptical, the officer guided the cup to his hand. Phillips had a flash of insight. He needed to convince this guy. So, he did the last thing the guy would expect based on his reputation. He cooperated.

Phillips opened his mouth and extended his tongue. The officer hesitated, then dropped the pills into his mouth. *Gel-coated. Finally, a break.*

He took a sip of water and spilled the rest on the floor, making sure it looked like clumsiness. He grabbed the officer's arm before he could leave. "Can you... Can you..." The officer had to believe it was hard for him to get the words out. "Take me to the bathroom."

The officer's eyes narrowed again, and Phillips let his own become flying-saucer huge. He hoped he looked like he'd been taking acid or smoking pot. Huge pupils disconcerted people, and his should do the trick. He noted the last name on the guy's tag, Warren, without recognition – he didn't remember any Warrens, so maybe this guy's family had moved here after Phillips was sent away. Maybe he hadn't gotten the full dossier.

The officer shook his head. "The chief said to keep an eye on you, but leave you put."

"Please." Phillips trembled. "The meds. They knock me out cold. Haven't been–"

"There's a toilet in the cell," Officer Warren pointed at the corner. Phillips knew almost no one was ever made to use that thing. In a town this size, that'd be tantamount to treason against a fellow citizen. Tourists, on the other hand…

"Not the tourist toilet." Phillips grabbed his arm again, struggling to his feet. "I don't have long. The meds. Take me."

Officer Warren's attention flicked back and forth between the cell toilet and Phillips. "Crap. All right. But don't tell your dad, OK?"

Phillips closed his eyes, flicked them back and forth behind closed lids with a moan. He popped them open. "I'll tell him you *helped* me."

A satisfied smile transformed the officer back to high school age. *God, he looks younger than me. In all the ways that count, he seems to be younger than me.* Phillips gave a moment's regret to the trouble this guy would be in when his dad came back. *Maybe they'll bond over it – I've tricked my dad enough times.*

First, he had to get out of here though. He bent as he stood, enough to dump the pills in his hand with a casual tired swipe across his mouth.

He leaned his weight against the officer, heavily. His timing had to be perfect.

They walked – the officer normally, Phillips half-stumbling – up the hall and into the station. The bathrooms were on the far side of the large open room, on the other side of the break area.

Officer Warren wasn't the only one left after all. A vaguely familiar man in a black suit that screamed FBI sat at the big coffee table in the break area. His head was tipped back to watch the muted ceiling-mounted TV.

The man's presence complicated things. Phillips traced the consequences – of both success and failure. Once he took the next step in this plan, he'd be in the kind of trouble he'd always avoided. The kind that wasn't so easy to get away from. The decision was his to make.

And in that moment, wrecking his future didn't matter. Only today mattered. Only tomorrow mattered.

The rest could storm down afterward and ruin his life. He'd take the chance.

The FBI guy was drinking coffee. Another cup rested in front of the vacant chair next to him. So he and the officer had been watching the coverage together, drinking coffee. Phillips had banked on both. After all, who wanted to miss the action? That guaranteed the TV'd be on. And all these guys had been working since the disappearances were reported, which meant the need for even more caffeine than normal.

On the TV, the brittle blonde reporter he'd watched

Miranda dismiss so perfectly was beaming. The scene behind her was of crowded chaos in the courthouse square.

Phillips raised his hand toward the screen. "Oh my god," he said.

The weight of Phillips' extended hand carried him forward, the FBI agent spinning with a moment's surprise.

"What is the kid doing out here?" The agent got up, agitated.

Phillips kept his eyes trained on the small square of TV, his hand shaking like an arthritic old man's. Officer Warren grabbed his other elbow to steady him, and said, "He's the chief's son and he's having a hard time of it."

Phillips really would have to put in a good word for Officer Warren. This guy wanted to stay local. He wasn't courting the fed's favor a bit. He was loyal to Phillips' dad.

The FBI guy must have reached the same conclusion. "That's not your call – that boy may have murdered an innocent man just because his girlfriend wanted him to. And your chief promised we could question him after the head count. Take him back."

The officer's shoulders squared. "Not yet."

The fed took a couple of steps toward them and Phillips knew the time had come. Act fast, or go back and wait for John Dee's main event. The voices in his head kicked up a notch in volume, roaring like they wanted him to act.

Phillips ignored the fed. He blinked like he was dazed by the images on the screen. He powered forward, breaking free from the distracted officer's grip. He slipped a hand into his pocket and then back out as he crashed into the table – hard enough to rattle the cups, but not hard enough to upend them. "Oh god, so sorry – can't control..." he said.

"Grab him," the FBI guy said.

Phillips reached out quickly, innocently, to slide the cups back into place. His hands floated over their tops before he released them, trailing the powder from the sedative capsules he'd crushed in his palms into the coffee cups.

The FBI guy moved forward to shoulder him away from the table. Phillips turned and gratefully grabbed the officer's hand.

"You think this kid's trying something, Agent Walker?" Officer Warren said, disgust in his tone, as he led Phillips toward the bathroom. "He's suffering is all. And I seriously doubt he's the murderer, since he has an airtight alibi. Down here, we require you to back up accusations with facts."

The fed stalked back to the chair, yanked it out and swung back into place. Phillips' teeth pressed into the flesh below his bottom lip to stave off a grin as the fed picked up the cup and drank from it. *Like a horse to water.*

He crossed his fingers that the pills didn't taste too strong or work so fast that Officer Warren caught on before the plan worked. After all, the officer had to suck down some coffee too, if this was going to work.

Phillips made it to the bathroom with a smoother step, indulging in a few deep breaths, as if the meds were kicking in. "The pills are working," he said, keeping his voice weak. He went inside, counted off an eternity of fifteen seconds, then flushed and opened the door.

The officer nodded. "Back to the cell."

He wasn't half-bad at his job. Phillips checked on the FBI agent as they passed, afraid he'd already be slumped over and the officer would bust him. But Agent Walker was upright, freshening his coffee cup from the half-full pot and eyeing the screen. He refused to look at them.

They reached the hallway with the two cells the jail possessed. The drugs had put Phillips out in only a few minutes, but he'd been in much worse shape. Still, not much time.

The officer removed his keys and opened the cell, hooking them back onto his belt. Phillips' hand spasmed as he grabbed a bar. He gave Officer Warren an embarrassed look. "I hate this," Phillips said. "Being weak."

The officer said, "Just lie down and wait for your father to come back. He'll get you out of this."

No one can get me out of this. Phillips grabbed the man in a clumsy hug. "Thank you," he said, meaning it.

Officer Warren frowned. "Well, not a pleasure, but... I hope you're better. And you'll tell your dad like you said."

"Bet on it." Phillips went inside and eased back onto his bench. "You better go check on Agent Moron."

The officer's face split in a quarterback grin, despite himself. "Babysitting detail," he said. "Not sure who I'm supposed to watch more – you or him."

He rolled his eyes and left, the cell door clicking into place. Phillips echoed the gesture, rolling his own eyes and laying his head against the cinderblock wall to wait. A key was needed to open the cell, but not one to close it. All part of Phillips' plan. The key warmed in his palm, and he slid it into his jeans pocket.

*You just dosed an FBI agent. And, soon enough, that
nice cop.*

But he would have sworn that the voices seemed upbeat.
The chattering had taken on an energy that felt like approval.
He'd never noticed the spirits reacting to anything he did or
that was going on around him before. The voices had only
talked *at* him.

Maybe, just maybe, the spirits would keep behaving while
Dr Roswell's bad medicine did its trick.

Hanging out with Polly and her friends was nothing like it
had been a few days earlier, Miranda discovered. Polly had
always been chatty and warm, but with a serious undertone
that made her competent and good at her job. Now the serious had overtaken the warmth. The other girls weren't much
for the BFF giggles anymore either. Miranda never would
have thought she could miss their endless in-jokes. She did.

Miranda hesitated before starting Polly's Taurus. "Are you
sure Sidekick will be all right here?"

Sitting in the passenger seat beside Miranda, Polly didn't
answer. Miranda had casually placed her messenger bag
between them, the strange concealed weapon inside. No way
was she leaving it behind again.

Kirsten had insisted on bringing the few remaining donuts
along, the sagging box propped on her knees in the backseat.
Polly's head whipped around at the sound of the donut box
opening. She frowned at Kirsten, "Get control of yourself."

Gretchen reached out to grab the last donut for herself,
frowning too. *Like she doesn't know what she's doing.*

Gretchen had complained in the house that the sugar in the donuts made her stomach hurt. Miranda told her that was because she usually refused to eat either carbs or refined sugar. Gretchen's reaction then had been like the one now, disapproval tinged with confusion. Miranda had felt the urge to explain what carbs and refined sugar were. Which was ridiculous.

The day the overly skinny and obsessed Gretchen Wolcott didn't know the definition of these things – along with descriptions of every diet popular in the last five years – was the day that Miranda's ancestors turned out to be witches, people who'd sold their souls to some weirdo with an Elizabethan mad science lab. *Oh.*

"Let me just go get him," Miranda said. She should keep Kicks with her, in case these girls forgot that dogs weren't something they ate when the donuts ran out. *OK, not fair. They're acting strangely, but surely they wouldn't...* Kirsten's cheek puffed with her fifth donut. *They might.* And Miranda was leaving with no intention of being the one who brought them home.

"Gretch is frightened of dogs," Polly said. "Best leave him here."

Gretchen offered no agreement or denial, but Miranda reluctantly nodded. She'd come back for him. *Before* these girls made it home, as soon as she could ditch them. Sidekick wouldn't know to worry anyway, was probably snoozing or nosing through the trash for wadded up napkins with donut residue.

She started the car and drove toward town as fast as she dared, meaning the speed limit. She hadn't forgotten that the feds wanted her, that they thought she and Phillips had murdered her father.

Her father. Her hands clenched for a moment on the steering wheel, then relaxed. Wearing the snake on her face made her feel closer to him than she had since before her mom died. He'd borne this curse too, and she was beginning to understand what that meant. It wasn't just a birthmark. It was something that snaked its way *inside*, too. Her father hadn't been strong enough to fight it. The curse had beaten him.

What if she wasn't strong enough either? She shook her head.

Polly barked a choppy laugh that barely sounded like her. "Having a conversation with yourself, Miranda?" she asked.

"Just an earworm." Miranda slowed the car as it entered a line of vehicles heading into downtown, refusing to glance over at her friend... Her friend who was being extremely weird. "We may as well park back here and walk it, don't you think?" Miranda asked.

"Fine," Polly said.

Miranda pulled up to the curb, wanting out of the car. Walking with the others to the courthouse square was a risk, but a crowd would be the easiest place to lose them. She tightened the slipping ponytail she'd pulled her hair into in the hopes of being slightly less recognisable to the agents if they spotted her. They'd only met her once, and Miranda didn't fool herself that her face was capable of launching a thousand ships or lodging in someone's memory. They were trained to remember, though. She wasn't fooling herself about that either.

Polly grabbed her arm before she could get out. "It *is* good to see your face."

Whatever fate Miranda was fleeing, these guys might have already faced. She'd wanted Polly to come back, and she certainly hadn't wished for the other missing people to be gone forever either. That they had returned should be a good thing.

"You too," she said.

Miranda slipped the strap of her bag over her head and they left the safety of the car. They joined the horde of townsfolk swarming toward the square. The air smelled of sunscreen and sweat, of summer's end. Miranda realised there was every possibility the town rumor mill already knew she was suspected in her father's death. Not that they had ever cared about him before. Then again, the chief would try to keep it quiet for Phillips' sake, and there was the return of the missing to fill the ever-present need for something – or someone – to dissect with the scalpels of gossip. Maybe no one knew yet.

Everyone left in Manteo had turned out, from the size of the crowd they joined in front of the courthouse. The news trucks squatted in the same locations they'd claimed before. Near one, Blue Doe had a microphone gripped in her hand and a wild gleam in her enormous eyes. The courthouse itself was cordoned off by police tape, setting a perimeter about fifteen feet past the columns and broad porch. A lesser mass of people were inside the cordon, standing with such patience it was clear they were waiting.

The local police had some help from state troopers keeping gawkers away from the tape, while one of the older officers on the porch repeated with a bullhorn, "Only the missing are requested past the cordon. If you're one of the missing, come up to the courthouse."

Gretchen and Kirsten moved toward the tape immediately, a state trooper shooting them a nod and smile as they slipped under the cordon.

When Polly didn't follow, Miranda patted her shoulder. "It's OK, you should go with them now," she said, trying her best to hide the shake in her voice.

"You will wait for me?" Polly asked.

I'm a terrible person. "Of course," she said. "Now, go. Your parents are probably worried sick."

Miranda thought they lived somewhere in upstate New York. Polly's lashes fluttered, and she said, "I forgot about them… My parents."

Where had Polly and the others been for the days they were missing? Where could they have been that she would have forgotten about her parents?

"They'll never know that," Miranda said. "Go on."

Polly blinked at her, and then finally walked to the trooper and under the yellow tape. Miranda turned away quickly when he shifted in the direction Polly had come from. Going into a crowd full of law enforcement was not among her top five smartest decisions ever. Had this been one of her favorite shows, she'd be screaming '*Get out of there!*' at the screen. She slipped back through the crowd, intending to do just that.

"Is that everyone?" officer bullhorn said.

The crowd continued to talk, speculating how much tourism would pick up after this, how it must have all been arranged, who was in on it and who wasn't. Spinning theories to make sense of the mystifying now that the missing were herded before them, no longer missing.

"Silence, please." The officer roared into the bullhorn. "Now. Do we have everyone?"

The crowd stopped talking, necks craning to see inside the cordon. Miranda stopped, afraid to keep moving when no one else was.

"Last call for members of the missing to join us behind the tape," the officer said.

Miranda turned her head and watched Chief Rawling come through the front door of the courthouse and stride over to take the bullhorn. "Welcome back, everybody," he said. "We knew the town would want to see you, to know that everyone is OK. That's why we're doing things this way. If you could just stay here, we'll be coming through to take your names and then take you inside for your statements. We'll get you back to your families as quickly as possible."

Miranda had felt like she was under a spotlight the entire time she'd been in the crowd, but suddenly the snake pulsed. She scanned the mass of people and, all the way on the other side of the square, saw Bone pointing at her. She read his lips: "There she is!"

He was with his friends, but his father was standing behind them and he cuffed Bone's ear. Dr Roswell focused on her location too. The crowd had begun a low buzz of conversation after the chief's announcement, and that saved her. She had to get out of here.

She took one last look at the courthouse where the missing were arrayed and stopped. They were arranged in a familiar formation. Some were higher, being on the porch between the columns, and some lower, down the stairs, on the sidewalk and lawn. In tidy rows, each of them turned to the other in sequence. They weren't wearing the gray cloaks from her dream, but their arms wound through the air in similar fashion.

The crowd hushed again, and Miranda had trouble breathing. This was no dream. She forced herself to look away from the movements of the missing and found Roswell cutting through the crowd toward her. He dragged Bone along by his arm.

Miranda shoved her way past people murmuring their confusion about the bizarre arm-waving actions of the no-longer missing. Phillips trusted Roswell, but she barely knew him. And she definitely didn't trust Bone.

She made it to the crowd's thinner edge, ready to head for Polly's car. She couldn't resist checking behind her, to confirm what she'd seen. Were they really doing the motions from her dream?

The missing were still clearly visible, on the raised porch and just below it in their rows. But they stood normally, arms relaxed, making her wonder if she'd imagined their actions. No. The crowd – they'd reacted. This wasn't like at the theater with the ship. Everyone else had seen their movements too.

Frowning, about to take off, she almost missed him. He walked under the police tape and entered the rows of the returned people. He stopped and looked at her, unmistakably *at her*. She wouldn't have been sure it was him if she'd never seen the photos from their wedding day. That suit had been from the Salvation Army, but this one was nicer. Better cut. He could have been a businessman.

Instead, he was her father.

18

No Escape

Miranda hadn't known her dad could clean up so well. His hair had been trimmed into a tidy cut, and no stubble shadowed his cheeks. His complexion was pale instead of ruddy, his eyes clear. He tilted his head down, as if to greet her.

She wanted to go to him, felt compelled by some magnetic force. She took a step toward him without meaning to.

"*Come to me.*" The whisper seemed to come from beside her ear. She stumbled.

"Miranda Blackwood!" Roswell called out, and a few people nearby noticed her.

"Poor girl. Her father got murdered – that family truly is cursed," someone said to the person next to them, and Roswell called "Miranda!" again.

She snapped out of the blind-need haze. No one else recognised her father. And why would they, when she barely did herself? They might gossip about him, but she doubted they ever bothered to look too closely. To them, this man was a clean-cut stranger in a suit. They probably thought he was a disappeared tourist.

The man who *had* to be her father – but who didn't *feel* like him, somehow – curved his lips in the slowest smile she'd ever seen. The expression was as foreign as his made-over appearance. She was certain the voice next to her ear had been his, even though his lips hadn't moved, except to offer that slow smile.

Even though she hadn't recognised the voice as her dad's.

A couple of rows away from him, Chief Rawling held a clipboard and talked to one of the returned. He paused to scan the crowd, which meant he'd heard the good doctor's shouts. The woman the chief had been talking to swiveled. It was Polly. The sun fell directly on her features, her face pinched as she followed the chief's lead and scrutinised the surge and press on the other side of the rope line.

Miranda shrank behind a large man in the crowd, hiding. *My father is dead.* She called up the memory of him laid out on the shiny table in the funeral home, the cold air and antiseptic smell of the room returning like a sudden sweat.

"Miranda!" The shout sounded nearer. "I just want to talk. It's about Phillips!"

Nice try. That crackpot was going to get her busted.

She made sure the keys were ready in her hand before she went for the car. There was no looking back this time, no Sidekick to get distracted by the evil phantom ship, no one but her. And then she was behind the wheel of Polly's car, tossing her bag into the back and turning the key in the ignition, jerking the car into drive and out of the spot.

She executed a three-point turn in the middle of the wide street, not willing to do a drive-by of the scene or risk getting caught on a throng-blocked street. She didn't miss Pineapple this once, because Polly's Taurus made a far more reliable get-away car.

In the rearview mirror, she spotted Dr Roswell on the street behind her. His hands were propped on his hips, head shaking. His face was as pink as Bone's when an insult landed.

It was too bad if she'd hurt Roswell's feelings. Phillips could apologise for her later. She didn't have time to worry about him. No, her worry was fixed on her father – or was that on the man who wore her father's body?

Dead men didn't hit the salon and go out for a stroll, not even on Roanoke Island. Or did they?

She barely knew where she was headed until she arrived, only to wonder if she might finally be losing her mind.

Phillips waited as long as he could, composing a symphony with the drumming he inflicted on his legs. But he couldn't sit tight any longer. Either the drugs had worked their sleepy magic, or his plan had tanked and he'd head directly back to his to jail cell without passing go. There was one way to see whether his fate was door number one or…

"Opening door number two," he murmured. He stuck his hand through the bars and fit the key into the lock. He clamped onto the door with his other hand, avoiding a clank by holding the metal in place when the tumbler released. Slowly, he eased the door open and slipped into the hallway. The voices lowered, like they were worried about giving him away.

So far, so not descended upon by angry young officer. He hurried up the hall, stepping softly, glad for his sneakers. He hit the end of the hallway, the front door of the station in sight, and judged it an acceptable risk with everyone else otherwise occupied.

The cough startled him.

In the waiting area, Officer Warren was slumped into a chair the powder blue of a bad tux. He looked like he was fighting hard to stay conscious.

Phillips checked the station floor and spotted the FBI agent. He laid forward on the coffee table with his head on his arms, like a kindergartener at naptime. If kindergarteners were bald and wore black suits.

Officer Warren's next sound was a massive yawn mixed with a frustrated moan. He said, "Don't... be... stupid."

Phillips noted the gun loosely gripped in the cop's left hand. "I'm not," Phillips said. "That's always been one of my biggest problems." *That and hearing the dead.*

The officer clearly put forth a massive amount of energy to get his next sentence out. He said, "You'll go to jail. For real."

Phillips nodded. "Probably."

"I hope whatever you're leaving for's worth... that."

She is. Phillips headed for the door. "I'm not leaving, I'm staying," he said, shocked to discover it was true. Under his breath, he added, "For once." He pressed the glass door, then crooked his head back. The officer might or might not have sunk into sleep, but he said, "You'll both be fine once the drugs wear off. I'm not *that* stupid."

Phillips hit the parking lot and considered his options. They weren't great – none of the things he needed to do meshed, and he had no idea where to find Miranda. He scanned to make sure the area was deserted and stopped.

Across the street in the station parking lot, the driver's side door of a maroon Taurus – he'd never seen it before, he was certain – swung open. Before he could take off, someone stepped out of the strange car, someone who wasn't a stranger. Her hand gripped the top of the door.

Miranda?

Blinking at the front of the jail from across the street, Miranda was convinced she *had* lost her mind. Maybe she dropped her brain somewhere in the courthouse square. The jail's front door had opened and Phillips strolled out.

He squinted in the sun, the wind punking his hair into messy pieces. The clothes he'd been wearing the day before were rumpled. And probably still rough with fine grains of sand worked into the faded T-shirt's green cotton and the grooves of his jeans.

The memory opened inside her, a raw wound. She'd shoved him *to the ground*. She'd shoved him *to the ground* when he was *in pain*. Getting to him had been her biggest goal an hour before, but she considered running again. Or at least ducking so he couldn't see her.

But they both just stood there, looking at each other.

Phillips moved first, jogging over to the car with easy strides that gave her the courage to leave the safety of the car door shield. She walked forward to meet him, putting her hands in her pockets to keep them from shaking. Correction: to hide their shaking.

Letting other people have this much power over you is dangerous. She thought it, but somehow, she couldn't care about that. Not with Phillips almost to her.

He stopped and she did, too. Half an arm's length separated them. She wasn't sure what to do next. He grinned at her.

"I'm sorry," she blurted.

When his brow wrinkled above the grin, the grin that stayed, she was afraid he'd ask what she was sorry for, so she blurted again. "We have big problems. Huge, really."

His eyebrows shot up. She'd missed those eyebrows.

"Well, yeah. You're a federal fugitive," he offered. "For one."

She thought of the missing, standing in their rows, lifting their arms, and her father walking among them. Or the man *wearing* her father, she corrected herself, feeling dizzy. Which possibility was worse?

She detected the shimmer of sand in his shirt. He was waiting for her to respond.

"Oh," she said, "I didn't mean *that*."

"I am too," he said. "Now, I mean. A fugitive."

She angled her head at the station house, "You *didn't*?"

His grin slipped away. "I did."

"You escaped from jail?"

His nod was short. "Guilty," he said, fidgeting.

So he really *was* a federal fugitive. But then so was she. How had he managed to... What if he got in *more* trouble? Because of her?

Her hand left her pocket before she knew what she was doing. She reached up and gave him a push with her palm. "Get in the car, Houdini."

His shoulder rolled away from her stupid shoving hand. But the shove had been light this time. A tap. A request.

He got in the car without a word. She joined him, shaking her head – *he escaped from jail* – as she put the car in drive. *He escaped from jail and I immediately shoved him again.*

He patted the dash. "Whose is this?"

"Polly – the stage manager at the show. A friend," she said. "Or she used to be."

"Are you OK?" His question came low enough that she could ignore it if she needed to. But she looked at him, giving him permission to go on, and he did. "Last time we were together you were... freaked. Understandably freaked."

"Fine. OK, maybe still freaked." She'd expected to have to apologise. "About yesterday..."

He touched her cheek, below the evil birthmark, the one she wanted to force off her skin. He didn't seem to hate her. She relaxed as much as she could manage.

He stroked his thumb over the curve of her cheek. She wondered if there might finally be kissing, and if that'd be how they got busted. *Well, judge, they were apprehended lingering outside the jail making out in a stolen car.* Still, she'd have stayed inside the moment, right where they were, no matter if the cuffs were coming. It was the first time in years she'd felt like escape might be possible.

Then Phillips crooked his head toward the back seat. "Your last donut spoken for?"

She laughed because she couldn't help it, the motion tossing his fingers aside. "That creepy donut is all yours. I'm never eating donuts again."

● ● ● ●

As they began a slow approach to his house through the woods, Phillips was still absorbing the bulk of what Miranda had told him. The voices in his head rumbled and rushed at each revelation, but the flow never reached an overwhelming level. It was almost like the voices were confused, too.

What she had to say didn't make any immediate sense to Phillips. So he focused on making another plan, isolating the steps they needed to take to figure out the endgame. He hoped whatever he came up with would work as well as the escape plan he'd eventually land in jail for.

He didn't want Miranda to know what he'd done to get free. Not yet.

They wouldn't be able to keep her friend Polly's car for long, but their options were limited. He pressed a low hanging branch aside so Miranda could pass in front of him. "We do this, then I promise we'll go get Sidekick. And return the car so they won't say it's been stolen. Is that OK?"

Miranda had wanted to go get Sidekick first. The green branches turned her into a haunted creature from some other realm when she turned to him, the kind who lured men into the forest to their deaths. She'd taken her black hair down and it hung wild with tangles.

She resituated the strap of her messenger bag, which had John Dee's weapon in it. Miranda hadn't seemed to want to answer how she'd gotten the gun out of the trunk of his mom's car and so he'd dropped it.

"You're sure we can't do this later?" she asked.

"It's just going to get more risky to come back here. People will be back at the jail soon. I need to get something from my room."

"Maybe we can still beat Polly and the others back to the Grove." But Miranda didn't sound sure of that.

They traveled another stretch of woods. Birds and insects chirped around them, as if it was any normal day. Miranda stopped near the tree line, the house's yard steps away. A quick scurry across, and Phillips could climb the tree outside his room and retrieve the letter. Simple.

Phillips said, "After the Grove, we'll head to Roswell's–" He caught the look Miranda tossed over her shoulder. "We need to question him more about your family history, right?"

Miranda rolled her eyes. "Yes. But I told you – I *ran away* from him at the square."

"You should have, I wasn't with you." He puffed his chest out and put his fists on his hips in parody of a superhero.

Her teeth bit into her lower lip, restraining a laugh as she turned toward him. "Captain Ego!"

"I prefer to go by…" He searched for a better name.

"The X-Prisoner?" she offered.

They didn't have time for this, but he dropped his mouth open in false outrage. "Not catchy enough."

"Mischief Man?" she tried again.

He tilted his chin down and gave her a look full of acid disapproval.

"OK, OK. That one sucks." She bit her lip again, thinking this time, and then thrust a finger into the air. "I've got it – Random Fact Boy!"

He considered. "Not bad. Except facts aren't random, you know–"

The front door opened. He moved to Miranda's side, pulled

her hand down. They crouched, wordlessly, letting the dense groundcover conceal them. His mom stepped out onto the front porch. She scrutinised the yard and trees where they were hiding, but she didn't come any closer. When she went back in and closed the door, he was sure she hadn't spotted them.

"Damn," Miranda said. "She's home."

Phillips frowned, more at Miranda's damn than at the news his mother was home. He'd expected her to be.

"I like your mom," she said. "Don't get me wrong."

"Not that. Why didn't you say 'frak'?"

Her cheeks flushed. "You noticed I do that?"

And he'd missed her saying it more than he was comfortable with. "I like it."

"Wait. You've seen my room. You already know that I'm an enormous nerd."

"I know." He smiled, encouraging her to draw the conclusion.

She straightened her shoulders. "Frak," she declared.

"My thoughts exactly."

The noise of the woods seemed to surge around them, a wall that melded with the chattering voices in his skull. This girl could steal him into the wild and he wouldn't mind.

"Anyway, I like your mom."

"Me too, but she's not on my side right now. Not how we need her to be."

"Because she cares about you," Miranda said.

"Why doesn't matter right now. So you'll wait here and–"

"No," she said. The levity of the past few minutes disappeared, the darkness around her eyes like an aura. "My father. He... I can't..."

She's scared to stay here alone. Bringing her along would make getting out dicey if anything went wrong, but he didn't want her to wait and suffer either.

They just needed to storm the castle fast, make it in and out before his mom had a chance to catch them. *My kingdom for a couple more sedatives and a cloak of invisibility, just in case.*

"I get it," he said. "You'll come too."

19

Last Wishes

Phillips insisted on climbing the tree outside his window instead of trying to sneak in the front or back doors. She could tell he was surprised that she didn't argue – and that she was proving to be an ace tree climber.

It was something she and her mom had done together when she was a kid. Her mom calling her a monkey and laughing, even though *she* was just as good as Miranda at finding holds for her feet at the right angle to avoid ankle twists, at gripping the bark without scratching her palms, at looking up and going there. Maybe they had an advantage in that a fair number of island trees tended to grow weird, with dips and curves, or with trunks split by hurricanes and storms. Bent, deformed, cursed trees. No wonder she'd always liked them so much.

Phillips reached the thick limb that extended almost to his window, and Miranda raised herself up behind him, staying near the trunk.

He scooted toward the window. The limb thinned near its end, and she wasn't sure it would survive his weight.

"You don't have to stay back there. It'll hold us both," he

said. He maneuvered into a crouch, just where the thin end began to bow.

She protested, "Wait, that looks–"

He hopped the space between the limb and the window, landing in an upright crouch on the ledge. As if he'd done this a million times.

"–dangerous," she said.

He grinned at her. "It is, I guess."

"That's not what I want to hear," she said. She stalled. "How do you *know* it could hold us both? Entertain a lot of girls when you were thirteen?"

"Of course," he said, "because most thirteen year-old girls would have no problem with what you're about to do."

She traced her palms over the scarred bark. He meant come across.

"What is it?" he asked. "You climb like a–"

"Don't say monkey."

"Leopard," he finished.

The limb swayed in a breeze.

"Maybe I should stay here and wait," she said. After all, what were the odds that the dead man who looked like her father climbed trees?

"What's wrong?" he asked.

She had to tell him. "Breaking into your mom's car, I tripped when there wasn't anything there. I'm not usually klutzy."

"Oh." He touched his cheek. "Do you think that's because of…"

"This thing?" She nodded. "I do."

He reached out. "Give me your hand. No matter if it's a snake moment, I'll catch you."

He'd catch her. OK.

She pulled her messenger bag's strap as tight as it would go, and then shimmied a few inches further until the branch began to bend with her weight. She grabbed Phillips' hand and climbed unsteadily to her feet. He took her other hand, and, rather than get across in any graceful way resembling what he'd done, she counted to three and jumped across to him. She squeezed her eyes shut, opening them when she landed.

He caught her, but they swayed on the ledge with the force of her jump. He grabbed at the windowpane with the curled fingertips of one hand. Miranda braced against the brick wall that formed the ledge. There was barely room for them both.

The swaying stopped.

Phillips was so close she could have tilted her head and bitten his nose. He held her elbow, steadying her.

"Not *so* klutzy," he said, "but a little."

He turned to the window. Miranda sucked in a breath, dismayed by the sight of the windowsill. "Nailed shut?"

He maneuvered a fingernail under the edge of one flat metal circle, popping out the nail. He did the same with the other. "It was a problem the first time, but after that…"

The window glided open under his hands, and Miranda accepted his help climbing through it. Having solid floor under her feet became the height of luxury, like maid service or a DVR.

Luxurious until she remembered they were in Phillips' room. Together. Alone.

With no time to do anything but retrieve this mystery item he needed. She knew it must be the letter, but she didn't want to press. His giant duffel bag had been transferred from the bed to the floor, and said bed was as rumpled as the shirt he was wearing.

Make that, the shirt he whipped over his head. He seemed to realise what he'd done as he tossed it toward a corner, standing frozen and shirtless.

The moment had an intensity that was ridiculous. Miranda wanted to laugh, but the air was too thick. She made her way to his duffel and picked out a black T-shirt.

Phillips stayed exactly where he was, and she walked to him, laid the shirt flat against his chest, with its fabric between her hand and his skin. His hand rose to cover hers...

And then she did laugh, too nervous not to. She lowered her voice, so his mom wouldn't hear and come running. "Now you put it on," she said.

"Right."

He took the T-shirt and pulled it over his head. A gray-silhouetted ninja raced across the front.

"And get what you came for," she said.

"Right."

He moved past her and bent before the bag, carefully laying aside the contents until he found a certain T-shirt and unfolded it to reveal a small cream envelope, tattered with time. Phillips' name was written on the back. He wasn't hiding it from her.

Miranda felt drawn to touch it, much like she'd been drawn to the gun. The gun in her bag. The gun she'd blasted Phillips with.

Black dust only. She hadn't hurt him.

The light from the window spilled into the room, dappled with the leaves of the tree branches. Both of them flinched at the sound of the front door opening, then slamming shut. Phillips held his finger to his lips, and they waited. Miranda wasn't sure for what. Then, faint but unmistakably, a car engine coughed and turned over.

"She left," he said, seeming confused about why. "She must have taken dad's old car. Hardly ever leaves the garage."

Miranda didn't want to mention that the likely reason she'd left was Phillips' jailbreak.

He filled the silence. "Means we have a little breathing room here now."

"So, what's that?" she asked, curious if he'd tell her. Her fingers still itched to touch the paper.

He said, "It's a letter from my grandmother. To me. She gave it to my dad and he just decided to turn it over. Because of–"

"Everything. I know," Miranda said. She needed to be honest with him. "The other night I listened in on your conversation."

He blinked at her for a moment. "From the top of the stairs. Exactly what I would have done."

He seemed pleased.

"So, what's it say?"

He gave her a helpless shrug. "I don't know. I meant for us to read it together and then everything went haywire."

He'd meant for them to read it together. She was afraid for him, afraid what was in the letter would end up hurting *him*. Afraid she would.

"Do you want me to read it to you?" When he didn't answer right away, she took a deep breath. "I understand if you don't. This is private and–"

"When gram died," he said, "that night was the first time I heard the voices."

"You loved your grandmother?" she asked. The answer might not be so simple. She'd never known either set of her grandparents.

"I did."

"And she loved you?"

His lips softened with his nod.

"It'll be OK then," she said. "Let me read it to you."

He handed it to her. The envelope opened with a whisper of old paper against itself. She pulled out a single sheet folded into thirds. Tidy slanted handwriting in blue ink bled through the back of the page.

"Dear Phillips," she read and paused, giving him time to change his mind.

He waited without speaking. She shifted closer to the light of the window, and read on.

"I'm sorry you were gifted with such a pretentious name–" when she stopped to gauge his reaction to the unexpected beginning he gestured for her to keep going "–and sorry about the gift I know now will fall onto your shoulders. But the most important fact about our family is our lineage. It is what makes us who we are, the keepers and protectors of this island, a ground with as many names as our gifted have borne over the years. You will not find their names written or their actions detailed, but know that our family line has a long history of service to this place. It would not have been safe to document that history. And so it has been a tale told by one bearer of the burden to the next."

Miranda cleared her throat, dry as if dust bunnies from under the bed had migrated there. These secrets were never meant for her.

"Go on," Phillips said.

"In the past, the gift has passed down through the women in our family, fate's way of ensuring its preservation in our line. When I was able to bear only one child, a boy, your father, I thought that meant that I would be the one to finish our task. That either we would end, or the island would. Your father never developed the gift, never understood it. But you, Phillips, you are different. I see now that *you* will be the last of us. We must have been very close to the edge when your father was born – maybe I was to be the final protector. But events were turned from their course. I don't know how long you have, and I know you were not properly trained. I have failed you on that score, afraid your father would remove you from the island."

"I removed myself," Phillips said.

Miranda continued. "Our line stretches all the way back to the first appearance of the devil on these shores. A child was left behind on the beach when the devil's cohort was forced to abandon its plan. Your ancestor, and mine, was taken in and protected by the Secotans. A child well hidden before that bastard John White ever returned, searching for his master's weapon. That child was freed from her parents' sins, left on the island's rough ground because she was too young to promise herself and follow his acolytes into the other world. The tribe knew that decision tied her to this land. Just as the traitor Mary Blackwood's line was to be, marked with the serpent as agents of betrayal."

Miranda choked out her own last name, barely stopping to wonder that she'd kept it all these years later. Being chained to a cursed name was a curse of its own.

Phillips said, "Are you OK? Is that the end?"

She flipped the page to read the last. "The devil and his cohort are bound to return, my boy, and it will be your task to prevent them from staying, to prevent him from bringing a black night over this world. He will claim his acts are of nature, but they are not. He is clever and powerful, and he will not be alone. But know, Phillips, that you are not alone either. Let your gift guide you. Use all your strength, and protect this land as we are sworn."

Miranda stopped. "It ends there. She didn't even sign it."

Phillips ran a hand through his already-messy hair. "So John Dee's the devil."

"And I'm a traitor."

20

Damned Truths

Phillips knew this was difficult ground to navigate. Land mine, trap door, quicksand ground. The late afternoon light traced shadows under Miranda's eyes, hollowed out her cheeks. He wished there was more light on her face, wished there was enough light to see inside her head. The letter his grandmother would probably be horrified to discover *anyone* besides him – not even getting into the Blackwood thing – had read was clutched in her hand.

"The letter did not say that," he said.

Miranda held her hand beside her face, flourishing like a showroom model. "Because the serpent is equal to light and sunshine, and agents of betrayal are all the rage." She lowered her fingers, the gesture tired. Not defeated, tired. "That's exactly what it said. Phillips... maybe you shouldn't be helping me. You have a job in all this, on the side of the angels–" her lips quirked to one side "–literally, I guess. And I have the exact opposite."

Phillips stepped toward her, coming close enough to lift the letter from between her fingers. He was careful not to snatch it away. The voices in his head were talking and talking and talking. He did his best to shut them out. This was between him and Miranda.

"I'm supposed to protect the island, right? How can I do that without protecting you? Your dad–"

"He's the devil in this now, isn't he?" She'd used the same flat tone when his dad told her about her father's death. "He has to be. He was dead. We saw his body."

Phillips waved the letter. Her eyes followed it like the single piece of paper had made solid everything she'd suspected about what her family curse meant. He folded the page quickly – better to put it away, out of sight – and shoved it inside his pocket.

"Gram never met a situation she couldn't add drama to. She and my dad had that in common. But that's *not* your father. You told me it didn't feel like him when he looked at you. Your father's gone."

"Like the people from town were gone?"

She was too smart for him to manipulate.

The beginnings of a theory about the disappearance and the return hung unspoken between them. What if the people who'd come back were ones meant to be long dead?

Miranda said, "If we're betrayers and traitors, then maybe it *is* my dad."

"Even if it is, or some part of him, or an ancestor..." Phillips reached for her hand, but she skittered away. "He isn't you. You aren't your family."

"No. We *are* our families. Both of us. We are the baggage twins. That much, I get." She blew out a breath. "If I do turn out to be the bad guy, you have to promise me something."

Phillips already knew he wouldn't want to. "What?"

"This town has never treated me like anything except its trash. These people – most of them – have never done anything for me, except call me a freak. Except make me feel like one. And that's OK. That's what people do. They whispered about my mother after she died. She wasn't one of us. She deserved better."

Phillips wanted to tell her she never had to do anything for the people she was talking about, that they didn't deserve *her* consideration. His gram's words stopped him. His family was sworn to protect the island, and that meant the people who lived on it too. His mother and father were among that number.

No one deserved to have their life hijacked by alchemists from beyond the grave.

Miranda wasn't done. "So they couldn't help themselves. So all that was part of my being a snake. If I'm the bad guy, you have to promise not to let me win. I've resented all this, all these people, for so long. But I can't be responsible for whatever Dee, my father, whoever has planned. I won't prove them all right."

He touched her shoulder. "I promise not to let you be the bad guy."

"Thank you."

"But what *does* he have planned? You have the weapon, which seems to be the key to everything…" Phillips broke off when he caught a hint of sirens in the distance. Had they just started or had he not noticed them before? He answered Miranda's questioning look with, "Sirens. You hear them?"

She pivoted toward the sound. They were both facing his mother when she stepped through the door to his room.

"I'm sorry," his mom said, "but what was I supposed to do?"

She had on gardening clogs instead of real shoes. He'd bet anything she hadn't gone much beyond the driveway. He'd underestimated her. His mistake.

Miranda's alarm was clear, which meant he needed to remain calm. Even if the sirens *were* getting closer. He asked, "You faked leaving?"

"I've learned a few things from you over the years," his mom said. "And you know how I hate borrowing your father's car. I drive a stick like somebody your age, not mine."

"Were you listening the whole time?"

"Your dad shouldn't have given that to you," she said. "I wouldn't have let him. And I won't have you sacrificing yourself for this island. Not for anyone on it. I love you too much."

"So you called Dad."

The false calm she wore dropped. "You drugged a police officer and an FBI agent?"

She was pissed. That he understood.

"You did *what*?" Miranda clamped her mouth shut, as if she hadn't meant to speak out loud.

"It's not good for Miranda to be mixed up in this either. Your father can protect her."

"Mom," Phillips sighed the word. "I know you're worried and feeling all maternal, but you have to let us go. If they take me in now, no college, no nothing. Jail. If we stop without finishing this then…"

"The devil?" His mother prompted. "The devil will come back and what?"

She'd waited to come in until the sirens were on the way. She was trying to delay them. She didn't want them to leave before the squad cars rolled in. "Why didn't you warn them not to put on the sirens?"

"The feds are a little too upset to go the quiet route."

Maybe he could use her worry to convince her to *let* them leave. "If we stop what's happening, then it won't matter so much what I did."

The tilt of his mother's head meant she was listening to him, but the sirens were getting close.

"It won't matter if you're dead, either," she said. "Will it?"

Sirens. Voices. All getting louder.

He looked with longing at the window, wished for time to plan an escape. The voices roared in his ears. When he looked back, Miranda was pointing John Dee's antique gun at his mother.

It would have been a lie to say the sight didn't make him uneasy. But he wasn't worried – the black powder wouldn't hurt her. He shoved the voices back.

His mother rolled her eyes. "That's clearly a museum piece and they'll be here any minute. Guys, I'm the adult here. I rarely pull rank. Listen to me."

Miranda ignored her, or pretended to. "Can you help me get over to the tree? You'll go first," she said to him.

She was buying them an escape. *Smart girl.*

"Yeah," he said, "we can make it."

He crossed to the window, and his mother moved to stop

him. Miranda blocked her, leveling the enormous jeweled gun. "No," she said.

His mother barely paused, and Phillips watched as Miranda's finger squeezed the trigger. Phillips shut his eyes, a reflex against the memory of the powdery burst, a burst that shouldn't have been possible from an unlit matchlock. *It's a magic gun, no fire necessary.*

Only this time, there was the immediate scent of burning. The first sign something had gone wrong.

The second was the way his mother fell, collapsing in a heap with her head rolled back against his duffel bag. A film of pale dust coated her upper body. Her face was white as a cloud.

Miranda tossed the gun on the floor, and dove for his mother. "She's breathing," she said. "Oh god. *Oh god.* I shot your mom."

Phillips struggled to blot out the renewed roar of the voices, the sudden rush of blood in his ears. He bent and put shaking fingers on his mother's throat, feeling through the chalk on her skin to find her pulse. Steady, if slow. Her breathing was regular, too, but shallower than normal. He gently smacked her cheeks, checked her pupils. No response. *Oh god.*

The sirens had almost arrived. At least two cars, maybe more. The occupants would swarm the house. He struggled to think, to breathe. *Mom.* Before he knew what he was saying, he asked Miranda, "How could you?"

"I didn't think it could go off again," Miranda said, and brought her hand up to cover her mouth.

He looked away from her to his mom. Whatever the gun had done, the cops wouldn't have a clue. He couldn't just leave his mom here. Roswell might be able to help them figure out how to fix it.

"We have to take her with us," he said, a snap decision. "There's no time."

The sirens were so close they screamed louder than the voices of the spirits. He swore he heard gravel flying at the end of the driveway.

He hefted his mother into his arms and cradled her against his chest. He wasn't sure he could make it down the stairs with her if the voices surged. And his dad's personal car – wherever she'd parked it – was the only possibility they had for getting her much further.

"I need you to be ready to help me, just in case, OK?" He knew his voice was cold. *She didn't do it on purpose. It's the snake. Not her.*

"No, that way won't work," Miranda said. She scooped up the offending weapon and jammed it into her bag, then motioned for him to release his mother's legs so they could each get under one of her shoulders.

"She's not nearly as heavy as my dad was," she said.

The sirens reached the house, followed by the sharp sounds of car doors slamming.

"We have to go now," Miranda said.

The roar and protest of the voices was excruciating as they went down the stairs. Not incapacitating, though. Just like at the station, it was almost like the voices were paying attention to what was going on around him. Was that possible?

They made it to the first floor. People were talking outside, and the cruiser lights flickered a colorless pattern against the walls in the daylight shadows.

"Back door," he said.

They reached it just as he heard the front door explode open on the other side of the house.

21

Betrayals

Miranda shouldered the door open. She and Phillips managed the extra surge to lift Sara over the threshold without speaking, neither of them looking back toward the noise of their pursuers entering the house two rooms away.

Twisting his body so he could use the hand not supporting Sara, Phillips closed the back door behind them. Miranda saw Phillips' father come around the side of the house before he did. Chief Rawling's weapon was unholstered, if not trained on her. Compared to Dee's old pistol, the handgun gleamed like a toy fresh off an assembly line.

Oh, the irony if he shoots me.

"Chief," Miranda said, "it's not what it looks like."

That was a lie. Well, not really a lie, since no one would leap to the conclusion that moments before she'd shot kind, funny Sara Rawling with an antique magic weapon. By accident.

But it hadn't been by accident, and Miranda didn't harbor any doubt that being a Blackwood branded her as a traitor. Not one part of *her* had planned to pull the trigger of John Dee's gun. She'd removed it from her bag as a phony threat.

This hadn't been like when she shot Phillips – there was no phone, no sudden jarring sound. Only the repeat of the sirens, and Sara moving toward Phillips. Only the snake on Miranda's temple crawling with fire.

Only a need to use the weapon.

She'd been powerless to stop the contraction of her finger on the rickety mechanism that had released the blast of white powder and smoke. Who knew why it had shot in a different color this time?

Phillips stiffened at the sight of his dad. "It's really not. Dad, you have to let us go."

Up close, Chief Rawling's face looked like a combat zone. His mouth dropped open as he realised whose body they were supporting. He rushed toward them.

"Sara... What's wrong with her?" He didn't forget himself enough to speak loudly, but his questions tumbled out one after another. "Will she be all right? What happened?"

"I don't know yet," Phillips said. "I think she's stable, but it's hard to tell."

Chief Rawling touched the pale skin of his wife's cheek, relief clear when chalky powder came away on his finger. His attention darted between Phillips and Miranda, taking in the smears of powder on their shirts and skin. He pointed to a small storage shed at the edge of the yard. "Bring her over here."

But he swooped in to carry her, lifting her easily. They followed him to the scant cover the shed afforded. Phillips didn't wait for a better chance to bargain. "Dad, we have to get out of here. I think... we need to take her with us."

The chief asked, "What happened? No, there's no time for that. What are you going to do for her that I can't?"

Sara's peaceful face was tucked in to Chief Rawling's chest, like a fairytale princess sleeping under some devil's enchantment.

The devil in me. *Or the wicked witch.*

"I'm going to take her to Dr Roswell's," Phillips said, "while we figure out how to stop what's going on. All this–" he nodded at his mother "–has to do with the missing people. You brought me here because the island needed me. I'm here. And I'm telling you there are things going on that do not follow your laws. Things that can't be explained."

The chief looked down at Sara's face. He said, "She parked my car in your usual spot – I won't report it missing. But you find a way to get me updates." His fingers raked across her hair, smoothing the powered strands back with a tender care that stole Miranda's breath. "I wish my mother was still here. She could fix this."

Miranda remembered the conversation she'd eavesdropped on the other night, and what Phillips' grandmother had written in the letter about her son's unwillingness to believe, his inability to understand.

"Dad, what convinced you?" Phillips' surprise was plain.

The chief looked at Miranda. "I saw the new and improved Hank Blackwood earlier."

Miranda chilled. The man wearing her dad's body wasn't bothering to hide his wrongness. And, of course, the chief would have recognised him even if nobody else did, after all the time he'd spent as her dad's personal police caretaker.

A woman not so far away shouted "Chief Rawling!" and the chief said, "Give me two minutes to get their attention elsewhere and then get out of here. Phillips, I know you'll help her. Do what you can to help us all."

Phillips took custody of his mother from his father's cradle hold. His dad left them at a fast stride, disappearing around the side of the gardening shed. Miranda nearly closed her eyes at the way Phillips was looking at her over his unconscious mother. His sympathy was plain.

"You didn't mean to," he said. "It was an accident."

She hadn't meant to. But there had been a terrible moment right after the shot when she'd felt two things in equal measure. The first was hers, her shock at Sara lying on the floor. The second was a gloating sense that she'd accomplished a goal. That wasn't hers, but she'd felt it all the same.

She'd betrayed Phillips and Sara. She'd betrayed herself. The letter was right.

When they reached Roswell's house, the driveway was vacant and the windows dark. By all appearances, no one was home. Roswell could be anywhere – in town eating dinner, doing interviews about the townspeople's miraculous return, roaming around Fort Raleigh working on his theory. Phillips looked into the backseat, where Miranda held his mom's head in her lap.

The voices in his head were a storm, but they weren't helping, no matter what his gram's letter said. They were distracting him, making it harder to figure out what he should do. When the adrenaline wore off, he'd be exhausted. The effort of keeping the voices back was too much.

"She's no better," Miranda said. She sighed, and then said, "I think you should let me leave you here and take the car back out to the Grove. You're better off on your own."

He turned off the car and got out, clicking Miranda's door open and leaning down to talk to her. He wouldn't let her get away with telling the back of his head. That made it too easy to run.

"Sidekick will be fine. We need to help Mom now."

He reached out to touch his mother's hair. He didn't know what he'd do without her.

"You're right. She has to be your priority, and you seem to be forgetting that *I* shot her. Phillips, you were right. What you asked back there… How could I do that?"

"It's not going to be that easy," he said.

Miranda frowned. "What?"

"Getting rid of me." He held up a hand to stop her from objecting. "When this is over and both my mom and you are safe, then you can get rid of me. OK?"

Miranda said nothing, which wasn't a no. A sudden gust of wind buffeted him hard enough that he pitched forward on his toes. A shadow fell over him. The voices prattled and he made out a word repeated in many of them *Look* look LOOK–

"At what?" he said, without meaning to.

"The birds," Miranda answered.

Above them, the sky filled with a wheeling mass of uneven shapes. The frantic noise of their beating wings and screamed calls filled the air. Miranda slipped from under his mother, placing her head gingerly on the seat.

He noticed Miranda brush at her hair, in what looked like a reflex. "Did this happen before?"

"No."

A few birds swooped lower, and the cries from the mass were like those of warriors in battle, the frenzy of their flight causing some of them to injure others. A small bird dropped from the sky to the ground a few feet away. In death, its dingy brown feathers drooped like autumn leaves clinging to a limb. Its eye stared at nothing, a tiny unseeing bead on an invisible necklace.

"They're so frightened," Miranda said.

"Something's making them panic," he said. The response of the voices confirmed it. Their chatter was of agreement. The mass of birds was already heading off, but he shut the door to leave his mom safe inside the car and said, "Come on. Let's get the door open, and then I'll come back for her."

Miranda looked a question to him, but followed as one last sad shape fell to earth.

No one answered his knock, and Dr Roswell's security turned out to be a laugh – Phillips managed to get past the front door lock with an ATM card and fifteen seconds. Old style locks like this barely existed anymore.

The house was dark, empty. "They're not here," he said.

Miranda called out anyway. "Bone? Doctor?"

No answer. Phillips turned to Miranda, and brushed the hair off her cheek. If he could just make the serpent under his fingertips disappear... What if his mother turned out to be right? What if he'd finally run up against a problem he couldn't outrun or outsmart?

"You would never have hurt her on purpose. I know that much." He dropped his finger to her lips. "Shhh. We'll figure out how to fix it."

The protest in her eyes was clear. She *wanted* to pay for what she'd done.

He dropped his hand. "But why was it different this time? Why the *white* dust?"

Where had all that powder come from? There'd been way too much for the gun to hold, especially having been emptied once already and not reloaded with anything. What sort of weapon behaved differently at different times? He wasn't sure what the white dust *was*, but it wasn't the sulphur and charcoal that had coated him before. Chalk and something else...

He went on, thinking out loud, "And why did it put her into a coma–" Miranda's eyes widened "–or a trance or whatever. Even a magic gun should be a little predictable."

Miranda finally spoke. "What's different now than the first time I shot it?"

What isn't? He intended to give her some answer, but she was nodding.

"The difference is that they're here," she said. "They're back. My dad – or Dee, the devil – he's back."

It was as good a theory as any. "Doesn't tell us how to wake up Mom though."

"Maybe there'll be something in Roswell's papers. I'll get started." She crossed the living room, pulling up the hatch that led to the library. "Go get your mom," she said.

And she was gone, feet thumping down the ladder.

• • • •

Miranda paused next to the table and chair where Roswell sat on their first visit. The book he'd shown them before lay open on the table.

It was turned to the page featuring John Dee's portrait. He was a perfect specimen of the kind of noble the actors in Queen Elizabeth's court at the theater were made to resemble. He had a thin face framed by a high collar. A flush of color lit his cheeks in the portrait, pinched spots like the waxy skin of cherries. His eyes stared up at her, two black beetles about to crawl off the page.

Maybe not *the* devil, but definitely *a* devil.

The *monas hieroglyphica* mocked her from beneath him. In addition to the name and the fact that it was Dee's personal mark, the text said that the design represented the "unity of the cosmos," each part standing in for the moon, the sun, or the elements.

She closed the book, and moved on to search Roswell's desk. Her neck warmed like someone was behind her, watching her. But the house was deserted, and Phillips would be down any second.

Behind the desk, she turned to face the room. Empty.

You're alone – alone with Roswell's fire hazard. The doctor's desk was a mess of stacks and volumes and handwritten notes covering pages and pages, some lined and some not. On the ones that weren't lined, sometimes there were diagrams and drawings, lines with arrows at the end, or circles. They made no sense to her, the content of his research notes as jumbled as the material heaped before her.

There was one tidy spot, at the exact center of the desk.

A single oversized journal with a weathered brown leather cover had been placed directly in front of Roswell's chair. It must be more important than the rest. She picked it up and saw that its brass clasp was similar to the one on the box that housed Dee's gun. Interesting.

She added another couple of legal pads and books to make a pile in her arms, just in case the journal wasn't the jackpot she wanted it to be. Then she selected a spot and sprawled on the floor, setting the notebooks and research materials in a semicircle around her. Her fingers traced the leather book's cover, the surface cool and smooth. She reached up and scratched the snake, which suddenly itched like a bug bite.

Snapping open the clasp, she flipped open Roswell's journal.

The man was insane.

She touched the page, wanting to press down the contents and keep them contained.

Heavy globs of ink formed scribbled out sections, bleeding into a sketch of John Dee. And notes. Lots of notes. "The key to their return?" bumped up against "The alchemist's promise." Names, including her ancestor Mary Blackwood's – small and circled, included in a short list of others. An arrow extended from the list titled *PRESUMED DEAD*. The words *SLEEPING POWER* were written at the side of the sheet in all caps, circled in a repeated spiral.

Above her, Miranda heard movement. What would Phillips make of the madman's scrapbook before her? She knew he respected Roswell, but this guy seriously needed a new hobby. It was no surprise that Bone was such a tool.

She turned the page, noting that he'd pasted in some of John White's paintings. Heavy ink highlighted some sections of the art, with notes written messily beneath. A sketch of a Native American hunter from the period apparently concealed a message that Roswell translated into: "The promised land was to belong to him. Become the New London. The home of the Great Work." The next page featured the detail of a flower, and the legend, "The boundary once crossed permits only one return. All must be in readiness."

"'Only one return' too many," she said.

Flicking past a few more pages, she caught photocopied reproductions of letters with words underlined – *weapon, prepare, bloodline* – and then another page with two words connected by an arrow:

WEAPON ⟶ IMMORTALITY

She advanced another page, and saw the one facing it was blank. This was the last page Roswell had used.

Phillips thumped down the ladder. She didn't look up until he spoke.

"That took forever…" he said. "I don't want you to think I don't work out, but well, who has the time?"

He was giving her a little smile. He was playing the normal game. She often played the normal game in her regular life. The one where you pretended your day was fine, that whatever happened didn't solidify your freak status.

Peering over her shoulder, he said, "Whoa."

"Nice surfer impression, dude," she said. The normal game only worked if other people played along. No one ever had for her.

"Is that–" Phillips' expression darkened.

"Yeah." Miranda wished she could calm the frak down. "It's me."

The sketch gazed up at them, rendered in Roswell's too-heavy hand, her eyes enormous and black, the snake mark circled on her cheek. The birthmark was more detailed than her features, and for that she was almost grateful. Almost.

But being grateful was impossible, given the words beside the arrow that extended from the side of her face:

THE CURSE SURVIVES.

22

Keys

Phillips sat in Roswell's chair, trying his hardest to decipher the meaning of the scrawls and artwork in the doctor's journal. He flipped through the book again, the sequence not making much sense to him. These were the questions – and some of the answers – that had surfaced in Roswell's research. But the notes weren't left for someone else to read. They were the doctor's notes for himself. Phillips didn't know his shorthand.

What he did know was that Roswell clearly had a better view of how the pieces of Roanoke Island's weird history fit together than they did.

"No matter how many times you look, it's still crazy," Miranda said. "We should get out of here. Just bring it with us."

"He's not crazy – this is his life's work. An obsession, but he's not crazy. I don't think."

Miranda was perched in the stiff leather chair beside the little table. She wasn't looking at Phillips, but at the jeweled gun. Her hands turned it over and over again, as she examined its mechanisms with steady, competent deliberation.

She peered down its barrel, and his heart pounded. "Miranda, what are you doing?"

Her focus on the twisted, hammered metal was complete. "This equals immortality. I'm trying to see how it works."

Phillips would never have spent time dissecting the firearm. He was better with books, with messes people made with their minds. His ancestors and whatever random spirits were around babbled, but he could have sworn they were talking to each other and not him. He pressed them to the back of his awareness anyway, so he could think.

"I don't get it," Phillips said. When Miranda frowned a question, he clarified, "Immortality."

She held the gun closer to the lamp on the table, a gem on the grip flashing under the light from the bulb. "What do you mean?"

"It's such a bad idea. If everyone lives forever – well, just imagine it. Imagine if every person lived forever. For that matter, add every creature." Phillips was aware of the fact he'd never talked to anyone like this, not even Roswell, without wondering whether they'd think he was nuts. "The earth would be overrun. We'd run out of resources to deal with it in a blink of geological time. And then you get all the doom and gloom. Rationing, wars, et cetera."

"Et cetera?" Miranda half-smiled, but she was completely serious when she looked over at him. "I understand it – sort of. It's not about living forever. It's about not dying. To be able to keep the people you love around forever? I understand that."

She shrugged and frowned at the trigger, rubbing her thumb across the hammered metal.

From what Phillips understood of Roswell's journal, love wasn't any part of Dee's motives. The alchemist had identi-fied the North Carolina coast as a place he could experiment on his band of witches and attempt to turn himself – and them – immortal using the weapon he made. If that worked, then the island was to be his launching ground to lash out at the world, to take down the queen herself. When his plan went south, disrupted, Dee and White hid the messages Roswell had teased out of the paintings and letters. Roswell had a number of White's personal letters to Dee, but only a few replies from the alchemist-in-chief.

Most people agreed that Sir Walter Raleigh and Queen Elizabeth had been a not-so-secret couple. Watching Miranda, Phillips decided Raleigh wouldn't have liked Dee going after his girlfriend's empire. Raleigh must have been Dee's unknowing pawn all along.

The page under Phillips' hand featured a sketch of a door-way surrounded by trees, bald cypress trunks like fingers reaching out of the ground. According to Roswell's handwrit-ing scrawled around the image, Dee had given the settlers – the ones who "followed him true and were promised" – detailed instructions for traveling past the veil of reality to the place of spirits. There, they could wait as long as they had to for someone to reassemble the plan, to bring them back and complete Dee's agenda. Their lives beyond were tied to the island, not so different than Phillips' and Miranda's own.

Dee intended to follow the colonists into the spirit waiting room after his own death, and he must have succeeded. His was a long game, and Phillips was afraid he was winning.

There wasn't enough here to come up with a strategy to even compete.

The sigh of frustration was out before he could stop it. "What's in here, it's not everything."

"How do you know?"

"These are mainly background details. Roswell must have another notebook somewhere," he said. "There's too many important things missing – like how to trigger the right conditions to bring the settlers back into our reality. And not much from Dee's own hand." Plus, the Blackwoods were barely mentioned in this journal.

He still wasn't sure how Miranda's family fit into all this, what the traitor thing his gram had written translated to. Dee had a grudge against them – or did he? Had Mary Blackwood been left behind just so he'd have a vessel to inhabit when he returned? Roswell had claimed she was an alchemist like the rest.

Evil dead guys having secret plans for girls you really liked and wanted to live sucked.

"You're right," Miranda said. "There's nothing too specific in there – it's more chaos than theory."

"There's also nothing too specific about the weapon." Which meant nothing about how to heal his mom from its effects. He suspected Dee was the only one who knew how the unpredictable gun in Miranda's hand worked. His magic had created it, after all.

"We can't put off leaving much longer," Miranda said. "It's too dangerous for your mom."

"Where will we go?" Phillips asked, though he knew the answer.

"Dee's got to be the only one who can help her. So I have to go to my 'new and improved' father and ask him."

What if Dee wouldn't or couldn't help? And if he did, what would be his price?

"I don't want you to. I'll go." There, he'd said it. For all the good it would do.

Miranda didn't respond right away, instead stashing the gun inside her bag and folding over the flap. She stood and paced along a bookshelf at the other end of the library from the desk.

"Phillips," she said, "I know this will be hard for you. You want to be my knight in... Well, we don't have any armor and that's part of the problem. We're way overmatched. I'm dealing with a curse hundreds of years old that makes this place loathe me and me loathe this place, and that makes you my enemy, sworn to put the island first."

"I'm not your enemy. I never could be."

At the end of the bookshelf, she turned to face him. The wide spines of reference works, dictionaries and encyclopedias, framed her on either side. None contained the answers they needed.

She said, "I have to go with you and you'll use me. You'll use me to bargain for your mother's life. You know why?"

He didn't want to hear anymore. "I won't."

"Because the part of me that shot that gun at your mother, that part enjoyed it."

Phillips rose from the desk. The voices buzzed, and he did his best not to listen. When he reached her, he pulled her toward him.

Their bodies touched, barely, the pressure slight. Pulling, repelling.

The raised voices in Phillips' head reminded him they weren't alone. That he was never alone. The jumble of words swallowed his own thoughts, leaving his mother's chalk-painted features.

He released Miranda. "You'll come then."

"I have to." Miranda looked away. Her eyes traveled down the shelves of reference books, down to...

He was confused when she bent, her hand exploring a gap between the bookshelf and the wall. She pulled on what appeared to be a plastic tarp. When Phillips saw the zipper, he understood what she'd found. She dropped the plastic as she realised it too.

"Is that a body bag?" she asked.

The hatch above them flipped open, light from the living room above brightening the space. She kicked at the body bag, trying to get it stuffed back into the corner.

Phillips shifted to hide her motion from Roswell, who plunked down the steps. Bone was behind him, his face pasty instead of pink.

"I found your girlfriend's father much more polite, Phillips," Roswell said. He walked closer to Phillips and peered around his shoulder at Miranda. "Of course, he was deceased."

Funny that Miranda wore the stupid snake when Roswell turned out to be one.

Sara's body lay across hers and Phillips' laps in the back seat of Roswell's hunter green Volvo, Bone riding shotgun.

Heading across the island had been their next move, but not like this. Not as prisoners.

Thick cords of rope, the kind used by fishermen in Wanchese, chafed Miranda's wrists. Bone had pretended to take pleasure in binding her. His shaking hands gave him away. He was wigged, but still being daddy's boy. Once he finished, she quickly determined that the restraints were too tight for her to loosen by working at them. These ropes were made to withstand the pressure of the Sound and the ocean, of high winds. She'd used them to secure enough sails on the faux ship at the theater to know all she'd accomplish would be tearing her skin.

"Doc," Phillips said, raising his bound wrists, "why are you doing this?"

"After the time we've spent together, you don't have a guess? You know this is my research, my life's work." Roswell seemed amused. "You've always been such a sharp boy, surely you can make a guess."

Bone shifted in his seat when his father complimented Phillips. Miranda was curious whether Phillips had been anywhere near the mark about Bone liking her – doubtful given the overkill on the rope, but they needed every edge they could get.

Phillips tapped his fingers together. "You've always been a crackpot, haven't you, Doc? Yeah, that's it. You think you won't be a crackpot anymore if you actually manage to resurrect history."

"I'm not a crackpot." Roswell's voice was clipped. "And I've already resurrected 'history.' One hundred and fifteen people, to be exact."

Right. Souls of one hundred and fourteen settlers inhabited the bodies of the returned, plus John Dee inside her father. There might have been others – Miranda wasn't clear on whether Mary Blackwood or Phillips' ancestor counted in that number. But these were the one hundred and fourteen people that history had bothered to record as missing.

Miranda said, "Which means you're now killing one hundred and fourteen other people."

"Well, in fairness, your father had to be killed for this to work, and technically the others are still alive. You've seen them for yourself."

Sara's breath hitched, shuddering in and out. As Miranda maneuvered to check her pulse, her breathing returned to a more normal, if shallow, pattern.

"She's OK," Miranda said. The words were a promise.

Sara Rawling had to stay alive, even if it killed Miranda. *Phillips will never be much of a poker player.* His body was too expressive. She couldn't see his eyebrows, but his fingers clenched. "What's wrong with my mom?"

"I knew you had the weapon," Roswell said. "It was obvious, once I considered it, that the Blackwoods would have it secreted away. And then fail to keep it safe, like they're destined to fail at everything." He paused. "Sorry if that sounds harsh."

Roswell had demanded she hand over the gun first thing. There had gone her bargaining chip. She'd planned to trade it to Dee in exchange for Sara's health. She wouldn't have handed it over until Sara was back to normal.

Roswell sure loved the sound of his own voice. "At any rate, the first stage is blackening," he said. "Gunpowder – sulphur, potassium nitrate, and charcoal. They used to call it black powder. Phillips had a hint of it around the edges at the courthouse, and that was when I began to suspect. Then, albedo, the whitening stage. Purification. Salt, chalk. The third is rubedo – well, we will all see that effect together. It is the Great Work. Only *he* knows its secret."

Next to her, Phillips sighed again. "This really is all about alchemy?"

Miranda watched the edge of Roswell's face as it angled into an approving smile.

"Nicely done, Phillips. Such a bright one, you are."

"What do you mean?" Miranda asked – asked Phillips, not Roswell. "I thought the alchemy stuff was all turning straw into gold. I thought Dee was magic."

She tilted her head toward Phillips. Inches separated their faces. His criminally long eyelashes were so close she could have counted them. She'd almost expected him to forgive her in the library, in those last moments they were alone. *I'm as crazy as Roswell.*

"Magic and science," Roswell said, "have never been in opposition the way we think of them now. Dee knew that and found the key to uniting them. To finally fulfilling the alchemist's greatest ambition–"

"Making the first home chemistry set?" she interrupted. She wouldn't give Roswell the satisfaction of holding court.

"Eternal life."

He said it with a huff. She was getting to him.

"Yawn," Miranda said. "Phillips? Will you explain? I like it when you explain instead of Doctor Crackpot."

Maybe she shouldn't be rude, but she couldn't think of any good reasons why. Phillips' lips tilted up in approval.

"Be my guest," Roswell said.

"You've got a funny idea of guest," Miranda said, and was rewarded with another puff of exasperated breath. Bone shot her a look over his shoulder, unreadable.

Phillips cleared his throat, flattened his palms together. "Alchemists were always looking for some kind of edge they could scheme out of the natural world. Making base metals into gold, sure, but their other great project was figuring out the secret to eternal life. Of course," Phillips rolled his eyes, "they should have known that eternal life is the opposite of natural. Why would nature provide a process to do that – it's a dream, nothing more."

"It's real enough," Roswell said, "the greatest discovery ever made. Does your mother look unaffected?"

Miranda realised what Phillips was doing – he was trying to make Roswell doubt that the process would work.

"She doesn't look *immortal*," Phillips said, quietly. "Is a failed experiment worth all this death?"

"The experiment won't fail, my boy," Roswell said. "I'm sorry your mother had to be a part of this, sorry you did. But this is my life's work. No one in my family has ever gotten this close to bringing him back."

"What family?" Miranda asked.

"John White's, of course," Roswell said.

Phillips head dropped. "Whitson – White's son. That's why you had access to his private letters."

So Roswell was related to John White. She pictured the stick-in-the-mud who overacted the part. Figured.

Flashing lights ahead distracted her. A smattering of police cars were pulled off next to the roadway, a few cops milling around outside. No one else in the car had spotted them yet. If she could just keep Roswell talking, distracted, maybe they'd get flagged over. Phillips' dad would help them.

"Why did you bring him back?" she asked.

"To finish his own life's work, the greatest work of all," he said, like they'd approve if they understood. "None of those people were doing anything with their lives. They weren't. Not like what he and his followers can accomplish."

Phillips said, "Lives aren't measured like that. Every person gets their own. One. Alchemy honors nature, and this is unnatural. It won't work."

She hadn't missed Phillips sitting up straighter before he spoke, and she knew he'd seen the cops too. Roswell *would* notice them, but would it be too late? Morrison Grove wasn't that far, which meant the officers were at the entrance to Fort Raleigh and the theater. Odd place for a roadblock.

It wasn't a roadblock. As the car got closer, she saw it was just a cluster of police at the lip of the parking lot. A couple of TV trucks too. Hard to say what they were doing there.

"Dad–" Bone said.

"Down," Roswell barked. "We're too close to fail now. Put your heads down." When they didn't react, he said, "Your mother is in a very precarious state."

He sounded like a nasty professor threatening a bad grade, but they couldn't afford to ignore him. Miranda and Phillips draped forward over Sara's body, ducking below the lip of the window.

The flashing lights reflected on the window glass and tan leather upholstery, and Miranda held her breath, hoping for capture.

23

Costumes

No one stopped them. The sand covering Miranda's sneakers might as well have coated her tongue. Her mouth was desert-dry.

She was going to see her father.

It wouldn't be her father. Not really. But the body would be his, would move and breathe like he still inhabited it. A lie dressed up like a miracle. She'd never forget the sight of him on that metal table. He might not have been the perfect TV dad, but he didn't deserve to have Dee wear his skin like a new suit.

Miranda and Phillips unfolded from hiding as Roswell took the right into the Grove's parking lot and selected one of the few open spots. The packed lot was a sharp contrast to the few abandoned cars left in a lonely tic-tac-toe that had been there the day before.

Roswell braced his hands on the steering wheel. "Dee's soul was waiting there for me. Hundreds of years he'd been past the boundary of our reality, and yet he slipped out of death like an egg from its shell, and into that man's body.

He understands how to unite the esoteric and the natural in a way the world has never seen before. He's used them to beat death. Think of the research we can do, the advances to be made."

"Research?" Phillips snorted in disgust. "You are the worst amateur historian ever. Eugenics, anyone?"

"Perhaps research isn't what I mean, but *knowledge*," Roswell said.

Beside his father, Bone hadn't moved, gazing out the window toward the rental units that made up the Grove. Something in the set of his jaw made Miranda suspect he'd been subjected to a number of these self-serving pep talks. *Poor Bone.* Her sympathy was genuine, if not total.

"Knowledge," Roswell said, "is all we have. All that separates us from lower animals. It is the basis of civilization."

"Bull*frak*," Miranda said. "It's for power. If you're pretending this is about something else, even to yourself, then frak you, you delusional murdering excuse for a nutty professor."

"I'd applaud if I could," Phillips said.

She wriggled her wrists. "I understand."

"This is bigger than any individual one of us," said Roswell. "He will build a shining city of light and knowledge. The New London. You'll see–"

But he stopped, and Miranda felt sure that meant he didn't know if they'd see. He didn't know exactly what Dee had planned for them. Maybe they weren't going to see anything for much longer.

She looked at Phillips, stung by the fresh reminder that

Roswell didn't matter so much anymore. He was just a henchman, the equivalent of the armed guard who opened the door to a bad guy's office on some backwater planet on *Firefly*. The mastermind behind everything, the man who'd defeated death, was the one wearing her father.

Getting out of the car was awkward because of the lack of skills Roswell and Bone had in dealing with captives – particularly when one was out cold. Miranda thought about old movies where people had to cart around someone unconscious and played it for laughs. There was nothing funny about Sara's white features, about how dead she looked.

Even Bone was surprisingly careful when he lifted her limp body from the car. Miranda was thankful for that, anyway. Otherwise, Phillips would have needed immediate payback. And she wanted him busy generating one of his grand schemes to end all this, to crack Dee's stolen shell and send him back to Eggsville.

It didn't feel like something a traitor would want. Still.

Dr Roswell headed for the trail that led through the trees to the houses. Miranda and Phillips marched behind him. They didn't try to escape. All paths would have led here eventually. Bone trailed them, his steps landing heavier with Sara's weight in his arms.

Dust particles flew in the millions wherever sun pierced the canopy of trees. What did they call twilight on movie sets? Right. Magic hour. Ha.

This was Miranda's chance to test Phillips' assumption, to see if she could sway Bone to their side after all. She caught

Phillips' questioning glance when she slowed, notched her head for him to go on ahead. He nodded and hurried to catch the none-the-wiser Roswell.

Miranda spun to face Bone. He was paler than usual, if not as chalky as the woman he carried. He wore another Tarheels shirt, this one with long sleeves pushed up to the elbow.

"What?" he asked.

"Bone, I just want you to know that I understand why you've treated me like you have. If it wasn't me, it would have been you."

Him with his crazy dad, him with no mother, him getting mocked.

"But I don't believe that's all you have in you," she said. "You're not just your father's son."

He blinked at her. She didn't need him to respond right away, so she trotted back to rejoin Phillips. Roswell continued to barrel ahead, in a hurry to get to his alchemical crush.

The trail was damp, though Miranda couldn't recall the last decent rain they'd had, and leaves stuck to the packed earth. The trees' shadows made the trail dark, and the houses were quiet given the number of cars in the lot. Being in the Grove when it was full of people and hearing such silence was worse than seeing it deserted had been. She didn't even hear any birds singing to each other. The forest could have been dead.

A rich throaty bay pierced the quiet. She'd know that lonely howl anywhere. *Sidekick.*

She darted around Roswell. "Stop..." he called, but

Miranda loped clumsily on, her tied wrists at her waist. She tracked the howl through the open door of Polly's. She stopped just over the threshold, uncertain how to proceed.

Her father stood in the middle of the common room. He was bent, a hand curled in the fur of Sidekick's neck.

The coffee table had been moved along with most of the other furniture, turning him into a circus master at center ring. Women Miranda vaguely recognised crowded the edges of the room, sitting in chairs that must have been raided from a variety of kitchens. Their backs were hunched over some task. Needles flashed in their fingers, sweeps of gray fabric draped across their laps. They were sewing. Several of them looked up, but none set their work aside.

Meanwhile, Sidekick struggled and whined against the fingers of the man in the suit. If she'd harbored the smallest doubt that her father was really gone, she knew for certain that he was now. Her dad might have complained about "that fool dog," but Kicks adored him, and he'd quietly rewarded that with belly scratches and the occasional table scrap. A piece of bread, a crumble of bacon.

The worst thing was that the man before her was a perverse picture of the sober, cleaned-up version of her dad she'd wished existed a thousand times.

John Dee gazed at Miranda through her father's face. "Mary," he said.

Well, maybe not the worst thing.

Dee gave her father's head a slow shake, and released his grip on Sidekick.

Her dog scrambled to her, nails scraping the hardwood

floor. He cowered beside her in a way that made her ache. Tail between his legs, ears and head down. As if he'd done something wrong.

Kneeling, she buried her face in Sidekick's fur, managing to loop her arms over his head to hug him in spite of her tied wrists. He shivered against her. Dee's footsteps came toward them, his approach measured.

She should cringe in fear. She shouldn't provoke him. She had to remember Sara, unconscious. They had no way to wake her that didn't rely on Dee's assistance.

And yet, Miranda would have considered alchemy as a career choice if it meant the ability to send this devil back to whatever hell he'd been hiding in for the past four hundred years. He'd scared her *dog*.

"Wrong girl," she said. "I'm Miranda."

Phillips knew he should make some effort to hide his shock, but the scene in the house Miranda had raced into was not something anyone could expect. No matter how weird their last few days had been.

A bunch of women were sewing – yes, sewing – or, rather, they'd stopped sewing to watch the drama in front of them. Miranda rose from a crouch next to Sidekick. Her father stood opposite her, a sympathetic expression on his face.

John Dee's expression, Mr Blackwood's body, Phillips reminded himself. What surprised him was that the sympathy the man radiated seemed... sincere.

"I would never hurt your pet," Dee said. "Animals are more sensitive than most humans–" he looked over

Miranda's shoulder at Phillips with curiosity "–and can sense when the forces of nature are in flux."

Miranda gaped at John Dee in her dad. She was clearly furious. And Phillips didn't want her talking to him when anger was in control.

He didn't believe Miranda had shot his mom on purpose, no matter what she'd said. He was still on her side, even though he had no idea what his gram would say about that. Protecting the island should come first according to her letter. Thankfully, the whispers of the spirits – and they *were* whispering – had quieted so he barely heard them. If his gram was among them, he couldn't hear her.

"You're Dr John Dee, then?" Phillips asked.

Sidekick gave a couple of quick thumps of his tail in acknowledgement that Phillips had joined them, but even the dog seemed nervous.

Bone had stopped next to Phillips, still cradling his mom's body. Roswell pushed past his son to get to John Dee. "I'll do the introductions–" Roswell started, but Dee sidestepped the doc without a hint of interest in him.

"I had no idea Virginia Dare had survived," Dee said, wonder and disdain mixing. "She was a seed of a thing, and the natives were… What's the expression? Restless. Owing to you." He focused the accusation on Miranda, whose only reaction was to continue to scowl at him. Finally he turned to Phillips, and then he frowned. "Why have you bound the hands of Virginia Dare's descendant? Why is he here at all? The child is not one of mine. Her parents are."

I'm Virginia Dare's *descendant?* The first English child

born in the Americas and, based on this and his gram's letter, the head of a line of psychic soldiers. He hadn't made the connection.

"I'm not one of yours either," Miranda pointed out, but Dee only looked at her again.

Phillips needed to distract him. He held up his tied hands, jerked his head toward Bone. "I'd like to take my mother now, please."

Dee reached into the pocket of the jacket he wore. When his hand emerged, long fingers held the handle of a short, sharp knife. Dee moved forward smooth as a shark, and sliced through the ropes that bound Phillips.

The thick cords fell away. *A single cut shouldn't have done it.*

Dee untrussed Miranda with the same quick motion. She backed away from him.

Despite that, Dee appeared to be pleased. Phillips watched the way he studied his hand with approval, before returning the knife to his pocket.

"Getting comfortable in there?" Phillips asked.

Dee considered Phillips. "It's a process. Like all transmutations, one does not simply achieve success in a moment. After being in the starless void for so long, I find I am in no rush. Each sensation is a new discovery."

The adoration Roswell managed to cram into his murmur of approval turned Phillips' stomach. How had he ever trusted that guy?

Miranda was edging slowly further into the house with Sidekick. Phillips didn't know where she was headed, but he could keep Dee occupied a little longer. Hands free, he accepted his mother's weight from Bone.

"What's wrong with her?" Phillips asked him.

Dee reached out with his borrowed fingers, his glove of another man's skin, and touched the side of her chalked face. Tenderly.

"She is unaffiliated," he said, "which means I can aid her, if you wish." He turned to Roswell then, and the professor squinted liked the sun was shining his eyes. Like he was seeing something holy. "You have the invention?" Dee asked him, sounding irritated.

"Of course." Roswell snapped open his leather valise and produced the bundle eagerly. He'd wrapped the heavy metal weapon in a fusty afghan throw.

"Remove the cloth," Dee ordered, long nose wrinkling.

Exposed, the gun lay flat against the nubby plaid throw. It was a dream made in metal. *This* man's dream.

One of the sewing women got up and walked to Dee's side. She wore a summer dress, long and flowing, small sandals that seemed out of place with such a stiff gait. The gun must have been difficult for her to ignore, but she did.

"Master," she said, "I will need to go now or he will suspect."

"Of course." He raised his voice. "Any of you whose vessels possess family should go to them now. You can return here tomorrow."

"I would rather not go back there," said a woman who couldn't have been older than her mid-twenties.

"I understand what I ask you is not easy, but one more day and then such concerns will leave us."

The woman nodded, and all but two of the others also left through the front door. They'd draped the materials they were working on over the chair backs, turning them into cloth gravestones.

Dee gestured for Phillips to follow him. "Bring her this way."

Phillips couldn't believe he was taking this guy's orders. He couldn't believe Dee was being so calm and rational. He'd expected fiery, beyond-the-grave menace. *Don't trust,* the voices inside his head said, *don't* and *trust* repeating. Sometimes it was hard to tell the difference between the other voices in his head and his own.

As they passed the kitchen, Phillips saw three donut boxes – nothing but a few crumbs of frosting left inside – on the counter. No donuts in the starless void, then.

"Eleanor," Dee called, his voice carrying through the silent house, "keep an eye on my M... Miranda, please."

Eleanor? As in Eleanor Dare, his ancestor Virginia's mother? But that wasn't what he really wanted to know. What he really wanted to know was why Dee thought Miranda belonged to him.

A woman answered from a room at the far end of the hall. "Of course, she's right here," she said.

Satisfied, Dee motioned Phillips through a nearby door. Inside the room, he laid his mom down on the bed. He straightened her legs on the pink bedspread, wished again that she wasn't caught in this.

Dee eased down onto the side of the bed beside his mother and touched her face again. The bedside lamp's light gave the white mask she wore hollows and shadows.

Phillips said, "Miranda shot me with your gun, too. It coated me with black dust, but that was all. Why didn't this happen to me?"

Dee turned and caught Roswell lingering in the door. "Leave us," Dee said.

Phillips watched the doctor swallow his protest. He left the room. Bone must be hanging out with the women who'd stayed. He probably wasn't much for sewing, though.

"She shot you?" Dee asked, his pupils large and black. "Of course, she did."

Phillips noted the moony quality that crossed Dee's face when he was talking about Miranda. All traces of it vanished as he went on.

"You were never in danger because Virginia declined her invitation to follow her parents through the veil, into the void. She stayed behind. Too young for a decision, so the decision was made by her inability. You share her blood... with a curiously strong tie given the years that separate you. Regardless, it protected you."

"Her parents just left her?"

"Mortality is fleeting. Immortality is a promise of the eternal, pure as light itself."

Phillips imagined a tiny girl on a huge beach, a wilderness surrounding her. They'd have assumed she would die in minutes, hours, days. A funny idea of light and purity.

"But my mother – she hasn't chosen?" Phillips was solving the riddle. "You said you can help her because she's unaffiliated."

Dee said nothing. He watched as Phillips put one together with the other.

"You can help her if you offer her a choice. If she chooses you." Phillips drew in a shaky breath. "You can only help her if she becomes one of yours."

Dee stroked his mother's chalky skin. She was so pale, a ghost, fading fast into nothing.

"Yes," Dee said.

Miranda found Polly. She was in her room, sitting on the bed and bent over a long swathe of fabric like the women in the outer room.

Polly cursed, her lips pinched in a universal "ouch."

Sidekick stayed so close to Miranda she felt him cringe at the word. She wished she'd been better at protecting what she loved, better at understanding that her circumstances were not of her own making. Or of her father's. She wished she could have seen all this coming early enough to stop it.

Polly had angled the shade of the lamp to give herself as much light as possible, but it clearly wasn't enough. She didn't appear to notice Miranda's presence until Dee's voice – her father's but deeper and more commanding, with a clipped accent – called out. He called the name Eleanor. And Polly's familiar face looked up, exhaustion painting it, and confirmed that Miranda was with her.

"You knew I was here," Miranda said.

"This body has excellent hearing."

Polly jammed the needle through the fabric she held, cursed again as she stuck herself. It was the most inept attempt at sewing Miranda had ever seen.

"You came in here because you didn't want the others to see how much you suck at this," Miranda said.

"Perceptive," Polly said. "I was not a housewife or a tailor or anything but my father's protégée. Of those of us who traveled to make the New London, to bring about the great transformation, I was the most skilled next to Master Dee."

Miranda was close enough to see the tips of Polly's fingers were coated with red where she'd repeatedly stabbed herself. She knew Eleanor Dare – a speaking part, not a footnote – was inside that injured skin, but somehow that didn't matter. It was Polly's body.

"Let me," Miranda said, taking the fabric before the woman could protest.

She sat on the bed and held out her hand for the needle and thread. She started to ask what they were making, but then realised, with a stroke over the cloth, that she knew. She remembered the returned people in the square, arms drifting through the air, reunited with flesh and each other after so many years.

Cloaks. They were sewing the cloaks she'd seen in her dream.

After a moment's hesitation Polly handed over the needle, the rough red of her fingertips painful to look at.

Miranda accepted the needle and fitted it through the cloth again and again. She'd helped out the costumers enough on similar pieces that it was old habit. Sidekick lay down at her feet, letting gravity pull his eyes closed. Polly watched her with a puzzled expression.

"Why are you helping me? Your friend is not in here. She is in the void."

"My friend," Miranda said, focusing on the easy motion of the needle, the satisfying push through the fabric, "still exists. That's enough."

If only it was true.

24

Places, Everyone

Miranda bit the thread loose and tied it, held up the garment. The fabric billowed like a storm cloud in miniature when she shook out the cloth. It was about the best a sinister gray cloak could be in her opinion.

Polly plucked the cloak from her fingers and swept it around her own shoulders. She hooked a wide loop over a button she must have struggled to sew on. Miranda hadn't done it.

"Very Salem," Miranda said.

"There is much to complete before tomorrow evening," Polly said. "Will you do another?"

Miranda found her head nodding yes before she remembered this wasn't the real Polly. This wasn't the person she usually helped without thinking, the person who let her have a stageside view every show.

The cape fluttered behind Polly as she left the room, before Miranda could take back the yes. What was tomorrow evening? And where had Phillips gotten to?

Before she could wonder the same thing about her father's

body and its make-nice hitchhiker, he materialised in the doorway with a bolt of gray fabric. He raised his brows skeptically. "Eleanor said you asked for this."

Sidekick woke from sleep and scooted behind Miranda's legs. She should have known a visit from Dee was coming.

She stared at the floor. "I agreed to sew another for Polly's sake."

Why did she feel this need to provoke him? *This guy came back from the grave. You wouldn't like him when he's angry.* But the insult of having to deal with her father's form was too fresh. She refused to look at him.

"Who actually killed him?" she asked, keeping her eyes down. "Was it you or Roswell? Or was it the ship?"

Dee laid the bolt of cloth on the bed beside her. He was too close. She didn't move.

He backed off, settling into a wooden chair near the foot of the bed. Miranda resisted the urge to put more distance between them.

"What if I told you it was none of those? That it was the curse he bore."

Miranda picked up the cloth, shook it into position. The snake on her cheek felt like it crawled. "Then that means you. You or your ship. It's *your* curse."

She unspooled a bit of thread – filched from the costume department, without a doubt – and threaded her needle. The fabric flowed before her, a gray flood. She wouldn't look at him.

"It must be difficult," he said.

Needle through fabric, needle through fabric, needle

through fabric. She pictured her mother hand-sewing, longed for the machine she'd inherited from her.

He went on. "Difficult to be so skilled but to continually experience setbacks. You do, don't you? The other night at the theater must have been one."

You haven't answered my question. Why would I answer yours?

Her fingers folded another length of cloth over on itself to make a hem, a flash of silver as she poked the needle through. The words were out before she could stop them. "How do you know that?"

"You'll have to forgive me," he said.

There were echoes of her father in it, memories of all the times he'd said: "Forgive me, Miranda-bug." "Forgive me, sweetie." Or just: "I'm sorry." But Dee's words were clipped, his accent and delivery crisp.

She stared at the cloth, realised he was waiting for an answer. She wouldn't look up. Her fingers were so dedicated to their task they ached.

"Forgive you for killing my father?" she asked. "I deserve a straight answer. You got his body somehow."

He didn't respond right away.

Then, "You were conflicted, weren't you, when you discovered he was missing? We are not blind beyond, not unless we wish it. Where the veil thins, we can see light leaking through, can watch the lives on the other side as if through a curtain made of glass. Part of you was relieved, in that first moment, to discover your father might have passed beyond. I was watching."

Miranda's teeth ground together. So what if her whole body had risen like hot air when she'd understood what Blue Doe's reporting meant – that her dad might be missing? That was one stupid moment, past in a heartbeat.

"I didn't know he was dead. I'm not that kind of person."

"You are a strong person. You knew it meant you could be free – or you thought it did. And isn't that what you've always longed for? For freedom?"

Miranda looked over at him, finally. The sight of her dad's face came as a shock, even expecting it. Talking to him wasn't like talking to her father. Looking at him was different, too. He leaned forward, watching her with his elbows poised on his knees and his hands clasped. He was like a preacher waiting for a confession. Her father never sat like that in his life.

"I *never* wanted him dead. Answer my question: Which one of you killed him?"

Her attention went back to her hands.

"I wish I could make the answer simple. But it isn't. Your father had to die. He bore the mark, the mark that allowed me to return to his body. The reasons he bore that mark – the one now passed to you – are complicated. Suffice to say, your family owed me a debt. I consider that debt paid."

She hesitated, then stood. She let the cloth fall, tossed the needle onto the bedspread.

"Then I can go? I can leave? Right now – and you won't follow me. None of this will follow me. My debt is paid?"

Her father's eyes burned with regret.

"I'm afraid not, not so long as you hold the mark. Your

family will be a part of this as long as you wear it, as long as my soul lives."

"That's what I thought." She dropped, defeated, onto the side of the bed. She left the stupid cloak-in-the-making where it lay.

"No," he said. "You misunderstand."

He moved at the corner of her vision. Her cringe away was automatic, but he eased down beside her on the bed anyway. The snake burned and squirmed against her cheek, but she barely noticed because her entire skin *became* the snake. Surely she would shed it, the way her arms and legs crawled at how near he was.

This was the opposite of what she felt when she was close to Phillips. Every instinct said exit, leave, run. *Sorry, instinct.*

She sat her ground, keeping some pride by making no effort to disguise her discomfort. He wouldn't need to spy through any glass curtain to see it.

"You look so like her," he said. He lifted a hand.

Miranda hoped he didn't have any designs on touching her with those fingers. She wouldn't meet his eyes. "Don't," she said, then, "You mean Mary?"

"It tells me that the grand design brought us all here. The angels spoke in my ear when I was alive, and they told me it would all come to pass as it was meant to. And now the boy with his connection to Virginia is here. And you, so clearly of Mary's line. The fullness of time has brought us to perfection. This moment was always the right one."

Miranda missed the meaning of some of what he said, but not that he was convinced everything was wonderful. Sara must still be somewhere sleeping. Phillips would have come to tell her if she'd woken.

"If you help Phillips' mom, Sara, it would make up for what you did to Mary. At least some." She hesitated. "Why did you curse her?"

And my family. Me.

"I was angry then," he said, and nothing more for a long moment. Then, "You are a fresh chance to be better than that rage. A gift for our homecoming. An auspicious sign."

"No, I'm not." She didn't trust the soft tone of sympathy he spoke with. Of *care*, she thought. He was making it sound like he cared for her.

"I can take this away." His finger traced the mark down her cheek, a bolt of heat smashing into her like a wall of fire. Surely her skin really was coming off this time. It would melt onto the floor at her feet and she'd be nothing but blood and bones, like the story her mother told at the Halloween bonfire the year before she died, the flickering light playing over her features and making them unfamiliar. *Bloody Bones, coming for you. Bloody Bones takes naughty children to his dirty pen, and they are never seen again.*

Dee said, "I can take it away. I can give you freedom."

Bloody Bones, coming to fetch you...

The feeling of being on fire faded as soon as he removed his finger, until Miranda's skin subsided to a scoured-raw feeling. He left the room without another word. What he'd already said lingered.

If he took the curse away, what would be left of her?

● ● ● ●

Phillips was outside on the deck when she finally went looking for him. He had his forehead leaned against the middle
bar of the wood railing, his feet dangling in space. He looked
out into the treehouse world of the Grove.

She admired him for a stolen second, unnoticed. He'd been
kinder to her than anyone ever had. Hope was an unfamiliar
thing for her to feel, but that was what she most associated
with him.

And Dee was killing that hope. Maybe it was already dead.

Sidekick breezed past her and over to Phillips, wiggling his
head under Phillips' arm. "Hey boy," he said, glanced over his
shoulder to find Miranda. "Join me."

That was the best offer she'd had in hours.

"What's tomorrow night?" she asked, slipping down next
to him. She left Sidekick between them, without letting
Phillips be too far away. Every moment they had felt like one
where she was saying goodbye.

"How'd you know I'd find out?" he asked.

"I didn't bother trying – I knew you'd figure out what
they're up to."

She won a flash of white teeth in the dark, a brief smile.

"They're going to mount the production, and conduct
some sort of ceremony. It will make all this permanent, from
what I can tell. I think they need the townspeople there –
they're calling it a 'special Dare County night.'"

She shook her head, snorted. "Wow. That's perfect."

"Why?"

"We have Dare County Night every year, at the beginning
of the season." Her vision had adjusted to the dark enough

that she caught his eyebrow quirk at her. "The play isn't exactly the same every year – it changes. Sometimes big changes, like the year the director inserted a bunch of people in animal suits – but usually smaller ones. Anyway, we have a town night every year, a free show, because they're the ones who make or break it. They're the ones who talk it up to the tourists – or not. They freaking quote along. It's a big deal. A special thing the town and the theater have together. We call it Dare County Night. This year's season is almost over, and tomorrow's an off night. No ticket holders to piss off. They can do a special one."

He turned his head toward her, temple propped against the railing. "You're right. It is perfect. This one, this performance, is supposed to be to celebrate the return. This is from Bone, but I believe him."

She'd swayed Bone's allegiance after all.

"Everyone will cover it," she said. That was why the cops were staking out the theater, security to keep everyone out until the big night. "When Grandmaster Dee does… whatever, won't they just think he's crazy?"

"This is John Dee we're talking about here. Crazy is just the beginning."

"Point taken. I've been sewing gray witch cloaks for the past two hours," Miranda said.

The moonlight waned over them, its light thin. Miranda said, "He told me he watched me when they were… wherever they were."

Thin moonlight or no, Phillips' scowl was unmissable. "What?" she prompted.

"I bet he was watching," was all he said.

Miranda let it go. Minutes squeezed by, before he spoke again.

"What did he offer you?" he asked.

Freedom. "The one thing I ever wanted."

"Oh," he said. "He offered to make my mom one of his minions."

"But he'll save her?"

"So he says."

Miranda didn't believe Dee either. But the hope, she had to honor it. "I can convince him to help her."

Phillips said, "No."

"I'm doomed as long as I wear this mark anyway. I can convince him. He wants me."

Saying it out loud made it worse. There was her skin, crawling again. He did want her. Maybe he wanted her as much as he wanted his New London. His angels. His alchemical madness. And he was dressed up in her father. Ew didn't begin to cover it.

"He is the devil," Phillips said. "He is."

Sidekick moved his head over onto her leg. She could have sat there forever with her dog and Phillips and been happy. Could have, if none of the rest of this existed.

"I know."

25

Ready, Set

Phillips woke to discover his legs tangled with Miranda's. Whispering leaves framed a soft blue sky. She'd fallen asleep sometime after they stopped talking, oozing into unconsciousness on the deck. He vaguely remembered giving in and stretching out beside her, closing his eyes...

How they'd ended up sleeping so close together that he couldn't move without jostling her awake was a mystery.

But not that much of a mystery.

Her fists were curled to her chest like she was ready to fight dream monsters, her hair tossed in messy fronds. From this angle, the snake mark on her cheek didn't exist. He could almost pretend none of the last few days had happened, that he'd come home for a visit and seen her again. That then they stayed out all night and soon they would have to deal with overreacting parents.

Reality sank sharp teeth into him. He needed to check on his mom.

Sidekick whined. Phillips had never had a dog growing up, but figuring out this was a plea for a morning bathroom

break wasn't rocket science. Still, he regretted not being able
to freeze this moment. Slow down the clock.

He meant to scoot a safe, non-awkward distance away
before he got up, but the whining jolted Miranda awake
before he could. She blinked, then slid her legs from his and
stiffly sat up. She stared out into the forest instead of looking
at him. Was she blushing?

"I better take care of Kicks," she said, the dog nosing
her arm.

Since the moment he wanted to freeze was past, he wished
for the ability to snap his fingers and resume normal speed.
He searched for something to say that would make her laugh,
relax. What he actually said was, "I don't know how much
sleep we got, if you're wondering."

Why had he said *that*? All they'd done was *sleep*.

"I can't believe I slept at all."

She climbed to her feet and stretched, her back curving a
long arch beneath her T-shirt. Then she pulled the screen door
open and Sidekick galumphed inside, his tail tucked down
between his legs. Miranda paused. "You hear that?"

The trees rushed like water in a gust of wind. Nothing else.

"No. What is it?"

"No birds or insects… It was quiet when we got here last
night too, aside from Kicks. It's like they're all in hiding. Or
maybe took off for less messed up pastures."

She went inside.

Phillips pushed to his feet. How had he not been the one
to notice the silence was unnatural? A forest should be full of
sounds. He was totally off his game, officially plan-free. And

he'd forgotten all about getting news to his dad, who would be well past freaking out.

A couple of voices whispered inside his ears, delivering the dead and unwanted's first troubling message of the day: *Don't worry about him.* He's *safe.*

Unlike him and his mom and Miranda, lost in the quiet forest. Dee had said the natural world could sense flux, but maybe animals were just smarter than people. You didn't see them trying to outwit death and build immortal societies.

Inside the house he encountered a handful of girls and women, dressed normally and back at the sewing. Several more people crowded into the small kitchen – a few men were mixed in with that group – involved in some other weird activity. Water steamed, and there was the smell of burning... was that wax? Four fresh cartons of donuts were propped open on a short bookshelf beside the kitchen. He grabbed one.

"Morning, creepy people," he said, to no reaction whatsoever.

He headed to the room where Dee had stashed his mother, taking a bite of what tasted like sugar and cardboard. The donuts were from Stop and Gas, for sure.

The bed where his mom should have lain unconscious was made. The puffy pink comforter was smooth and vacant. Bone sat in a corner of the room staring at it, wearing another of his lifetime supply of Tarheels T-shirts. Phillips swallowed, throat stuffed with dry dough.

In his head, a voice said: *Worse than you think.* Another echoed: *Much worse.* He pushed the voices away.

"Where is she?" Phillips demanded, fighting to keep his panic theoretical.

Bone rubbed a hand over his cheek in a gesture that made him seem more mature. Maybe his actual age. "She's fine – I mean, awake. Doing better. A lot better." Bone stopped, seeming to choose his next words carefully, possibly the most frightening thing that had happened yet. Finally, he said, "She's with him. The 'master.'"

"*What?*" Phillips raked a hand through his hair.

Dee entered the bedroom. He'd changed into a fresh suit, and his skin glowed like a commercial for skin cream.

He's getting stronger.

Phillips wasted no time being polite. "But I didn't choose. You said it was my choice."

"I believe I told you I could offer *her* a choice, help *her*. I could not stand by watching the poor woman suffer through the purification cycle any longer. Now she'll have time to build her strength before tonight."

"Where is she?"

"Come see for yourself. She's much improved." Dee swept out his arm and left the room, obviously meaning for Phillips to snap to and follow.

Bone got to his feet. "This is bad, isn't it?"

Phillips nodded. His feet felt inches off the floor, the surfaces around him distant and unreal. As he left the bedroom to see his mother's miraculous recovery, he felt like a ghost.

Dee preened on the tree-shaded central lawn outside, lifting a hand to point out his mother in the swarm of people.

His mom's health *had* improved greatly. There was no arguing that.

Phillips assumed the people around her were members of the returned. Maybe some of them were from her rook club. Whatever, the group was solemn and mixed in age and dress. But his mother chatted and gestured, her energy at odds with the subdued people around her.

The entire one hundred and fourteen settlers must have been accounted for between the people outside and the ones in the kitchen. Phillips scanned the scene.

At the edges of the main group, a few uneasy people lurked. He had to assume they were confused family members. He considered trekking over to them, casting his own confused lot with theirs. There was also a smattering of other people. They gave a wide berth to the lawn, toing and froing among the houses like they belonged. They must be the regular theater workers.

Dee really was going to put on a show.

Miranda was near the door with Sidekick. She was staring at his gabbing mother. Scratch everything: Dee already *was* putting on a show.

Phillips' mother saw him and smiled. He lifted his hand, gave a forced wave.

He was glad she was awake and smiling. But not like this. Not if it meant she had to cozy up to these body thieves.

She made her way to him, members of the group moving to let her pass. She looked like this was some sort of town event and she was heading over to say hello and catch him up on the gossip. She still wore her sweats, clog straps dirty around her heels.

He had to admit she looked great. After they moved to the island, too often she had worn exhaustion like a second skin. The weight of her worry was plain as coffee stains and cigarette smoke. All because of him.

That weight appeared not to exist anymore. Her happiness taunted him. Dee had given her this. Dee had repaired the damage he'd done.

"Phillips," she said, and pulled him into her arms.

He let her, but it didn't feel right.

"I called your dad," she said, speaking louder than she needed to. She pushed him back to arm's length, keeping a hand on his shoulder. "He knows we're both here and that everything's OK now. He'll keep the others away until it's over."

Dee grinned at his mother, who gave him a stiff smile back. Getting a closer look at her, Phillips decided what he'd read as happiness was simple relief. She'd made a deal with Dee.

"Everything is most definitely not OK," Phillips said, quietly.

Miranda walked over, Sidekick close on her heels. The other people outside pretended to be ignoring them, but they were as nosy as the people whose bodies they wore. And the normal people at the fringes, they were nosier. Their town drunk commanded the scene.

He was supposedly dead, though, so they must believe this was some stranger. They'd still want to know why their mothers and sisters, brothers and sons wanted to hang out with the theater people. Dee must have conjured a convincing story, if they were content to stand by and watch.

"Master" Dee chuckled. *Chuckled,* and said, "Does your

mother look harmed? She will be one of mine now, Phillips, an immortal. It's almost like Virginia has come back to us – not in blood, of course, but you *are* her family. It's as if you are one of us, too. There will be a place for you in New London."

The stiff smile remained on his mother's face. He wanted to grab her shoulders and shake her.

Miranda appealed to her. "Sara, please. Think. You know Phillips can't be part of this."

His mom dismissed Miranda's objection. "He can't stop it either," she said. "We are *all* a part of this now, and we've come too far to stop now. The world is going to change. Tonight. And no one has to be hurt for it to happen. We can all get what we want."

Her certainty sounded like a little kid's. So did her logic.

"What about your rook club?" Phillips asked. "Your friends."

"There are some things I'm willing to let go of, and some things I'm not. You're my son. They would understand."

Doubtful. But his mother was too scared to listen. Nothing he could say would change her mind. He knew just how Dee would have manipulated her to his way of seeing things. As long as she thought Phillips and his dad would come through this unharmed, she'd go along.

Phillips had to try anyway. "Mom, you can't give up your soul–"

"I value those who are mine, Phillips." Dee stepped closer and placed a hand on his arm. "You need not worry for your mother any longer, unless you try to disrupt the ceremony. *I* would never willingly give up anyone who belongs to me."

Phillips didn't miss where Dee's eyes landed – on Miranda.

"You see, Phillips. This is fine." A slight falter in his mother's voice, but he didn't bother to believe she'd do anything to cross Dee, even if she changed her mind.

A short, square-jawed man joined their small, unhappy group. His face was tight with barely-concealed anger, and a gray-haired woman Phillips had never seen before was at his side, frowning at him.

"Master, I apologise for the interruption," the woman said.

"No need, Eleanor," said Dee. "What can I do for the director?"

Phillips turned to see Miranda studying her sneakers. This must be her boss. And she'd said Eleanor was inside her friend Polly – so he was the gray-haired woman's boss, too. *Not anymore*, the voices whispered soft, so soft, overlapping. *They are trapped. We feel them.* They whispered as if they were afraid Dee would hear.

"Who is Eleanor? Wait, I don't care." The director was clearly used to holding court. "You have to understand one thing: I won't have my name associated with a sham production. Not while the whole town is watching. If we're going to put on the show, I need my employees back," he said. "That includes my intern, too." He looked past Miranda, where Bone was lurking. "And my other intern. I need all my people. Now."

Beside Bone was his father, holding his leather valise. Roswell smirked at the director trying to direct the dead man.

The dead man who smiled, slow and cold. "They are not yours any longer and–"

"This is Polly's support group," Miranda interrupted. "And Kirsten and Gretchen. Surely you can sub in someone for them this once?"

Dee watched Miranda with naked admiration. He stayed silent.

The director cracked his jaw. "And you? *You* need a support group?"

"Me, well... I..." Miranda seemed lost. Her shoulders ticked down a fraction, and Phillips was probably the only one who caught the movement before she lifted them. She shrugged. "I quit."

"Me too," said Bone, though *he* sounded happy about it.

The director wasn't trying to conceal his outrage anymore. He opened his mouth to respond, but Dee lifted his hand and touched the man's shoulder. "Leave us in peace. You have work to do."

Phillips braced for a fight, knowing the director didn't have a clue who he was dealing with.

But the director gave a simple nod. "I agree," he said, scowling like he wanted to argue with himself. He turned and left.

What just happened? Dee must not want any of them thinking about it too hard. "Now, Sara, you'd best continue with the others," Dee continued. "The director is not the only one with work to do. Today is all we have to finish the preparations."

Phillips watched as Dee ushered his mom away, Eleanor trailing them like an obedient puppy. "I can't believe I quit," Miranda said. "Or that your mom's decided to go along with this. What are we going to do now?"

Before Phillips could answer, wavering music began, swelling into something like a waltz, swooping and old-fashioned, grand and polished. The song came from within the crowd. As the gathered people moved back, he saw a handful of the returned men were playing instruments while Dee looked on with approval.

Dee strode back toward them. He grabbed Miranda's hand in his, and swept his other to her waist.

Miranda stumbled, but managed to stay on her feet as Dee drove her in a clumsy dance around the circle formed by the crowd. Phillips' mom looked worried, and Roswell disapproving, but the rest smiled in muted approval. Dee himself was blissed out.

Turn after turn, the dead band played on. When Dee and Miranda neared Phillips' side of the cleared space, he took a step forward. Miranda's eyes were wide and panicked when she met his. She shook her head slightly: *No.*

But Phillips migrated closer, dodging Dee's practiced step to avoid getting mowed down. "Mind if I cut in?" Phillips asked.

Miranda stumbled again.

"I do," Dee answered, and wheeled her away.

Phillips was unsure how to force the issue. His mother walked over and looped her arm tightly through his, to prevent him from trying to interfere again.

At last, Dee circled Miranda back to where he'd grabbed her. He lifted her hand, bent to drop a light, respectful kiss on her skin, and deposited her at Phillips' side. His mother said, low, "Just one more day. One more," and left before Dee's attention fell on her.

Phillips didn't know what to say. Neither did Miranda. She opened and shut her mouth a couple of times. The crowd retook the lawn. The music wavered and halted. Finally, she said, "Did that just happen?"

Phillips held her hands in his. They were cold as seawater in winter. He said, "You know, insects can't just stop making noise. And a lot of them have no way to get out of here. They can't fly or swim."

"Then where are they?" she asked, seizing on the change of topic.

"There's another possibility. They might be dead."

26

Dead Things

Miranda trailed Phillips along the path to the furthest edge of the Grove's property, Sidekick loping ahead of them. Her hand vibrated with invisible ick she would never get rid of.

He touched it. *He* danced with her. *He* wanted her. She officially had devil cooties.

After the nightmare dance, the body snatchers and the theater crew went to work. Mounting the production after a few days off was always harder, and preparing for the 'transformation' apparently had its own pages-long to-do list. Dee left Miranda and Phillips to their own devices. It annoyed her that he was so sure they wouldn't try to escape, wouldn't be able to do *anything* worth preventing. Especially since he was right.

Where could they go? Miranda had no way to get anywhere but here. This island. This day. And if Phillips tried to stop the preparations, he'd be risking his mother's life.

Maybe it *was* a good thing Miranda had never made life plans.

Phillips had said he wanted to test his dead insect theory,

so that's what they were doing. She also suspected he wanted some distance. So did she. Breathing the same air as Dee was like having FREAK written on the outside of her car a million times in a row.

Not anything like how nice waking up on the deck with Phillips next to her had been.

Stop, you'll blush again. Silly girl, all the way.

They reached the final house of the Grove. Just past it was a stretch of mowed grass that led down to the shore, thick forest bordering its other side. Phillips knelt at the edge of the trees and rummaged around in the undergrowth.

"Got one," he said.

He removed his hand, cupping it to brandish a dead insect at her. She wasn't sure what kind of insect it was – had never been that great at any kind of flora and fauna school projects. Leaf collections were a special nemesis, and carapaces all looked the same to her.

"Dead bug," she said. She pretended to fan herself. "For me?"

He rolled his eyes, knelt again and rummaged some more. When he opened his hand this time, there were several tiny carapaces, like small damaged robots.

"Oh," she said. "You think he killed them."

"He has to be getting energy from somewhere, enough to keep himself breathing in that body until it's really his. I think he's pulling on nature to get what he needs, for him and for the rest of them. I have nothing to back this up, really, but–" he held up the handful of bugs "–this. And you said animals were being all weird that first night too, right?"

She eyed Sidekick, worried. "The dogs all went crazy, like

they were, um, barking mad about something. Even Kicks. Do you think Dee hurt him?"

Sidekick thumped his tail at his nickname, at Miranda's attention. He looked fine.

"You said he told you he's been watching you. I don't think he'd hurt Sidekick, because he'd be afraid you'd find out. And I'm afraid he has control of this. Killing these insects, no one will care, notice. The birds, they'll make up explanations for. He needs everyone to hang around until he's really in power. He can't go scaring the locals *too* much before then."

Miranda flexed and unflexed her fingers. She needed to tell him about the dance.

"I don't waltz," she said. "Or foxtrot or whatever that was."

Phillips' eyebrows drew together. "You didn't have much of a choice."

"I didn't have any choice. Actually."

"What do you mean?"

The dead silence around them didn't make it any easier to talk about. She walked a little further around the side of the last house, through the patchy trees. The Sound flowed toward and away from the beach nearby, almost visible from where they were. The cadence was usually soothing. Not now.

"I mean that he was controlling me. Like a frakking puppet. A marionette. I wasn't doing the moving."

Phillips stood there, not doing anything. Finally, he said, "When I tried to cut in, you stumbled. Because I distracted Dee. You were fighting him?"

"Trying, especially at first, but he was too strong. The

mark–" her fingers fluttered near it "–burned on my face the whole time."

He laid his hand lightly across the snake, and she sucked in a breath in surprise. Not bad surprise. They looked at each other.

"He said he could take it away," she whispered.

Phillips left his hand on her cheek, inclined his head closer. "But he didn't, did he?"

"It wouldn't matter if he did, I don't think."

His forehead rested against her own. She experienced a weird sensation – an easier time breathing, a harder time breathing. The Sound washed against the shore behind them in its own easy rhythm. She leaned her head slightly, resting her cheek against his hand.

And she kissed him. A hungry kiss, filled with her need to get away from dead bugs and dead fathers.

Then filled with something more, something that only belonged to them.

His hand slid into her hair, gripping lightly at the roots. Hers gathered the cloth of his T-shirt in her fist, holding him to her.

"Uh, sorry," Bone said, from somewhere nearby. "Seemed like the best time to talk. They're all busy."

One thing she'd never say about Bone: That he had good timing.

Heavy footsteps clomped toward them, and she drew back, releasing Phillips' shirt. But he didn't turn to Bone right away, watching her instead. His face was still near hers.

Frak. She was blushing. She knew it.

Phillips leaned in to touch his forehead to hers. "I asked him to come," Phillips said, making it clear he now regretted that. She nodded, "It's okay."

He stepped away from her, motioning Bone closer. "What can you tell us? Anything?"

"My dad is nuts," Bone said. "I never thought any of it was real. Dude, I thought he was *just* nuts."

"I liked your dad," Phillips said.

"I didn't," Miranda said.

Bone became solemn. "I'm sorry about your dad," he said. "I never thought mine would do something like that."

Interesting. "So it *was* him who killed Dad? Not Dee?"

Bone shrugged. "I only know from the bragging, but I think he... called Dee here somehow. I don't know how they did it, but your father had to die and lay empty for so long. Then..."

Miranda wrinkled her nose. "He went to the body and helped Dee take possession of it."

Bone nodded. "I'm sorry. Until I saw the body bag when we came downstairs, I thought it wasn't real. But that's the kind of thing he'd keep. For his collection. I didn't know."

She couldn't deal with the idea of her dad's body bag as part of someone's collection. "Do you know what they did with the gun?"

"Dee looked it over last night while Dad told him what a genius he is. He put Dad in charge of it until tonight, his reward from 'the master,'" Bone said. "I should have known he was like this. I should have done... something."

The shame was clear on Bone's face. She hated feeling sympathetic toward him, but there it was. She understood him too well at this point not to.

"I just danced with the devil. None of us have choices here."

Phillips raised his hand. "About that. Do you think Dee's been able to control you all these years?"

Miranda had been trying to figure out the same thing. "No. Just since I got the mark. But my dad – definitely. It would have been easier with him after Mom died. I wonder if it's why he drank so much. You can feel it, when he's making you act. You can feel that it's not really you."

"It's hard to believe your dad stayed sane," Phillips said.

Miranda didn't trust herself to say anything. She'd stopped cutting her dad slack so long ago, given up on him. And she'd been wrong...

Maybe he's watching you through that glass. Maybe he knows you're sorry.

Phillips came over to her and she let him tuck her into his side. He was the one good thing in all this mess.

One more thing she was going to lose and never get back before this ended.

His nose crinkled. "You smell that?"

She sniffed and, even with the wind blowing in the other direction, caught something rotten.

Bone said, "I do."

They hurried toward the smell. After a few more feet, Sidekick lay down on his belly and whined, refusing to go along.

The scent trail led them to a small bank that overlooked a slice of beach. When they reached the overhang, Miranda turned away almost immediately. She'd seen enough.

Dead fish covered the shore in heaps. Silver, black, red scales shone in the sun. Their empty eyes stared, sightless.

She couldn't name the types, but she knew the smell shouldn't be so strong, not so soon. Dee had killed these fish. He'd sucked out their lives. The bodies were decomposing faster than normal.

Miranda staggered back toward the forest. She heard the boys behind her. Phillips caught up, touched her shoulder. It was a small comfort against the sight of that shoreline.

"Dee went into a room alone 'to prepare,'" Bone said. Then, "Dad says he talks to angels."

"Satan was an angel," Miranda pointed out.

"No," Phillips said, "this isn't something any god would be involved in. Or any fallen angel. The devil is just the kind of word my gram would use."

"What do you mean?"

"The forces he's calling on... You've felt it when he looks at you, when he touches you. He was just a man once, a mad scientist who wanted to believe he was talking to angels. A man who believed in progress, in the dream of a New London on this island. But he has become something else. Worse. More."

"Death," Bone said.

They left it at that.

Miranda sat next to Phillips on the sidewalk in front of the house that formed the main hub of activity for the returned, and they watched in silence as the returned and the theater types bustled around. She'd asked Bone to fetch her messenger bag from his dad's car, and she got up when she saw him carrying it toward them.

Phillips said, "Where are you going?"

"Just to freshen up," she said. "A girl needs her secrets."

He smiled at her, but he still looked worried. And that's why she couldn't tell him where she was going. He'd only worry more. He'd want to help. It was better for him to stay out here in relative safety, in case she got caught.

She met Bone and took the bag. "Thanks," she said, then lower. "Follow me inside. I need one more thing."

Bone did as she asked, without drawing attention to it. He really wasn't so bad.

In the apartment, the bizarre prep continued with women sewing their fingers raw and a mix of men and women in the kitchen drying candles. The room smelled like burnt wax. A couple of the women glanced up at them, and went back to work. Unconcerned.

And why should they be. What threat could Miranda pose to them?

"What?" Bone asked.

"Your dad, where is he?"

"He's in the bedroom next to the one Dee's in, I think."

Good. "Can you distract him?"

Bone looked at her. "What are you going to do?"

"Better if you don't know." When he didn't answer, she leaned in close to his ear, "You said you should have done something."

He hesitated, but said, "Give me a minute."

"I'll wait in the bathroom across the hall."

Miranda kept her bag tucked against her side. She went into the small bathroom, softly shutting the door, while Bone broke off into the room across the hall. The mirror called out to her, and when she saw what a mess she was she swiped at her hair in an attempt to smooth it. She made sure her face was angled so she didn't have to see the snake. Then she got closer to the door so she could listen while she rummaged in her bag.

Bone and his dad were arguing. Bone raised his voice, no doubt so she'd hear him. "Dad, I get that you have *things to do*, but I need you for a minute outside. Just a minute."

Miranda waited, taking a handful of change from the bottom of her bag and transferring it to her pocket. She resisted a fist pump when she heard them enter the hallway, Roswell complaining as he went.

She opened the door by degrees, and rushed across into the bedroom once she was sure it was clear. She hoped against hope that Roswell hadn't taken the gun with him.

He hadn't.

It rested on the center of a pillow on the bed, like a crown in some king's chamber. She walked over, put her bag down next to it. She knew she didn't have much time, and this was a long shot at best. The gems on the grip flashed as she picked it up.

She stuffed the coins from her pocket into the long barrel one by one, using a pen from her bag to press them deep inside. For the capper, she crumpled the page with the picture of Dee she'd ripped from Roswell's book earlier and added it. When everything was in and she was satisfied a casual examination would reveal nothing, she hurried back to her hiding place. Roswell harrumphed his way back up the hall seconds after she closed the door.

She had no idea if the coins were enough to jam Dee's weapon. Probably not. But she'd tried.

Phillips observed the rest of the day from the edges. Next to him on the sidewalk, Miranda stroked Sidekick's head. The desiccated insects in the forest and the rotting fish washed onto the beach were never far from Phillips' thoughts. The voices of the spirits snuck and insinuated, and he did his best to block them.

"I should be helping the techs," Miranda said. "They'll be down several staff. Polly... It's still the show."

Phillips shook his head. "No. Way."

He'd attempted another conversation with his mother, but she waved him off. She whispered, "He'll find out. We can't talk. I'm doing this for you." He'd considered calling his father, couldn't figure out how that would help. So he sat and watched and tried to locate an exit strategy.

Whatever the wrong thing inside Dee was, Phillips knew they would regret forever the moment when it got what it wanted, what it had waited for all this time.

Immortality. With forever, with powerful followers in forever, Dee could do anything.

He must not succeed. You must stop this. Must stop. Must.

He shoved harder, shoved the voices away – either he was getting better at blocking them, or being near Dee made it easier. He wasn't sure how he felt about either possibility. But he didn't see how the chatter was supposed to help him; his gram's gift must have acted differently. How was he supposed to think with so many voices talking at him? What strength did spirits have to give?

The early evening stole in like a cat burglar, and brought Polly – who had been Miranda's friend before. She emerged from the house where they'd spent the night in a long cloak that matched her hair. Her fingers were red, bloody raw, and she sucked on one absently, as if she felt the hurt from far away.

"Dinner inside," she said. "Miranda, I need you to come with me."

"You're Eleanor, right?" Phillips asked. "My ancestor?"

The gray-haired young woman nodded. "You're one of Ginny's descendants. Such a surprise that she survived."

"She hated everything you stand for," Phillips said. "She passed that on down the line."

Eleanor smiled. "We have been misunderstood all along. I'm not surprised to hear it from my daughter's spawn. Come inside. Soup for you. And Miranda gets a bath."

Miranda climbed to her feet, and told him, "Have your soup. I'll do the bath because I smell." Polly smiled again, and Miranda clarified, "But if you try to stick me in some wedding gown or something, it will not happen. Got it?"

Phillips' smile was real, but gone as soon as Miranda left. *What if they do try to put her in a wedding gown?*

Sidekick stayed with him, looking hopeful.

"All right, boy. Last meal, it is."

In the kitchen, a few fat candles sat on wax paper, burned down to their wicks. They were black. "Subtle," he muttered.

The people who'd been working in the kitchen had slowly made their way out to the common area over the past hour. He discovered an enormous kettle of normal-smelling beef and vegetable soup on the stove, a stack of bowls beside it that must have been collected from several kitchens. Phillips scooped soup into one, noticing how loud every noise became in the lack of bustle.

He ate a bite, realised he was starving, but waited to see if he keeled over. He didn't, so he put the bowl on the floor for Sidekick to slurp in gulps. His own bowl went almost as fast.

Phillips expected Polly and Miranda would be the first to emerge. Instead, Dee joined him.

If Dee had been a skin cream commercial before, now he was an ad for youth itself. Vitality. Strength. Even the body he wore seemed in better shape.

He was also wearing yet another suit. This one had thin gray pinstripes. Some devoted follower, or his lackey Roswell, must have shopped until they dropped to make sure he'd be coordinated with his coven's capes. Dee's own gray cloak remained folded across his arm.

"So, what's your big dastardly plan?" Phillips set down his bowl on the counter with a clatter. Couldn't hurt to ask.

Dee looked at him, eyes black and blank as if he were a painting that walked.

In that moment, Phillips felt sure he'd been right about the forces Dee was accessing. They were unknowable, beyond understanding. Maybe they were using *him*. Maybe he wasn't fully in control either.

Those eyes made the murmuring voices in Phillips' head go

quiet. They made it hard for him to breathe.

Or maybe that was the invisible fist squeezing his lungs–

He couldn't breathe–

"Shall we go?" Dee's lips formed the words, and the flatness left his eyes. A boundless dark energy replaced the two-dimensional death glare.

Phillips knew who he'd see before he turned, gasping, lungs released.

Miranda stood in the middle of the common room with her arms crossed over her chest. Her hair was loose and almost dry. She wore a fresh outfit – a vintage western shirt, a pair of jeans, and dusty sneakers. This was the girl he wanted to go anywhere with, anywhere except wherever Dee went.

Beside her, Polly and a couple of women Phillips didn't recognise wore heavy cloaks. Polly who was really Eleanor said, "Master, I apologise for the state of her. She wouldn't consent–"

Dee held up a hand. "Mary–" He paused. "Miss Blackwood is a vision. It will be my honor to escort her to the birth of New London."

Polly's mouth closed. She nodded.

"I'll walk with Phillips." Miranda crossed the room to him.

"That will be fine." Dee responded with a don't-care elegance he could afford, with everything else going his way.

Phillips could not fathom how the man had become so divorced from reality that he thought Miranda was not only into dead guys, but that she'd *ever* be attracted to someone who looked like her dad. Merry olde England hadn't been *that* backward.

Phillips' thinking must have showed on his face. The squeeze of his lungs was more than a warning this time–

He coughed, hacked–

Miranda gripped his arm, concerned. "What's wrong?"

The pressure eased at Miranda's question.

Phillips sucked in a breath. Dee was waiting to see how he'd respond. He choked out an answer, "What isn't?"

Dee's black eyes left him.

Still, Phillips wasn't breathing easy.

27

Break a Leg

The trek to the theater began at sunset. Dee, Polly, Roswell, and Sara were in the lead, followed by Miranda and Phillips. The rest of the returned formed a dark cloud behind them. The visual of familiar figures wearing the unfamiliar gray cloaks was guaranteed to freak out any friends and loved ones attending the Dare County Night to end all Dare County Nights.

They didn't walk along the main road, but took the back way. Miranda had always considered the path somewhat enchanted, because only people in the show used it. It hugged the coast, the waters of the Sound in full view, before dipping through the corner of the Elizabethan Gardens and on to Waterside Theater's backstage.

The actors and technicians had left a few hours earlier. Dee wanted them to put on the show, though Miranda still didn't understand why. Couldn't he clap his hands and make thunder and lightning strike and drop birds from the sky and take his stupid gun and force her to betray everything she was?

She didn't know about the other stuff, but the last one was

coming. The moment when Miranda was made into the traitor he'd branded her as. She touched her cheek, an absent
gesture that was becoming habit. Her last-ditch effort at sab-
otaging the gun seemed like a bad joke with the entire parade
of body-snatching alchemists around her.

"What did they want you to wear?" Phillips asked.

These were the first words he'd spoken since they left
Polly's, after that weird choking incident. He'd tell her if Dee
had hurt him somehow, wouldn't he?

"Gray isn't my color." They'd gotten a tray of make-up
from somewhere, and a sack-like too-long baby doll dress
made in the same gray of the cloaks. Polly had attempted to
force a cloak onto Miranda's shoulders, but she'd locked the
bathroom door and put on her own clothes.

Miranda refused to look over at the Sound, in case it was
dead fish fiesta from here to eternity. Dee looked far too
strong, leading his favored companions toward the theater.
Or Eleanor was favored, anyway – Sara was as much a pawn
in this as Miranda, and Roswell just had a bad case of hero
worship.

The wind tossed Miranda's hair around her face. She
wanted to tell Phillips how much his sticking with her had
meant. She wanted to tell him lots of things. But she didn't.
He didn't say anything more, either.

She reached down to pat Sidekick's head, where he trotted
along beside her. She hadn't wanted to bring him, but she was
too afraid to leave him behind. If she never made it back, she
didn't want him trapped with *them*.

The silent party finally reached backstage, winding along

the stone path between the small buildings that housed everything from costumes and props to lighting gels and tools. A
stagehand leaving the costume shop called out to Polly. "Poll,
where have you been all day?"

Polly ignored him, fixated on Dee.

The man in the pinstriped gray suit didn't stop until they
left backstage behind and reached the amphitheater. He
stopped in front of the stage, waiting for the mass of his followers to file out behind him. The audience watched, their
questions murmured.

The event had packed the house. Every seat was taken,
aside from a large vacant section down front blocked off by
strands of police tape.

Once his cohort was complete, Dee crossed to the first row
of empty seats. He swept on his cloak with a flourish. He
called out, words loud and clear as if they'd been broadcast
through a wireless mike: "Welcome tonight's guests of honor.
Your beloved have returned to you!"

The confused applause quickly gathered force as the
returned claimed their seats. Miranda spotted Blue Doe at the
back of the house with her cameraman, beaming as they
caught the entrance on film.

The applause and Blue Doe's presence were all the confirmation Miranda needed to prove her theory that Dee had
billed tonight as tourist fodder. The people here would see
their annual income triple from the bump in interest caused
by the disappearance and reappearance. The show's next season would probably be its biggest ever.

This night was about dragging out the attention on the

new mystery, adding to the local legend. Next year's dollar signs were in everyone's eyes. *Except they don't know we'll be living in "New London," then, with our creepy mayor, aka the devil of Roanoke Island.*

When she finally looked at him, she realised Dee had been waiting for her. He leaned forward, giving her a small bow. "You will do me the honor of sitting at my side."

It wasn't so much a question. The snake burned, and her lips opened, "Yes, delighted," she said. He made her say it.

"I'll stay with you," Phillips said.

"Yes, and our Sara will be right beside you," Dee said, scanning for her, "in case you need motherly guidance."

Dee looked around for his wayward recruit, and Miranda located her at the same time he did. She was engaged in a heated conversation with Chief Rawling, who was in uniform. Sara met Dee's gaze and walked back to them, not another word to her husband.

The chief shot a worried look in Phillips' and Miranda's direction. Miranda matched it, as Dee's cloak swooped in the air. He urged them into their seats. Front row center, of course.

Blue Doe appeared as soon as they were seated, teetering in front of Dee. Her eyes narrowed on Miranda, trying to place her. Miranda craned her neck in the opposite direction.

"Sir, can I have a moment of your time?" Blue Doe asked. When she got no response, she said, "Anyone else care to do a quick interview? Come on, now. Don't be shy. America wants to hear your stories… What is that *dog* doing here?"

Without looking at her, Miranda reached down and tugged Sidekick in front of her feet.

"What do the capes symbolise?" Blue Doe asked, exasperated. "At least give me that much."

Miranda shifted to catch Dee's response.

"Ceremony. The connection between souls who have been among the lost," Dee answered, nailing the reporter with a look that would have shut Miranda up.

It must have had the same effect on Blue Doe, because she took off, clicking away on her high heels. But Miranda didn't get a chance to enjoy the reporter's retreat, because Dee placed his hand over hers.

The hunk of flesh was cold as ice cubes. The summer night's humidity stuck to her skin, and she half-expected mist to form where his hand made contact.

The lights swelled then dimmed. The crew was readying for curtain.

"We're really watching the show," Miranda said, disbelieving.

"I know this version of history means much to you," Dee said. "And what better way to bring reality to our new home? We will show it to them."

Miranda's mouth opened to ask what he meant – not that she would've expected an answer, not after the way he dodged admitting he'd helped murder her dad – but His Royal Majesty came on stage then. She didn't miss his dirty look at her and Polly in the front row.

He hates us. Great.

He gave a stiff speech about what a relief it was to have everyone home safe, how the theater wanted to mark the return of everyone's loved ones in a special way, with a special island tradition.

Miranda heard every word, but processed little of it. What did Dee mean 'we will show it to them'?

His Royal Majesty exited stage right to another round of applause – this one merely polite – and the show began. Miranda tried to lift her hand from Dee's in the guise of covering a yawn, but he exerted a steady pressure that kept it under his own. Noticing the struggle, Phillips propped his forearm on the armrest, so his shoulder touched Miranda's.

She had death on one side, and life on the other.

The first group of actors marched onto the stage, decked out in the most elaborate Elizabethan costumes *The Lost Colony* had to offer. They bustled with pomp, and Miranda settled into her seat despite the reality of what was happening. She dipped her head back to take in the sky above. Those familiar, clear pinpoints of light stared down. The stars were watching tonight's performance, too, and she wanted to warn them. *New scenes, little rehearsal. This night might well go down in flames.*

The play began with Queen Elizabeth and Sir Walter Raleigh in London, agreeing that he should colonise the new world. The settlers came next. They voyaged and arrived, argued and suffered. Musical numbers hit in perfect time, the chorus not a note out of tune. No one forgot a line or stepped on a cue. Mean little Caroline was a rosy-cheeked angel.

It was one of the best performances Miranda could remember.

And none of them knew what lay ahead. Not one of the actors giving it their all, celebrating this messed-up island. Not one.

She chanced a look next to her, resigned not to hold it against Phillips if he was smirking or bored. But he seemed taken with the production too, something that pleased her more than she'd expected. She felt more tied to the theater than any other part of the island. She had always belonged here more than anywhere else.

But the show was also long, too long for Dee's patience to hold apparently. Just as the second act closed – after the actors left the stage, but before the lights went down and intermission started – he released her hand.

Watching the play had been a reprieve. That ended when Dee rose to his feet, and the rest of the returned stood on his cue. The mark on her face burned, and he made her stand.

Sorry, stars, we have to interrupt this program.

Phillips got up, too, said, "Miranda... Mom..." But Sara was already walking away with the others.

The returned filed out of their rows in neat lines, as choreographed as if they'd rehearsed for a few hundred years. They climbed the stairs on either side of the stage. Some lingered on the steps facing the audience, while others took over the back half of the stage itself. All of them left space for someone else to pass by. It was a makeshift promenade.

The crowd buzzed in confusion, not sure how to react. But they stayed in their seats.

Miranda fought as hard as she could, willing her limbs to be under her own control. But her elbow jutted out at a wide, proper angle to allow Dee to slip his through it. Her feet walked her forward, her pace matching his perfectly.

The cloaked figures Dee paraded her past were curled in a

generous half-moon, a cupping shell that mirrored the *monas hieroglyphica*. They climbed the steps onto the stage.

When they reached the top of the short flight of stairs, she managed to look into the crowd. Locating Phillips was as easy as finding the flash of movement. Agent Malone and Agent Walker had come to the show. Phillips was being hauled up the aisle by them in slow degrees, his father attempting to intervene while Phillips argued. Neither of their protests seemed to be meeting with success.

The crowd itself barely noticed that disturbance, despite all the busiest busybodies in town in attendance. They were too busy watching the stage – there were a few confused murmurs, but far more wide smiles that assumed this was all part of the show. The disappearances themselves were part of it, they must have been thinking. What a grand idea this was.

No one was going to intervene. No one was going to save her.

Her head notched back to what lay before her, and her feet moved forward. Cloaked arms extended, marking a gray path across the stage for her and her father's body.

The audience murmurs kicked up a notch then. People wouldn't think *this* was part of the show.

"That's the Blackwoods!" someone said. It was a man in the middle section, starting to rise from his seat, gesturing toward the stage. Was that Mike from Stop and Gas? As the seller of the cheapest six-pack in town he *would* be the other person besides Chief Rawling to finally recognise her father.

As quickly as he said the words, his mouth clacked shut, his seatmates shrinking away from the loud noise of it.

Dee called, "Stay in your seats."

And the audience did, obviously bewildered that they couldn't do otherwise. The feds and Chief Rawling trotted back down the aisle, sinking into seats left empty in the returned's section.

The breeze brought a rank smell to meet her nose. More dead fish. They must be washing up on the beach behind the theater.

His Royal Majesty appeared at stage right. "What is this?" he demanded. But the director was silenced as quickly as the others.

The words Dee spoke weren't any she recognised, but they brought forth a trembling-in-ecstasy Roswell. He hadn't rated a cloak, but he did carry the pistol. The dulled metal and its bright jewels lay flat on his extended hands as he walked up the stairs. A paler-than-ever Bone broke away behind him, not climbing onto the stage, but taking a seat down front instead.

Roswell crossed the stage, stopping across from Dee and Miranda. The three of them were obviously the main event, isolated from the mass of gray cloaks. Her own position placed her at exactly center stage, under the main spotlight.

Miranda cringed at how loud her voice was when she spoke – was made to speak. She said, "I have a story to tell, of a night much like this, on a shore not far from here, many years ago. A young woman, Mary Blackwood, was brought out from the safe walls of the Colony's fort at night to meet the ship of the man who loved her. A man who had spent long months in the traveling, navigating by patterns in the stars, on the most auspicious of schedules. A great man who would have given up his greatness had she but asked. A man who was coming to deliver his promise to the colonists sent on Raleigh's voyage. To deliver his promise to Miss Blackwood herself."

Miranda was held rapt by the story like everyone else, despite the fact she was being used to tell it. She didn't know where the story would end, just that she expected humiliation.

When she stopped fighting for control, her tongue moved easier. The words slipped freely from her lips. "She was an enchantment, a brave dream, emerging from the night forest in a dark hooded cloak. The girl met him with a kiss – as beautiful as she had ever been, after those long months away. The colonists were ready, she said, ready for their final journey, the journey of forever. She asked to see the mechanism of their transformation."

She paused, not of her own accord, but because Dee needed a pause. Apparently a sizeable one.

The surf sloshed behind them. The wind sang in her ears.

"The weapon was a variation on a new creation. A pistol. No wonder now, of course, but then the processes were still being perfected. And the man had let the words of angels and pure intentions guide him as he perfected this weapon, so that it gave not death, but life. Eternal life. The alchemist's – *humanity's* – final challenge would be met. His love asked, and he showed her the product of his work. He placed it in her hands himself, to let her hold it."

If there'd still been any insects alive, they would have seemed loud in the hush of the theater.

"But Mary had not – as the others – agreed to the voyage, to the prospects ahead, with a pure and true heart. She was pledged to the queen's stooge, Raleigh, the purse behind the colonist's voyage, but not the power. The man had always been the power. Mary stole the weapon and hid it. The stars were only auspicious that night, the preparations in place nearly impossible to recreate. She made his promise a lie. Even so, the alchemist was too noble to let her meet the punishment she deserved. So he joined their fates forever, with a simple mark. Made it so he could never lose her. She would still have the weapon, and one day she would bring it to him, and assist in the last great work that ever need be done. She would do so willingly. She would keep her promise."

Miranda wanted to protest with some comments of her own, but of course she couldn't. There was no *willingly* about any of this.

She wasn't a betrayer of good. She was a betrayer of evil. Her ancestor Mary Blackwood had tricked John Dee, had beat him.

Winning was possible.

It. Was. Possible.

But Roswell came closer, and her hands reached out for the pistol and gripped it. Phillips' shout of, "Miranda, fight him!" was sweet but meaningless. The surf and the air and the night around her were as unreal as her ability to exert her own will.

She leveled the pistol, her arm steady, pointing it at Dee. Her lips formed a final pronouncement: "And now I will make this man, and with him these colonists, the first immortals in a new world."

Her finger curled around the trigger, pulled hard...

The metal vibrated in her hand with enough force to push her back, and she waited to see the spray of dust emerge.

But nothing else happened. Nothing.

The barrel was blocked. Not even magic could force the contents out until it was cleared. Her sabotage had *worked*.

As Dee understood, her father's face twisted and he howled in rage. The colonists shouted to each other, surging forward in their borrowed bodies. Miranda found she could move enough to fling the gun off the stage, in Phillips' direction. Maybe he would take it behind the theater and throw it in the Sound to drown it in the waves, lose it forever, carried out to the ocean beyond.

Dee lunged at her, and her heart froze. Because Sidekick danced across the stage barking and snarling, snapping at Dee's legs, trying to protect her.

"No, boy," she said. She intended to get him behind her, but Sidekick began to wheeze. Dee had to be the cause.

He stood blade straight in still concentration, his black eyes fixed on Sidekick. Death rattles twisted Kicks' long torso, and he didn't seem like her big, goofy dog at all. He seemed so very small and fragile, so easy for Dee to break, to end forever.

Miranda thought of her father, how her father would never have hurt Sidekick. She thought of her father who hadn't gone crazy, and she hoped he was on the other side of that glass wall, hoped for him to break it.

She called out to him, screaming, "Dad! Dad, you have to stop him! Dad!"

28

Forgetting the Lines

When Sidekick leapt onto the stage snarling Phillips knew that no federal agents could keep him off it. "Dad, I have to go," he pleaded. His father thrust an arm across the feds' chests and said, "Let him," in a tone that left no room for argument.

Phillips' bounded from his seat, pausing to say, "Sorry about that whole drugging you thing. Desperate times, desperate measures. Etcetera." The agent started to respond, but Phillips didn't stick around to hear what he had to say.

As he rushed the stage, the voices in his head were a raging river of sound. He battled to build a wall and dam them behind it. He needed his mind clear, or clearer, anyway.

The crowd was on its feet, but he was the lone one heading *into* the action. The audience was more confused than anything, thrown by their inability to move during Dee's pathetic monologue using Miranda as mouthpiece. Invisible hands had held them all in their seats.

Miranda had messed with Dee's magical weapon somehow. She was amazing.

Phillips put his hands on the edge of the stage and vaulted onto it. He immediately had to dodge a few angry cloak wearers, who were forming a protective circle around their outraged master. The returned would have grudges against Miranda, wouldn't they? Her ancestor had trapped them in mortality, had been the reason Dee put them on hold behind death's veil.

Dee was essentially a jilted fake boyfriend. Phillips wasn't comforted. Anyone who carried a torch after this long would be dangerous even *without* the power over life and death.

A middle-aged cloaked woman attempted to block Phillips' path, but his mom pushed her aside. He expected her to try and stop him too, but then he saw how her watery eyes gleamed under the stage lights. She said, "I just wanted to protect you."

So she'd finally understood that signing on for this had been a mistake. Too late was better than never. He said, "You need to get out of here. Go find Dad."

"I'm a bad mother, the worst. You help her. You…" She squeezed him into a brief hug. "You be careful. I trust you."

His mom let him go and Phillips maneuvered through two more cloak wearers, past the boundaries of their imperfect circle. He was just in time to watch Miranda lunge at Dee and beat his chest with her fists. She was screaming. Dee didn't fight her. He stood vain and proud and tall.

Sidekick wasn't fighting either. He'd lain down, rolled onto his side. From this angle, it was impossible to say whether he was still breathing. Maybe Miranda had managed to distract

Dee before he could do permanent damage to the dog's lungs or heart. What he'd done to Phillips had hurt like hell. Poor Sidekick wouldn't even know where the pain came from.

Roswell dove toward Miranda and Dee, latching onto her like a tick. He was trying to pry her off his hero. She elbowed him in the face.

Phillips ran the rest of the way to her, and shouldered Roswell away. "Time out, professor," he said, satisfied when Roswell skittered back several feet.

With Miranda no longer pummeling Dee, the alchemist bent double, the pinstripes of his suit folding in a crease at his waist. Phillips wondered if she'd managed to injure him.

Dee unfolded to a standing position, his arms flinging out. The motions reminded Phillips of a puppet on jerky strings. They weren't the least bit fluid. Was Dee not able to control the body? Why?

Miranda sucked in a breath. "Dad?" she said.

Two sharp bobs of the head for yes. His limbs flew in a fight with the air, with himself. With Dee.

Miranda's dad *was* back in his body, but Dee was still on board. The body turned, looked at Phillips. The chorus of voices erupted from behind the flimsy wall Phillips had built to contain them. The man's eyes went flat and black for just a moment, and he spoke to Phillips, "She wants you. She gets what she deserves."

Phillips didn't have time to prepare for the force that slammed into him. Not that he'd have been able to. All the air left his body. The spirits roared, rising in an endless cocoon of sound, until Phillips was the one behind the wall.

He was the one clawing to get to the surface, trapped among the voices he'd only ever wanted to ignore.

John Dee occupied his body.

"Dad? Why would you say that? Dad!" He barely heard Miranda's voice through the others around him. They were much closer than she was.

Phillips watched from a distance as an invisible ribbon of energy like an arm or a tentacle emerged from his body. It was searching... Seeking...

Dee lifted Phillips' arm. He waved the hand at a cloaked figure blocking the crowd. "Step aside," he said.

The man dropped his cloak and moved, saying, "Master."

Phillips had no choice but to look as Dee swept his eyes over the audience...

Nice, brave, loyal Officer Warren did not look afraid. His weapon was in his hand, and he was in the aisle making for the front of the house. The ribbon of power smashed into him. He fell to his knees like he'd crossed a goal line.

In a way, he had. Officer Warren's death filled Dee with a rush of power.

A woman wearing a long white dress crumpled as the ribbon moved on, adding the energy of her life force to its own. To Dee's.

Phillips felt Dee revel in the rush of power. He felt everything Dee did.

Dr Roswell wobbled into the edge of Phillips' vision, and Dee noticed him. Phillips knew that Roswell was next. The ribbon entered his chest.

Roswell's death was his punishment for touching Miranda.

Inside Dee, Phillips discovered a vast rage that might once have been love. It was cold and absolute and centered on Miranda. Dee couldn't separate her from her ancestor. Mary, Miranda. Both were Blackwoods.

Phillips located Miranda's voice, still distant. She was talking to her father. "Dad, you know you're dead, and we need to keep it that way. Is he inside you?"

"He…" The man's words in response were weak, shaky. "He left."

She didn't know Dee had taken over Phillips.

Roswell fell, then, wearing a dreamy smile as he died.

Crazy as he was, he didn't need to die. No one else needed to…

In the first second, Miranda didn't move, busy gaping at Roswell's glassy dead eyes. In the next, she turned to Phillips in confusion. "What happened to him?"

Dee was barely aware of her question, busy making his way through every cell of Phillips' body. Phillips had to retreat, back inside the cocoon of voices, the spirits talking to a version of him that wasn't home anymore, telling that him things he couldn't understand.

Dee learned his new vessel quickly. When he noticed Miranda's attention, it was like a spark flaring into fire. He wanted her. He shifted Phillips' body toward her, close enough to use one of his arms to grip the back of her head.

Miranda frowned, still confused. Phillips' heard his voice say, "Such a beauty," felt his arm pull her closer.

The spirits he hid among were talking and talking and he had no way to warn her.

He didn't need to. She figured it out, tearing free of his grasp. But she didn't run, not this girl. She put her hands on Phillips' shoulders and shook them. She snapped her fingers in his face. He barely heard. Within him, Dee's cold rage surged.

"*Phillips.* Your grandmother, remember what she said – you need to use your strength, all you have. Don't let him win."

Dee was ready to punish Miranda now. She'd rejected him for the last time. Her lips were still moving, but no matter how Phillips scratched and clawed against the voices to get to the surface, he couldn't hear her. Phillips' effort only revealed the voices – and his hiding place – to Dee. And Dee knew the spirits for what they were.

Dee didn't try to push the voices of the spirits back like Phillips usually did. Instead he wrenched power from them, and turned it on Miranda. Phillips could suddenly see and hear everything, sharp and clear. He wasn't hidden any longer, only trapped.

"You may not be her," Dee said, using Phillips' lips to deliver Miranda's death sentence. "But you are just like her. I had hoped for redemption for you. But it is not to be." The last words were whispers. "Alas. Goodnight."

The wide ribbon flooded out of Phillips' body and into Miranda. She gasped, her father's hand still clutched in hers. He stood ashen and confused beside her.

Miranda choked out, "*Phillips.* The letter," and bowed like a weak branch under Dee's onslaught.

Dee was using Phillips' gift to kill her. Miranda was going to die while he watched.

Phillips searched and found the corners of the memory. What had his gram's letter said? But he lost his grip on the crinkled page fluttering in his mind as he experienced a wash of intense pleasure. Dee enjoyed watching Miranda suffer. He showed Phillips a flash of what he had truly wanted with her. Mary melded with Miranda. There was more punishment. And sickness.

Sickness.

Dee's satisfaction increased as she faded. Her heart squeezed in his unseen fist, her lungs emptying like bellows stomped by his heavy feet. Her soul tasted sweet to Dee, like honey wine. He rolled Phillips' tongue over his teeth, across his lips. Tasting her.

The letter. Phillips tried to grab the memory...

It had said to use his gift, and that he wasn't alone. What gift? All he'd ever had was voices. Chattering. Telling. Helping in theory, but not in practice. In practice, they were too strong for him. The letter didn't help.

And Miranda didn't have much longer. She reclined on the stage, her eyes wheeling. Sidekick was stretched out an arm's length away from her. Her father knelt beside her, jerky in his own body, saying his daughter's name over and over.

All Phillips could see was Miranda. His place inside his own mind was so small. The voices that were left surged and swam against him, crowding him, as Dee pulled on them. Used them.

He used them through his control of Phillips' body.

In that moment, Phillips finally stopped fighting and *listened* to the voices that surrounded him. The spirits were attached to this island. They were desperate to be free of Dee's influence. They wanted him and the colonists gone.

Phillips had an army of ghosts. He just had to control them.

He stopped listening, and talked back to the spirits. *Whatever part of you he's got hold of, use it to shove him out. Get your hands on his slimy soul and shove NOW...*

Phillips forced his limbs to lunge in front of Miranda's father, to grasp his shoulders. The man was too weak to push him off.

At Phillips' command the spirits' energy stopped draining into Miranda and crashed *against* Dee. Phillips combined his own strength with theirs, pushing against the invader Dee's hold, pushing him *out...*

Phillips exhaled, then held his breath.

Mr Blackwood's head ticked down as Dee returned to his body.

Phillips experimentally moved his arms, but he knew it had worked. The voices were a soft chorus in the background of his mind, because he controlled them now. But Miranda still lay on the stage, not moving.

Phillips tumbled down beside her, his fingertips against her throat to find a pulse. "Live," he pleaded. "Live."

His gram's voice then: *Lay on hands.* For the first time, an image in his mind instead of just words. *His grandmother in the kitchen of their house, a woman on the tile floor not breathing. Gram placed her hands on the woman's chest, eyes closed, and...*

He pressed his palms over Miranda's heart, called on the spirits to provide whatever energy they could. He didn't know what he was doing. There was no ribbon of power leaving him. But he willed her to wake, to fight. He lifted his hands.

The not-CPR was all gram had shown him. He looked over at Roswell's glassy stare into the sky. Dee's cloaked followers didn't seem to be sure what to do, or maybe their master's weakening had an effect on them too. Whatever the case, they had hushed, walling off the action on the stage again. Phillips heard his father barking commands somewhere not far off. They wouldn't be isolated for long. Miranda's dad was wheeling, flailing, struggling against Dee while Eleanor grabbed clumsily at the body.

And still Miranda lay, peaceful. A sleeping beauty. He put his palm against her face, brushed his thumb over the cursed mark. He wanted to tell her that he'd finally figured out how to use the voices. He wanted to tell her everything.

He pressed his forehead against hers. The touch felt so natural. If only he didn't also feel like his own heart had stopped in his chest.

29

Till Death

At first, Miranda saw nothing but darkness. Her eyelids fluttered, and it took a universe-sized effort to see. Blinking, she made out a face above her.

Phillips' face. A flicker of light and hope shot through her, before she remembered that he'd tried to kill her. He'd nearly succeeded. He wasn't Phillips anymore. He was Dee…

She dragged in a ragged breath, lungs protesting like she'd been underwater. Raising her arms, she pushed him as hard as she could. "No!" she shouted.

She attempted to roll her body away from him, but his hands pressed her into place.

"It's me," he said. "It's me."

She looked up at him. Brown-black eyes. Not flat and black. Worried.

"It's you," she said. "But where's…"

She turned her head to find her father nearby, his arms flailing again. "Help me up," she said, clutching at Phillips' arm. She found she could tell her body what to do and it mostly

311

followed orders. *He* wasn't controlling her, and she didn't seem to be broken, just bruised.

Phillips said, "Dee's in there, but I think your dad's holding his own. Miranda, I put him back in your dad."

"Thank you," she said.

She paused, standing over Sidekick. He looked far too peaceful.

"I don't know if Sidekick's OK," Phillips said.

"After this," she said, cringing at the way her voice broke. She dragged in another breath. "After I do this one thing. I can't until then."

"What one thing?" Phillips asked. "Miranda, I'm sorry I had to… Your dad was there and I knew Dee's soul could go into him."

"Don't be sorry." She didn't have time to explain.

Polly's arm was around her father, who was caught in a fit of mighty flailing. Miranda stumbled toward them, and told her, "Let go of him. Now."

Phillips was there if Eleanor protested and Miranda knew he had her back. But Eleanor's expression was slightly dazed, and her protest was weak.

"He can't keep the master at bay for long," Eleanor said, releasing him. She looked like *she* might collapse.

Phillips said, "They're not as strong because your dad is fighting him."

Her father's arms windmilled, but Miranda quickly had an arm around him, supporting him. He stilled, trembling. She looked at him, discovered her dad there in the eyes. "He's in you, and he must stay in you. You have to hold onto him, keep him there," she said. "Understand?"

Chief Rawling thundered onto the stage, shouting, "Clear this area." He had a host of uniformed helpers with him.

"Phillips," she said, "we need to take Dad to the water. Can you keep yours out of the way?"

Phillips' question was clear on his face, but he yelled, "Mom!"

The chief and some officers scuffled with the cloaked figures of the returned – to them just townspeople – trying to get them off the stage. Sara must have been with them, because she was at Phillips' side in an instant, no longer wearing her cloak. Miranda could tell she wasn't under Dee's influence any longer. And Phillips must be right about the returned being affected by Dee's struggle with her dad, because the cops were making serious headway.

It gave her hope.

While Phillips talked to his mom, Miranda got her shaky father's attention again. She wished she had time to talk to him about life instead of death. "I'm going to walk you to the edge of the surf and you will… you will leave this island. Dad, you have to keep going. You're not alive any more. You can't be alive. And neither can he. So you're going to walk right off this island. OK?"

She gripped her arm around him harder, held one of his hands in hers.

"Those stories. Dad, they were all true. You understand?"

Her father's head nodded, a quick jerk, then smoother as he got better control of his body.

Phillips had heard what she'd said and, by the look on his face, figured out what she meant to do. He moved to help when Miranda slowly started across the stage with her father.

They were headed for the beach that gave Waterside

Theater its name. The sour, rotten smell of more dead fish washing out of the Sound stung her nose.

Miranda talked to her dad as they went. "You can do this, Dad. It's not so far," she cooed. "I'm your daughter. I'm your good daughter. You said so yourself." It couldn't hurt to help her dad keep hold of reality. In truth, it was a comfort for her too. "It's not so much further. This will all be over soon."

"Miranda, this is your dad," Phillips said.

"I know. And we're going right down to the Sound, aren't we, Dad? You're going to drown in the deep water. But it won't hurt, because you're already dead."

Please, let that be true.

Phillips managed his side of the support, but said nothing more. They stumbled down a short flight of stairs at the back of the stage with her dad, curving around behind it.

The rocky beach met them, a long pier thrusting out over the water nearby. Stinking heaps of dead fish lay stranded on sand and stone. The chunk of moon above reflected on the Sound like a long mirror, fading into the pinprick lights from the shores of the outer islands in the distance. The sloshing of the waves drowned the shouts from the stage.

Phillips said, "Miranda."

"He's dead, Phillips. This is the right thing."

"Right. Thing." Her dad choked out his agreement.

They had to hurry. Dee's soul might be confused, depowered, but that wouldn't last. She wasn't sure this would work, but Roswell's notes had said the transition from death to life could only be made once. They had said that the boundary wouldn't allow more than a single crossing.

And Dee's curse meant that her father's body shouldn't be able to leave the island and survive.

"It's a good plan," Phillips said.

She wasn't surprised he'd figured it out, given a handful of minutes. Their eyes met behind her dad's head.

"I learned from the best."

The surf lapped the beach, the waves a few steps away. Slimy fish slicked under her feet, and she righted her steps. Her father's body began to flail – Dee was resurfacing. Maybe he knew what was about to happen.

They had to make it.

They careened over the rocks and sand and fish, tripping into the water. Miranda held onto her father as he jerked.

"Phillips," she said, "give me a sec."

Phillips didn't look like he wanted to, but he stepped back onto the shore. He left her alone with her father.

"Dad," she said, "go." She took his flailing arm, fought to get his hand in hers. And she walked her father's body forward into the surf...

"Miranda," Phillips called a warning.

But she knew. She only had a few steps to travel with him. She stopped with the water at her knees, splashing up her legs. She wasn't far enough out yet for it to hurt.

Miranda squeezed his hand. Her father looked at her, and then Dee was there, flat and black, lip curling. But the eyes gave way to her father again. His features calmed. Even in the near darkness, she knew it was him. He was coming through for her, after all these years.

"Let go," he said.

And she did.

Her father walked, and kept walking, until his head sank beneath the waves. White foam broke over the spot where he disappeared, broke all around her. He didn't resurface.

Phillips waded to her, pulled her against him. She said her goodbye in the silence, wondering who her father would have been without the curse they bore, and who she'd be if she made it through this night.

"It's over," she said, finally, when he didn't resurface. "I think maybe it's over."

The shouts from back on the stage spiked, frantic, reaching them.

"It's not over," he said.

"Something's happened." She palmed tears off her cheek, not embarrassed by them. She was surprised that she *wasn't* embarrassed.

Phillips held her hand tight in his as they navigated through the dead fish shoreline and back up the steps to the stage. The reason for the noise became clear.

The bodies of the returned had wilted like so many flowers. They lay sprawled where they'd fallen across the stage. The police officers were checking for pulses, for breath. Other townspeople had joined them, hovering over loved ones. The rest of the theater was hushed, the people still left in the audience not knowing what to do.

"It worked," Miranda said, dully. "He's gone. And so are they. I did this."

She spotted Chief Rawling then, kneeling beside a fallen form. *Sara*.

"Mom!" Phillips released her hand, moving through fallen bodies to reach his parents.

Miranda followed, afraid the death wasn't over. What if she'd made everything worse?

Then a wave of sound rolled across the stage. Sudden intakes of breath – gasp after gasp – as the returned stirred back to life. Some sat up drowsily. Others stretched, and climbed onto unsteady feet.

Miranda listened to their laughter, to confused questions.

"It's really her," someone said. More laughter. The buzz of happy conversation. Shrieks. Miranda called out, "Polly?"

"Here," a weak voice said.

On the other side of the stage, Polly was touching her shoulders in confusion, like she didn't know where or who she was. She reached back to tighten her ponytail in a gesture Miranda knew well. She seemed surprised to find her hair was down instead of up.

"They're really back," Miranda said.

Her grin died when she turned back to Phillips and Chief Rawling. Sara was still unconscious.

Phillips shook his mother's shoulder, gently as if she was breakable. He moved to check her pupils. Her eyelids fluttered beneath his fingers. Her eyes opened.

"Mom, you OK?" Phillips asked.

In answer Sara climbed unsteadily to her feet, folding Phillips and his dad into her arms. "I'm so sorry," she said it over and over. "I'm so sorry."

Phillips shifted his head over her shoulder to meet Miranda's stare. *We did it.*

Miranda nodded. *We did.*

But she didn't linger there. They were a family. She needed only to look over at Bone, sitting shell-shocked beside his dead father to remember that she didn't have that. But it existed, and that was something.

Miranda reached down to squeeze Bone's shoulder as she walked past him. Her steps were slow, but they brought her to Sidekick. She eased down beside his furry yellow body, stretched prone like he was sleeping, but too still for dreaming. She placed her hand against his ribs.

She felt no movement, and part of her died. Part of her followed her father off the land, into the deep water, and met the fate of the Blackwood curse.

At first, what was left of her thought the slight rise and fall beneath her fingers was wishful thinking. It was what she wanted, but not reality.

But Sidekick *was* breathing. His ribs lifted against her hand, then fell. Lifted, fell.

She held her own breath in to better feel his, relaxing when he groaned and wriggled against the pressure of her hand. *Belly scratch.*

"My good boy," she said. "Welcome home."

The missing returned, the natural order salvaged, and gentle waves embracing the shore. The time to mourn what had been lost would come, but not tonight. Tonight, the island was all around them.

And that was good.

30

Curtain Call

Phillips had talked to Miranda once on the phone since the night at the theater. That was two days ago. The phone conversation had been like a blind date – frustrating and stuttering like they'd just met and had nothing in common. Jokes had met with expanding pauses. At the end of the "talk," when the silence became too much to endure, too many dead fish and insects swimming between them in its gulf, he'd said, "I'll come by on Sunday?"

She had Sundays off, he knew. The theater was closed that day.

"Sure," she'd said, in a weird tone he had analyzed over and over and come up with a thousand theories to explain. He didn't know what to expect.

He still wanted to see her.

So when he knocked at the front door of her house why did he feel like he was about to walk in and discover Dee sitting at the breakfast table? *If she doesn't open the door pointing a gun at you, it's progress.*

She didn't.

"Um, hi," she said.

She smiled at him, tentative. Nervous.

He had never been happier to see a dog in his life than when Sidekick bounded past Miranda and jumped up on him. Heavy paws thumping into his thighs gave him a furry face to pat and focus on. "I'm so glad he's OK," he said, looking up at her.

The smile was real this time. "Yeah. So," she said. "You want to come in?"

"That's the plan."

Phillips followed her to the couch, but decided not to give Sidekick the advantage this time. When Miranda sat down, he carefully eased down beside her. Not touching, but an inch or two away. Sidekick hopped up on his other side, licked his hand until Phillips petted him.

"You're not in jail," she said.

He snorted. "Because the feds had no freaking clue what to put in their report. They got out of here as fast as they could. And Roswell having your dad's body bag at his place... it was enough for Dad to close the case. But I'm sure he told you about that."

Her nod was tight. "He called."

"We went to Officer Warren and Delilah Banks' memorial services yesterday. Bone's not having one for his dad. He's going to live with his mom in Ohio."

"You know that wasn't you. You didn't hurt them."

"I didn't kill them. But it's still hard. Knowing..." Knowing that if he'd learned how to cope earlier, he could have stopped their deaths. He didn't know if he'd ever get over that.

"Yeah. How's your mom?"

Miranda must have sensed he needed to move on.

"She's atoning," he said. "Even though we keep telling her we understand."

Miranda pushed her hair behind her ear. He couldn't help it – he reached out and untucked it. Finally, the beginning of a flush.

"I like it loose," he said. "It's nice that way."

"Loose women are the most popular, that's what I've always heard."

He really wanted to kiss her again. "Miranda–"

"Wait," she said. "I have something for you."

She leaped to her feet and hurried up the hall. *Screw waiting.* He trailed her the short distance to her room, meeting her at its door. He walked forward, and she backed up with each step. They ended up in her room, standing close, which was all right with him.

"What's that?" he asked, pointed at her hands.

"I wanted to make you something." Her head angled toward the small sewing table in the corner of the tiny room. It was set up so she'd have to sit cross-legged on the bed to use it. Scraps of fabric were discarded next to it.

"Please tell me it's not a gray cloak."

She thrust her hand out. He took the fabric bundle from her and shook it out.

The T-shirt was blue – Superman blue, really – and the block lettering she'd stitched on was made of a motley collection of fabrics. The words stacked on top of each other said: Random Fact Boy.

He grinned. "I still think we could have come up with something better."

"Check the label," she said, still sounding too anxious. The gift had made him a lot less nervous.

He pulled the neck down and checked it. Stitched in black thread, twined in script: *My hero*.

She didn't say anything, and it took him a moment to figure out how to react.

He said, "Best present ever. Up there with the Statue of Liberty."

"Really?"

"Really."

Her smile was real, then, and finally he kissed her.

Miranda had been convinced that Phillips would have decided the girl that put him through all that was damaged goods. Convinced that what was between them would turn out not to be real without the constant threat of death and destruction.

She *almost* couldn't believe she'd been wrong.

He stopped kissing her, and she wondered why. She chased him back onto the bed, but he held up his hand. "This is going to sound weird, but... I just heard a voice and I want to know if what it said means anything to you."

Miranda straightened. Her immediate worry that it would be something terrible kicked into hyperdrive. "You're still hearing the voices then?"

"When I let them in," he said. "But a lot of them seem to be gone. Like they don't need to hang around anymore. But this voice, it just kind of showed up, just now. Bad timing. But, do you know the song 'Heartbreaker' by Blondie?"

Miranda swallowed. "It was my mother's favorite song."

Phillips reached out, casually put his hand against her neck, cradling it. She was distracted, but not distracted enough not to notice how nice that felt. "What else?"

"The voice – I heard it once before, when I first came back. When we were at the cemetery at your mom's grave. I heard it say *'Curse-bearer, curse-born child'*."

"Me," Miranda said. "She was talking about me."

"But just now, when she stopped singing that song – which I'll have stuck in my head for days now, thank you very much, Miranda's mom – she said *"Curse-breaker, curse-broken child'*."

She traced a finger along the snake, which had lightened to a pale pink.

"Do you think? I still have this."

"I think we should take a drive and find out. A scientific test."

"Me too. Plus, I'm too freaked out to stay here right now."

"Why?" He applied slight pressure against her neck.

"Um. My mom was watching us make out."

"She's gone now," he said.

But that didn't matter. She wanted to know if it was true, if she was free.

Miranda convinced Phillips that Pineapple was superior to his mom's sedan, what with the plastic covering the window she'd smashed. And she asked him to drive, not wanting him to croak if it turned out the voice from beyond the grave hadn't been her mother.

But she believed. She could feel the truth of what he'd said. Plus, Blondie.

"I forgot to tell you," Phillips said, "I'm doing senior year here."

"Congratulations. You're dating the school freak."

"Oh, I am?"

Why had she said *that*?

But he cut the tension by laughing. "I am, I am. You think you're *still* the freak? After the way you saved everyone. I don't think so."

Oh boy, he's got a lot to learn. Small towns didn't reclassify people. She'd just be the Blackwood freak who saved everyone. That was fine. "This is going to be a fun year. Assuming I survive the next five minutes."

They were heading out I-64 toward the new bridge, not the site of her previous attempt to leave and the shoving incident of shame. And they'd know whether she could make it over and keep breathing a lot quicker in the car than on foot.

"It's good luck that the bridge's named after Ginny the good," he said. "Did I mention I really like my present? You should go to fashion school. Or straight to 'Project Runway.' 'My hero' could be your label."

He was chattering to distract her. She appreciated the effort.

"Let's just see if I'm still cursed." But she felt an unfamiliar flutter inside her stomach at the idea. If the curse had been broken by Dee's real, final death, then she could. She could go to fashion school. She could go on reality TV (and not be the villain, not ever say the words of infamy – "I'm not here to make friends"). She could do anything she wanted.

"Ready?" he said, as the bridge came into view ahead. "You sure you want to chance it in the car?"

Phillips eased up on the gas, waiting for her answer. She took a moment to admire the nice view she had of the side of his face, before looking ahead. The water sparkled on both sides of the asphalt and concrete like a sea of diamonds.

"Don't slow down," she said.

Author's Note

This story was inspired both by Roanoke Island's history and its present-day reality. As in most mash-ups of history and reality with fiction, I've taken some major liberties. Locations have been altered in many cases, and some have been invented or moved (the courthouse and the jail, for instance). I also tweaked the structure of local law enforcement. And I hope it goes without saying that nothing in this story is meant to reflect on the real people living on the real island. Sources differ about the final tally of missing colonists, so some books may give a different number than one hundred and fourteen.

Also on the historical side, I enhanced John Dee's role in the colonization effort. That said, Dee actually was the title-holder for the land and was consulted by Sir Walter Raleigh in developing the route for the journey. In fact, I had the odd experience of finding *some* historical support for just about every outrageous leap here. We really do know very little about the colonists and why they made the voyage. And it turns out that alchemy was a bigger influence in the early New World than we're taught in history class (at least, *my* classes tragically neglected the subject). I discovered from Walter Woodward's book *Prospero's America* that John Winthrop, Jr., who was elected governor of Connecticut in the 1650s, actually did found a "New London" in America intending it to be a great center of alchemy. He even used Dee's *monas hieroglyphica* as his signature.

Of course, it's still unlikely that the majority of the lost colonists were alchemists who longed for immortality and world domination... or is it?

Acknowledgments

Like most first novels, this one wasn't born in a vacuum of just girl and computer. That means there are many people to thank.

For looking at very early versions of this story, my thanks to Write Club (Melissa Moorer, Katherine Pearl, Christopher Rowe, and honorary member Melissa Schwartz) and the Left Door Workshop. Thanks are also due to the entire wonderful community at the Vermont College of Fine Arts' Writing for Children and Young Adults program, but especially to my last semester advisor Martine Leavitt and to my last workshop group (Kelly Barson, Kari Baumbach, Liz Cook, Pam Watts, Rachel Wilson, and leader Cynthia Leitich Smith) for comments on the beginning of this novel. Emily Moses was invaluable in offering insider theater dirt and gave me Dare County Night. I also offer many thanks to Holly Black, Sarah Rees Brennan, and Scott Westerfeld for help as I was finishing up. And, of course, thanks to my fabulous editor, Amanda Rutter, for making the book better, and to the best agent in the world, Jennifer Laughran, for everything.

A few closer to home: George the Dog, Poster Boy for American Values, aka the original Sidekick; the current menagerie (Emma, Puck, and Hemingway); my parents, who always believed I could do this; and to my husband, Christopher Rowe, for talking me down and reading more drafts than any person should ever have to.

I've been lucky over the years to have the support of more people than I could ever possibly name here. I appreciate each and every one of you.

STRANGE Chemistry

EXPERIMENTING WITH YOUR IMAGINATION

"It's like the best kind of video game: full of fun, mind-bendy
ideas with high stakes, relentless action, and shocking
twists!" – *E C Myers, author of* Fair Coin

CASSANDRA ROSE CLARKE

the
Assassin's
Curse

STRANGE
CheMISTRY

"Unique, heart-wrenching, full of mysteries and twists!"
— *Tamora Pierce*

"*Ghostbusters* meets *Sabrina the Teenage Witch* with a dash of *X-Files*. A magical spell with equal parts humour, adventure and surprise." — *Sara Grant, author of* Dark Parties

MORE WONDERS IN STORE FOR YOU...

- ◆ Kim Curran / SHIFT
- ◆ Cassandra Rose Clarke / THE ASSASSIN'S CURSE
- ◆ Sean Cummings / POLTERGEEKS
- ◆ Jonathan L Howard / KATYA'S WORLD
- ◆ AE Rought / BROKEN
- ◆ Laura Lam / PANTOMIME
- ◆ Julianna Scott / THE HOLDERS
- ◆ Martha Wells / EMILIE & THE HOLLOW WORLD
- ◆ Christian Schoon / ZENN SCARLETT
- ◆ Cassandra Rose Clarke / THE PIRATE'S WISH

EXPERIMENTING WITH
YOUR IMAGINATION

strangechemistrybooks.com
facebook.com/strangechemistry
twitter.com/strangechem